Rotrud's
Rebellion

The Carolingian Chronicles, Vol. 3:
Rotrud's Rebellion

Copyright © 2020 Marilyn Lary. All rights reserved.

Published by At Last Communications

Printed in the United States of America

ISBN-13: 978-0-9842768-3-7

ISBN-10: 9842768-3-1

Library of Congress Control Number: 2019910237

The Carolingian chronicles, vol. 3

Rotrud's Rebellion

Acacia Oak

At Last Communications 2020

Members of Charlemagne's Court in Rotrud's Rebellion

Charlemagne: King of Frankish Realm

Alcuin: Anglo-Saxon scholar who established
                   academies for educating the people of the
                   Frankish realm
Angilbert: Adopted son of Alcuin, love interest of Bertha
Bertha: Charlemagne's second daughter
Charles: Charlemagne's second-born son
Count Janlur: Original friend/adviser (Peer), military
                   commander
Desiderius: King of the Lombards, Charlemagne's enemy
Fastrada: Charlemagne's fourth wife
Gizzie: Charlemagne's youngest daughter
Gisela: Charlemagne's sister, a nun
Hadrian I: The Holy Father, the Pope
Hildegard: Third wife of Charlemagne, most beloved
Himiltrude: First wife of Charlemagne, Peppin's mother
Leo III: Pope who crowned Charlemagne emperor
Liutgard: Fifth wife of Charlemagne
Louis: Charlemagne's third-born son, king of
                   Aquitaine
Count Norico: Love interest of Rotrud
Oliver: Most peace-loving of the original Peers, has
                   left the court
Pepin: Charlemagne's fourth son (first named
                   Carloman), King of Italy
Peppin: Charlemagne's first-born son, the Hunchback
Rinaldo: Original friend/adviser (Peer) to the King

Dedication

This book is dedicated to all who yearn for a true leader, one who works and dreams for his people, whose vision for them drives his decisions and his ambition. Who better to use as a model than an eighth-century barbarian king, one far ahead of his time? Charlemagne absorbed his conquered enemies into his realm, expanded trading opportunities for his people, established copy centers to preserve Greek and Roman literature, and established 'academies' throughout his kingdom to educate Frankish boys and girls. He overcame constraints and decrees from his manipulative mother, surrounded himself with advisers he trusted, and looked to the welfare of everyone in his kingdom. He was truly a hero of the Dark Ages. If only we could be so blessed today.

Chapter 1

QUESTIONS BUT NO ANSWERS

King Charlemagne shook his head, his eyes misting with unshed tears. He had no idea how to talk to his eldest daughter. And, oh, he was so weary of Rotrud's constant criticism. She was unable to forgive his marriage to Fastrada, his current wife. True, he married much too soon after her dear mother's death those four years ago, 783 it was. But no one knew of the compromising position Fastrada built for him.

Dear God, he knew the marriage was too hasty. He knew it then; he acknowledged it now. But, at the least, he remained faithful to his wife...and his vows. But once Hildegard was gone, no one imagined Fastrada's behavior: her offers to visit him nightly in his chamber, her smirks and sultry looks at table, her bragging references to 'the King and I.' He gave up and married her. Aye! He knew he responded too quickly. But the decision was made years ago and could not be changed...not for a Christian king.

"Everyone, except my children and my sister, accept the marriage. Rotrud must learn to adjust; she cannot hold grudges all her life." He murmured quietly. "Thank God, Rotrud doesn't know of those innocent Saxon soldiers I murdered just last year. For no reason, I snuffed out 4500 lives. Surely, in God's eyes, such a stain is much worse than the sexual dreams of a widower." Charlemagne sighed. "If I can only earn God's forgiveness for those murders, I will have overcome that biggest sin. Rotrud's distress is nothing, compared to it."

Hearing his daughter's knock, he stood up, girding himself for the tongue lashing he knew was coming. He smiled as she came into the library. Seeing her face, he knew his smile was of little use this day. The King encouraged his children to question and was always willing to discuss their own points of view. But this marriage question should have ended years ago. As time passed, he became more and more angry with his daughter. No one else dared question his morals nor his vision of Christianity. Even Alcuin - the scholar who designed the schools for the realm, the man Charlemagne most admired - seldom questioned his choices. His friends/advisers, the clergy of his far-flung realm, his court, the natives and the conquered peoples of Frankland, all embraced his religion.

And he did his best to lead them by example, to consult with the Pope, to encourage a Christian realm. Charlemagne regularly rewrote church laws, rituals, procedures, and, in some cases, theology. He even changed the chants which the monks' sang during high holy days. Alcuin argued theology and philosophy with him and praised his command of church doctrine. True, he forced the conquered people to accept Christianity, even on pain of death, but that was necessary for the realm.

Who would believe my own child would criticize me constantly? King Charlemagne held his temper and did not swear out loud. *I must answer her.* He vowed, again, to keep Rotrud's love and her obedience. He reminded himself to control his temper and speak quietly. Rotrud arranged her shawl around her shoulders. She frowned into his face and, without any greeting, she launched her questions.

"Poppa, why do you force the people you conquer to become Christians? The priests say men must answer only to God. Why, then, must the people answer to you as well? Aren't they free to become Christians themselves? How can you demand their conversion? The very idea, it is surely unchristian!"

Charlemagne took a step backward. He sighed, saddened and weary of Rotrud's sustained contempt. Her sad obsession with his marriage to Fastrada never seemed to lessen. She must leave this anger behind. They still needed to talk about his vision for Frankland, about the life their people deserved. In some respects, she was the most informed and realistic of his advisers, better able to analyze the benefits and expenses of a growing realm. Some participants of the Philosophy Club were much less able. But his marriage to Fastrada dominated her thoughts. She would tie her definition of 'forced Christianity' to the marriage; he had no doubt.

Rotrud waited for her father to answer. She twisted one long, black curl around her finger. Her eyes probed her father's, watching for any hesitation, readying for a confrontation. Her questioning sprang from her disappointment in him, from their long-standing disagreement. Her anger fed her needling. He must admit that his behavior after her mother's death was unconscionable. Try as he had over the past three years, he was unable to break through her rage, her judgment of him. Charlemagne saw the anger and, aye, the disappointment in her eyes. He opened his mouth to speak but, then, closed it. There was nothing to be said.

Rotrud shrugged carelessly. *When he gives me an answer which makes sense, I will stop aggravating him,* she promised herself. Rubbing her stomach as it clenched and roiled, she felt the beginnings of a headache. She glanced around the library.

"Once, this was my favorite room, Poppa. As Ma-Mam wrote her long missives to family and friends, I spent many mornings drawing and scribbling When I was small, Ma-

Mam was the only woman in the court who could write; remember? I was always so proud of that. It was one of our special gifts to each other—praising Ma-mam's writing. Her characters were so beautiful!" The king nodded, a slight smile on his face.

Now, the library - reflecting Fastrada's touch - feels cold and austere. Even the candles are barely serviceable, burning with thin, wavering light. The room is dull, the opposite of the bright, light-filled room which always greeted us those years ago. The room welcomed everyone then.

"Rotrud," Charlemagne swallowed his irritation and spoke to his oldest daughter. "I believe Christian values will aid in the governing of the realm. As we absorb many different people into Frankland, friends and former enemies, we need something to unite us all, a shared belief. With such a belief, diverse peoples can become one. Christianity serves that purpose; it unites. Its message is filled with hope and with values which exert control--obedience, responsibility, and concern for one another. These three teachings will forge kinship among the many peoples of the Frankish realm." He gazed at her steadily, wishing he could spank her as he did when she was small. But Rotrud was not to be won easily.

"And if you expect conquered peoples to accept Christian teachings, mustn't you embrace these Christian values yourself?" She asked him. "It's not acceptable to demand people accept your beliefs and, then, not live them in your own life, Sire." Rotrud spat her words at him. I will never forgive you for this marriage to Fastrada, she thought. *How dare you hold others to God's laws but not yourself!*

"The people rely on God's judgment, not on yours." She replied. "How do you explain His injunction not to kill... when your life is full of killing?" Charlemagne ignored her jump to another subject. He could scarcely counteract her argument. He did kill, God help him; but to the people, it seemed to make little difference.

"Rotrud, you know the church allows remarriage at the death of a husband or wife." King Charlemagne decided to speak directly to his daughter's problem. "I have not broken holy teachings. Were you truly worried for the rights of my conquered peoples and less with this perceived slight of your mother, we might have a useful discussion." He almost told her his marital status was not her business but caught himself just in time. "I am weary of your constant criticism. You either bait me to make me look inept or you discount everything I say."

"Mayhap. But you didn't allow a decent interval to pass before you took another into your bed. Better to have a sexual romp than to sully my mother's memory, Poppa! Why could you not rut like other men...and leave marriage out of it?" Rotrud caught her breath and changed her tone.

"You seem controlled by lust, Sire. The court nobles never tire in speaking of it. Will it never be left to the past, this need to examine your sexual needs?" Although Rotrud's face burned red with her reference to sexual exploits, her contempt vibrated in her voice and her pain showed on her face. "I HATE your choice, Poppa! ...such beastly behavior!" And she ran from the room, seething with indignation and resentment.

***

Charlemagne sighed. He shook his head, back and forth, more than aware of his hasty, precipitous marriage to Fastrada. He had no adequate response to his daughter's criticism and no explanation for her or for his court. "I am THE King!" He muttered. "I do not explain myself to any of them."

"How do those Saxon lives compare, I wonder," the King mumbled, "to my sordid love life? Mayhap, Rotrud could place it all in perspective for me." The King shook his head, recalling the court's interest in and, then, judgment of sexual exploits. Sexual misbehavior seemed the worse crime by far, even worse than mass murder. "Where do the people's values comes from? Their shock and wonder make no sense!"

Try as he might, King Charlemagne could not understand his court's puerile interest in his marriage bed or in any bed he might visit. His first two marriages - Himiltrude and Desiderata - were for the interests of the realm, not for his own needs. His marriage to Hildegard was for himself, though it became the best partnership he could have chosen for his people. This last marriage to Fastrada...aye, it was a mistake; but one he could not change. He might put away a wife, even two of them, for lack of an heir. But, now, with Hildegard's three healthy sons, Fastrada was his for the rest of his life, no matter how unattractive the prospect.

"What is this gross concern?" Charlemagne returned to his confusion. "...the peoples' frenzy of interest in their King's sexual habits? No one considers the murders which battle demands. No one questions my appropriation of land, of courts, of people. Very few of my critics give a thought to my assurances that God is on our side. Who knows? Mayhap, HE is not. Does this God who teaches love and forgiveness condone my murdering, my stealing, my callousness, my control of others' lives, my insistence they live as I command? Surely the Lord judges more than sexual appetite in men. Mustn't we answer for other sins as well - murder, abandonment of the sick and old, adulation of our battle commanders, cursing and damning God's will? No one ever questions the other commandments I repeatedly break."

"But they condemn a sexual liaison. One tumble is more loathsome than a battle that kills hundreds? The seduction of a married countess is more sinful than the maiming of untold numbers? A season of lustful encounters is more wicked than a careless battle command which risks many lives: squires, arrow carriers, and horses? Why is this sin of lust more despicable than any other?"

Charlemagne yearned to share his thoughts. He decided to bring this subject to Alcuin's attention, the next time they were together at Aachen. *Mayhap, the scholar can shed some light on the people's attention to a single commandment. They, for certain, appear to have no concern for the other nine.* King Charlemagne rubbed his temples, trying to block out his daughter's words.

If she were to overcome her anger, she might soon outwit me. As a young girl, Rotrud mimicked her Aunt Gisela, my sister, even in the toss of her head. But as a young woman, her mind is the equal of anyone in the court. Her mother would be so proud of her! King Charlemagne startled and tried to pull his mind away from Hildegard, his most beloved wife, the queen of his heart. *How I regret my lack of attention to her! … if only I had spared her more.* He thought back to the last few weeks of Hildegard's life.

***

With everyone in good health and the Saxons temporarily under control, Hilde and he relaxed. The closer the impending birth, the more they spoke of a permanent home. Hilde already had a name for it - the' Soldier's Manor.' "She wearied of the ceaseless rotations through the realm, but I was reluctant to discontinue my journeys. Still, she bore the rotations for twelve years with endurance and good humor; so I felt a permanent court site might be attempted. When I suggested it, her eyes brightened, lessening the dark circles beneath them. And her face glowed, almost as if she drank strong wine. But, alas, she looked so weary."

This pregnancy seemed overlong to everyone in the court, even the midwife, and Hildegard's health suffered greatly. Not even twelve hours after he and the Queen relaxed, the birth pains began. All in the court celebrated, relieved the pregnancy would soon be at an end. But, hours later, Hildegard labored still, resting between contractions but growing progressively weaker. The King left the birthing chamber to check on Rotrud, Bertha, and Gisela. He thanked God they were stopped and were in a manor for Eastertide, instead of in their traveling tent. Charlemagne ate the evening meal with his children and tucked them into bed. Hours later, he checked with Gisela. She and the women assisting thought the baby would soon be born. In Gisela's room, he heard the single cry of his new-born daughter.

"It rent my heart." He said later. "The shrill, high-pitched cry was followed by absolute silence." He hurried toward the birthing chamber but knew before he ever reached it. The babe was dead. As he stepped inside, he saw Hildegard moan softly and stretch out her arms. She understood the meaning of her child's cry. The midwife grabbed both her hands and held them gently. But Hilde whimpered, pulled her hands away, and stretched her arms out once more. Her face was filled with yearning. Then, with a small tremble, she fell back against the coverlet. His wife and his baby daughter, both were dead. He slipped away to console himself.

Just down the corridor, exhausted herself, Gisela heard the babe's cry. She startled. "Oh, dear God, please don't take them both." She hurried to Hildegard's side and stiffened. Hilde's arms still stretched toward the mid-wife, a worried look on her still face. Gisela lay her head on Hildegard's shoulder, sobbing over the loss of her friend and her newborn niece. "This birth appeared blemished from the start," she later told her brother. Hilde seemed so weak, so lacking in strength and energy during her entire confinement." Her thoughts jumped to her nieces and nephews.

"Oh, my sweet children, what will you do? No one can fill the place of your dear mother."

Gisela knew she must stop weeping and go to her brother. "It's best if he hears this ill news from my lips. He came by, just a half-turn ago, to kiss Hildegard's forehead and asked if all were well." She made an effort to stop weeping. "We did not prepare him for this. Despite the length of the labor and so much blood, we believed all would end well." She wept afresh, struggling to contain her pain and to force herself to go to King Charlemagne.

***

News of the Queen's death spread through the court. The tears of the wet nurse dropped copiously on little, two-year-old Gizzie's face. The toddler blinked rapidly, trying to escape the small splashes. Her face wrinkled in perplexity and, then, she began to cry: short, staccato bleats which begged for comfort. At Gizzie's first cry, little four-year-old Bertha, in a nearby bed, also, whimpered. The two young children seemed to feed on each other's sounds for both were soon crying together. The wet nurse wiped her tears hurriedly and began to change the little girl's soggy garment.

"Did anyone change this babe in the last week?" She asked as she replaced the absorbent mosses wrapped in a worn patch of cloth with fresh rectangles. She tied them in place with thin leather strips around the baby's legs, and tied them, again, around the baby's body at the waist. The child's sleeping shirt, now short for her and torn, was left open, not tied at the bottom with her feet inside. No longer chilled nor wet, Gizzie ceased crying and smiled at the nurse.

15

"I do believe Queen Hildegard's babes just got sweeter—the more she had," the woman observed.

"But none as tender as herself," a younger woman added as tears leaked from her eyes. "We must finish our grieving; it does no good for these dear babes. Our attention must focus on these two. They are sure to be neglected."

Just as the young woman settled the twenty-month-old child in her arms, King Charlemagne entered the nursery room. "I felt the need to hold my youngest children. Their poor mother is resting now. None of us will ever truly recover from losing her, I most of all." His eyes red-rimmed and sorrowing, he sat down heavily and held open his arms for the youngest child. She reached a small arm toward his face and patted his cheek very gently. King Charlemagne settled the child, holding the baby close on the left side of his chest.

"My sweet Gizzie," he murmured as his red eyes rimmed with unshed tears. "My sweet Gizzie, what shall we do—alone and broken-hearted?" He walked with the little girl, patting her back and swaying slowly. In moments she was asleep, holding his giant thumb in one tiny hand. With practiced movement, the king laid her in her bed.

Immediately, he went over to little Bertha who was trying to catch a small puppy. In the past, the girl's clutching hands grabbed the puppy once too often; he was always just out of reach now. "Are you having trouble, Bertha?" Charlemagne asked as he caught the puppy and held it out to the toddler. Bertha screeched with glee and turned toward her father. "You must be gentle with the puppy. He won't run from you if you're gentle. See, rub his head this way and he will stay closer to you. Be careful! Don't run too fast; you'll fall on the puppy and squish him."

Charlemagne smiled at the delight on young Bertha's face. He moved the child's hand slowly, encouraging the little girl to curb her enthusiastic rubbing of the pup's head. "You know, I believe your pup needs to sleep. Why don't you lie down? Here, I'll make you a bed on the floor. If you are very, very still, your pup will sleep beside you." As Bertha lay on the floor, Charlemagne brought the puppy close and began rubbing its head and patting Bertha's back. He knew Bertha was fighting sleep—she always did—and the pup was right there in the thick of the action. Soon, both small 'pups' were sleeping quietly, lulled by the steady comfort of those big hands.

"Thank you, King Charlemagne," the younger woman said. "Bertha insisted on staying awake, waiting for her mother and her goodnight kiss." The nurse wiped away tears as she covered the sleeping child.

"I suspect this place will become my refuge," the King answered her. "Even though they will miss their mother, they cannot hurt like you or me. I'll send someone to relieve you, Mistress Roe; thank you for your kindness and care."

Charlemagne left the nursery, the first stop on the route of checking on all his children, now motherless with the death of Hildegard in childbirth. He had, also, lost his last daughter, whom he named Hildegard after her dear mother. The King mourned the loss of them both. He steadied himself against the wall, sobbing into his hands. He must see his children each day. Each one of them had at least one of Hilde's mannerisms. He wished to keep those fresh in his mind. He continued down the corridor, wobbly and exhausted, his feet fumbling from his great sorrow.

***

Gisela, the King's sister, postponed her return to her abbey to console her nieces and nephews on the death of their mother. She stayed as much to comfort herself as to comfort them. Over the years, she and Hildegard became true friends, bonded in their love and concern for these offspring. Their presence and their need of her helped Gisela overcome her own grief and strengthened her dedication to Charlemagne's family.

Within the court and, as the couriers went forth, around the realm people of all stations tried to absorb the ill news. Nowhere was it more difficult than among those who loved and depended on the good queen, those who learned belatedly her true value, now that she was gone.

***

"Where is Hildegard?" Queen Mother Bertrada demanded of the woman who brought her breakfast. Lady Douglas signed inwardly. There was no use repeating the answer again. The Queen Mother would not remember.

"She cannot come to you now. She worries for her horse's new colt. I'm sure by mid-morning, she will return."

Queen Bertrada shifted uneasily. "It's not like her at all," she complained. "She always checks on me in the mornings. I need to see her." The grumbling continued. "My porridge is lumpy and thick. This is rye bread, not the barley she always brings me. And the spread for this bread is too thin. She knows I'm not over-fond of blackberry spread. Where is the apple spread for this bread? Why can't Hildegard be..." In mid-sentence, Queen Bertrada stopped. A flash of memory passed before her eyes. She saw Queen Hildegard lying on her sleeping bench, her eyes shut. "Nay! Nay!" She remembered her daughter-in-law was gone. "Nay, it cannot be! It cannot be!"

Lady Douglas was moved by the Queen Mother's obvious sorrow and hurried over to pat her shoulder. "I know, I know," Lady Douglas murmured sympathetically. "None of us can believe she's gone. What a mother she was! Only last week she was 'patching up Charles,' as she dubbed it. Hardly 'patching up;' she was surely strengthening the boy's soul." Lady Douglas came back to the present and poured Queen Bertrada a cup of tea. "Here you are." She placed the cup into the old queen's hands. "We won't bring her back with all this." Seeing the Queen's grief, Lady Douglas' heart ached for Queen Hildegard's children.

At that moment, those very children were comforting each other. "Charley, 'member Ma-mam to me?" Bertha asked, her eyes filling with tears.

"Remember Ma-Mam? What is the matter with....?" Charles looked up at his younger sister. Her face was white, her eyes huge. He held open his arms. "Come right here to me." He softly ordered. "Come on, hurry!" Bertha came straight into his arms and began to sob. Charles felt an overwhelming sadness for his little sister. *There's so much she'll never know of Ma-Mam,* he realized. *She will never have talks like Ma-Mam and I did. Ma-Mam won't be here to help her puzzle things out or to hold her close.* Charles knew his mother sometimes gave him her love in secret gestures. He remembered gentle kisses to his forehead, a firm hand rubbing his back and a caress on the head when he pretended to sleep. He promised himself to check on Bertha every single day, to be a more loving brother to her. *I've seen Louis tease and pinch her, when he visits,* Charles thought. *And he's unkind to Gizzie, too. He so likes to tell us all how to behave. He can never just enjoy being home. But I need to comfort Bertha now and forget Louis.*

"Ah, 'Berta, you remember. It seems long to me, too; but Ma-Mam hasn't been gone very long. I didn't remember Uncle Ro's face when he died. I was so sad and cried so much; I just couldn't think of his face. You will remember Ma-Mam, I promise. The hurt is just in the way right now." Bertha stirred slightly at his chest but did not answer.

Instinctively Charles rubbed Bertha's back and patted her. "Can't you just see that one curl, the one always beside her ear? Or the way she pointed with her finger when she was scolding you?" Charles laughed. "One day I caught her finger and tried to bite it! I told her that without that finger, she couldn't be mad at me." Bertha gave a muffled laugh and held tighter to her brother.

Coming across the yard, Charlemagne spotted his children in the lee side of the wall. Though shadows covered that entire wall, he saw his oldest son holding his small sister, talking intently into her hair.

My dear children, the King thought, *how can I help you with this sorrow - losing your mother before you even knew her? I know not if I can even speak of her. Oh, God!* The King's thoughts became speech. "How can I go on? How might I comfort my children when I can find nothing to comfort me?" He stopped to wipe his face and rubbed his eyes furiously, trying to wipe away the pain. The King looked again at Charles and Bertha. He was surprised to see Charles smile broadly and laugh. *Whatever he is doing, he is moving forward. Let me go to them. Their dear faces, so much like Hilde, may give me the comfort and strength I seek.*

"How are my oldest and my almost baby?" He asked the two children as he walked over to them. He picked Bertha up, put her on his shoulders, placed a hand on Charles' shoulder and began to walk with them. "Let's go to the cook tents for a delight. This is just the time that a sweet will be the best thing in the world." Charles put his arm part-way around his father's waist and walked close. From her perch on high, Bertha looked down on the world, quietly and solemnly.

"Poppa," Charles spoke. "Tell us stories about Ma-mam. Bertha and I are afeared we'll forget her." Charlemagne squeezed his son's shoulder.

"There's a portrait of your mother which the artist,

Monstral, is completing. It was to be her surprise to the court at Christmastide next. We'll put the portrait in an honored spot where you may see it as often as you wish. And, if you will both keep this secret, I'll ask Monstral to make a copy for each of you, a portrait of your mother which is yours alone. We'll have him make those smaller, so you can keep them with you."

Charles looked up at his father, tears standing in his eyes. "It's so hard, Poppa," he said. "I thought I cried all my tears for Uncle Ro; but they're back."

Charlemagne steered his son, now almost eleven years, into the woods where a small stream ran among the trees. The father and his two children sat beside the stream, talking of Queen Hildegard, each one grieving for the woman recently lost. And, then, Charlemagne began telling the two children stories about their mother: tales which showed her lively, happy view of the world; her concern for all who hungered; her worry for all who wouldn't have the chance to learn; her love for her family; her care for any sick or damaged animal.

***

"I should fetch Bertha from the king," one of the court ladies said as she spotted the king and children at the stream. "She has grieved deeply for so young a child."

"Nay, I think not," her companion replied. "They are comforting one another; leave them be." And so, she did.

***

Although all the court was in grieving, preparations for Queen Hildegard's funeral required even more labor for the court workers. Political alliances, favor of the King, and respect drew many nobles and their wives to the burial. This group was small though, far out-numbered by the hundreds who just loved the Queen, some from her reputation but many whose lives she touched with her humane concern.

Olvan looked around the cooking tent. The serving girls turned suckling pigs on splints; sweetened apples and dried berries bubbled gently in honey sauce. The ever-present roasts of boar and deer, the pear and apple mix, rounds of cheese — all were ready to feed the mourners. Olvan's clothes were damp from exertion. *Wonder why people keep calling for bread?* Olvan asked himself. *We've baked enough bread to feed three kingdoms! Oh, for true, I understand,* Olan puzzled it out. *When people are grieving, many don't want heavy food. Just the idea of eating can be painful. But bread and honey seem to soothe away the hurt feelings.* So thinking, he hurried to knead more oatmeal cakes.

The cooking tent's workers began last midnight: skinning, baking, roasting, boiling--preparing for the great horde of people who would attend Queen Hildegard's burying. *There seems to be no end to their numbers,* Olvan thought. *But there is no choice. If the court eats ill for weeks hereafter, these visitors must be well-fed: yet another reputation to keep afloat but, better still, an assertion of our regard for our Queen.* A page hurried up to Olvan, reciting an order from yet another high-born lady who wished refreshments in her tent before the service.

"Where is Mathilda?" Olvan queried. "Is she serving in the banquet tent? I've not seen her since yesterday's evening meal. We need her quick feet."

There was a shuffle at the door as one of the king's guards entered the tent. Work stopped in the kitchen. It was seldom a soldier came into the cooking area. If they came on an errand, most waited outside.

"Thought you'd like to know, Olvan, seeing she worked here. Mathilda is dead, hanged herself in the orchard last night. I don't know how she found her way there in the dark, but the lads discovered her body at sunrise. Sorry to tell you this way. I figured you was wondering 'bout her." The soldier stepped quickly out of the way of the busy cooks.

Olvan was immobile. *Dear Lord, help us. Death seems to have moved into this court. Lord, help us all.*

"I appreciate your trouble, Dunstan," Olvan replied. "We all are overcome with grief in here. Aye, Mathilda did so love the Queen. Somehow, I'm not surprised she took her own life. There be several others who feel the same loss. My thanks for letting us know."

Chapter 2

Internal Threats

In less time than one would guess, Charlemagne's court returned to its normal routine. Gisela, seeing her nieces and nephews comforted, left for her abbey. And King Charlemagne, eager for sunshine and activity, turned outside to evaluate brood mares for a new horse-breeding program. Alcuin, busy as always, was overseeing the education of the realm's children. He lived permanently in the castle at Aachen, welcoming the mobile court whenever it traveled through the northern part of the realm.

On this early, bright morn Queen Mother Bertrada's maid, Hroda, burst into the kitchen. Her shoes, worn and weathered, almost fell off her feet. She patted her chest while taking deep gulps of air.

"The Queen Mother is dead!" All activity stopped. The kitchen workers stared at her. No one said a word. It was scarcely four months since Queen Hildegard's death. "The Queen Mother is dead," Hroda repeated. "She took her last breath as I took tea in from the herbalist. The King and Scholar Alcuin are at her bedside."

Cooks and servers stood quickly, their early morning tea forgotten. The responsibilities of another funeral sliced through the air as the kitchen workers absorbed the news. None of them were overfond of Queen Bertrada. She was often unpleasant and always demanding but the reputation of Charlemagne's court must be maintained. The kitchen workers would bake bread, cook jams, dress meat and scour the countryside for provisions. As they worked, the stablemaster and grooms would retrieve and pack traveling bags, load carts, and begin herding cattle and goats toward the Aachen castle. All worked in a consistent rhythm honed by years of traveling around the realm. Once at Aachen, all the court workers and some nobles began cleaning; preparing stables and yards; cooking meat, fish, and venison; and preparing chambers for those attending the burial.

Bakers, cooks, and servers moved quickly in the cook tents. Extra pots found their way to the preparation areas. Bakers pulled their pans out and began measuring flour, lard, and salt. Serving girls pulled flagons and trenchers from the pegs. They all understood there were, again, to be endless days of cooking. Oh, no, there'd not be as many mourners for this funeral; but many pretend mourners would arrive, some not long after tomorrow's sunrise. There were sure to be far fewer of the common people this time - no doubt of that. None of the people – nobles or commoners – ever loved Queen Bertrada as they loved Queen Hildegard. But less people was a relief as well. Thinking of the last funeral, Orvan remembered Mathilda.

Queen Mother Bertrada had no one who loved her so well as Mathilda loved Queen Hildegard. He thought. *Oh, I know very well of Mathilda's debt to Queen Hildegard. Still, there'll be no one mourning the Queen Mother even half so well. Queen Bertrada, full of her own importance and querlous, earned no positive feelings in the court. The King will be devastated. But I predict he will find some good relief in the Queen Mother's passing.*

"Ha!" Olvan laughed. "Do you remember when Queen Hildegard discovered farming?" He shrieked in delight, thinking back to the cook tent during the days of the food wars. Even in his sadness, his face reflected happy memories of the time.

"Do tell us all about it," one of the young wenches begged. "I know naught of this happen'."

"I have to give you some history," Olvan smiled. "Understand that the Queen Mother directed Queen Hildegard to 'see to the food,' wanting her to supervise the preparing and serving. The Queen Mother always told us what to cook; but, sometimes, she remembered to do it just at the time all the court sat down to eat!" Olvan shook his head at the memory of the Queen Mother berating Queen Hildegard because the meal she wanted did not materialize. "The young queen would come to the cook tent each night just before the evening meal, and tell us her choices for the morrow's meals. She was very serious; she took much time questioning the master cook, being certain the food she named was available and could be prepared. Nearly every morn, Queen Mother Bertrada came to change the food choices for the day. Then, she would complain to King Charlemagne about the poor quality of the meal. Each day was misery for us and for Queen Hildegard." Several others, while smiling at the memory, shook their heads in agreement over Olvan's recital of the situation.

"It 'twas a battle, it was," Ristad agreed. "And meal times 'twas the worst part of the day." "Queen Hildegard," Olvan continued, "she always be the kindest heart of any in the court. She had no solution for the situation. She even came to the cook tent with Queen Bertrada and listened to her pleasure and agreed with every word. But Queen Bertrada would turn on her. It made no sense." Olvan saw the listener's impatience. "It made no sense. One spring morn, Queen Hildegard described one of her ideas to King Charlemagne. She wanted to grow two crops in every row during the planting season. He was not certain such planting would work but directed it be done. Our lady enlisted the aid of the monks. They spread her idea to the farmers. Monks traveled through the realm praising the new practice of 'crop rotation.' Lo and behold, the farmers got more yield at harvest time! The queen was so busy, spreading her idea, she had no thoughts for meals or court concerns. The Queen Mother had to oversee food preparation again!" He looked around at the grinning faces as they, too, remembered. "We've not heard from Queen Hildegard about meals in years and years." He smiled at the memory but noticed his workers standing about.

"But, now, this be enough stories. We must get to the cooking! This death will bring visitors from everywhere. All of them must be fed. I even hear a caliph is making his way here. Hurry! There's much to be done. Make every food you can that uses oatmeal; it can be stretched to fill many mouths," the master cook directed.

***

Much of the food prepared that day, and for many days that followed, was the best the court ever offered. The kitchen workers, determined to support and respect Queen Hildegard's memory, used the only means they had—preparing meals that would have been a credit to her hospitality. The Queen Mother, on the other hand, had been a long trial for the kitchen workers, cooks and servers alike.

"For her sake, I'm glad the old soul be gone," Olvan stated everyone's thought. "She was too long in this world, plotting and moving events to her liking—no matter the harm to anyone else."

***

Charlemagne shook his head and came out of his reverie about the past. His confrontation with Rotrud and his sad memories of Hilde's death made him eager to begin the evening meal with a group of visiting clergymen. As his guests, none of the visitors would dare question or aggravate him at table. Difficult subjects, questionable decisions, or past wrongs would not arise at a meeting of king and clergymen. As a result, the King welcomed the visitors-- even though the meal was late; the court was tired; and he himself longed for a bit of time alone.

He ordered Queen Fastrada to feed the guests well. His court's reputation for hospitality was wide-spread. He would never be so niggardly as to provide less food and drink for monks than for nobility. *After all,* King Charlemagne thought, *I have a reputation to uphold. I do hope Fastrada is serving squash and acorn soup. Somehow such soup always whets my taste for venison and boar. Mayhap, there will be a bit of fish this night as well.*

The guests, a group of initiates and monks, joined Charlemagne's court for the evening meal. They were following the road to Parma, the monks sent to oversee the young initiates' journey to the holy church there. They were, one and all, eager to meet Abbot Fulrad who had been in the King's court for many years. Fulrad was a well-known cleric, famous throughout the land. In addition to having been the King's teacher and adviser, he had been the arch-chaplain of the Church and was highly regarded. When King Charlemagne answered their inquiries about the Abbot, they were dumbfounded, never having thought not to see the Abbot. When Charlemagne explained that the Arch-chaplain had been felled by an illness in the head (though actually imprisoned for his betrayal of Charlemagne), their disappointment threatened to undermine the entire evening's delights.

Their mood, though, suddenly shifted as the King's children joined the banquet feast. The two older princesses were beginning to blossom and attracted much attention. Although the young monks were dedicated to their vows, they delighted in being in the midst of a large throng, joyously celebrating an upcoming Eastertide again. As the young monks ate, they were peppered with various theological questions, complimented for their insightfulness, and generally overwhelmed with attention. Their glistening eyes and wide smiles repeatedly thanked the courtiers and nobles for their respect.

Months before, as preparations for this visit were made, Abbot Fulrad reported that Paul the Deacon traveled with the monks and would share the King's table. Charlemagne, eager to enlist support for his educational ideas, made an effort to speak with each monk, as well as to remember the monks' final destinations. He begged them to take seats, sup at his table and enjoy the night's entertainment. He and Paul discussed the church's effort to educate through its monasteries and abbeys.

King Charlemagne was a gracious host. He was generous in sharing his table and diligent in providing entertainment. In the company of these religious pilgrims, conversation easily turned from church law to interpretations of existing religious tenets, or, even, to theological explanations from the King. Such pronouncements often reflected the King's blending of Germanic, even pagan celebrations, with Christian ones. Eating huge servings of tart plums and honeyed bread, the King and the initiates took turns interpreting various verses of scripture.

***

The following morning, rising from his sleeping linens, King Charlemagne was surprised to see his Queen, Fastrada, enter the room. "You are out and about early, my dear."

"It seems to be the season for visitors," Queen Fastrada commented, not acknowledging his kiss. Her lips tightened with disapproval. Her hands fidgeted, her forehead shone with a slight film of sweat. She brought the King a bowl filled with blackberry sauce and flat, baked dough.

"Fastrada, what's this?" Charlemagne's face beamed. "I have yet to break my fast. Do I get a special 'delight,' before I completely waken?" the King asked, taking a quick taste.

"It's warm from the cooking, Sire, the very best time to enjoy a serving of fruit," his wife replied. "I wish you to have the first taste. The berries are scarcely ripe; but we all know how much you yearn for them."

Charlemagne's mouth puckered. "They are tart," he allowed, "but delicious. Thank you for this 'delight,' as Poppa called them."

Waving a parchment that the courier delivered the night before, the King laughed. "We shall have another visitor arriving from the Middle East, in a fortnight," the King announced. "He's bringing a drawing of this 'elefant' which I first heard about many years ago. This must be a stupendous beast! I cannot wait to see its size. Oh, how I would love to have one for the Aix-la-Chappelle gardens. I wonder if the Caliph would gift me one?" King Charlemagne's eyes were shining.

"Charlemagne," Queen Fastrada hurried to deflect his next sentence. "These foreign visitors are eating up the court's resources. Must we entertain so lavishly when sojourners are here?" Seeing Charlemagne's irritated face, she amended, "I beg your pardon, Sire. If not that, we must decrease the number of guests from the Frankish nobility at the evening banquets. Our food stores are not so well-stocked that we can continue to feed so many. Might, also, the succulent sweets be eliminated? Their costs are so dear for the treasury."

"Nay, of a certainty." Charlemagne responded decisively. "These visitors are my guests and must be treated in a certain style. I would not seem small in my welcome of them, not after they have made this long journey. We are the most resplendent court in this part of the world. Our reputation must be maintained, my dear, and consciously supported. Nay, Fastrada, we spare no food or courtesy in this hall."

Changing the subject, the King added. "From now until the evening meal, I will be closeted with Alcuin, discussing our educational plans. Please, Fastrada, see that I am not disturbed. Be sure the cooks' servers gather more of these splendid berries for the banquet three days hence. And might some mint be found to improve the stews? Thank you, my dear."

***

After the King assured himself that adequate preparations for the expected guests were underway, he summoned Alcuin to the library and prepared to enjoy a day with the scholar.

"Ahh, it affords me much delight to be in this room," he commented to his friend. "These books represent such knowledge. That we all might feast on them--this is the aim of my empire. I know, I know, Alcuin." Charlemagne deflected Alcuin's move to interrupt and, then, dismissed Alcuin's negative nod. "Most people in Frankland have no interest in a feast of books. But, mayhap, hyperbole in speaking of books or of learning will emphasize my love for them and win us some converts. Do you think it possible?"

"Sire, I applaud your love of books, for a certainty. Truly, how can men not be intrigued by all the wisdom of the ages, even the conflict between different thinkers on the same subject? It, too, makes my heart glad to look around this room, not to mention the tomes you're sending out, both far and near. I receive copious thanks from brothers all over the realm. I do believe that some church brothers have begun learning to read, wondering at the mysteries in all these scrolls." Alcuin's enthusiasm reflected that of his King.

"If we haven't generated enthusiasm for reading, Alcuin; I do have force. And the nobles' sons, at least, will be forced to attend your school." He shook his head as Alcuin opened his mouth to speak. "I know what you're about to say. Isn't this your argument? Those that do not learn of their own choice learn poorly? Yes, but, if they are pushed, let us hope they will learn something." The King's lips firmed. His voice strengthened. He shook his head in confusion, not understanding those who didn't wish to learn.

"I have summoned you here because it is time, is it not, for my correspondence to be answered? I have neglected these loyal letter writers! I had a letter from Offa of Mercia almost a fortnight ago. His Anglo-Saxon views are insightful, don't you think?"

Alcuin nodded without enthusiasm. "Aye, Sire, but keep in mind: we are all victims of our homelands. I do try to remain open to new experiences." Charlemagne laughed with delight. He loved to bait Alcuin because of his own Anglo-Saxon heritage.

"Fear not!" the King laughed. "I cherish your values and your wild Britannia training, and you know it. Who else do I trust with the education of my children or of the children of my realm? It matters not that you come from and espouse those very 'Anglo-Saxon' views from time to time. Come, let us respond to these letters."

"My first letter must be to the caliph of Baghdad, Harun-a-Rashid. Doesn't that name roll off the tongue, Alcuin? Harun-a-Rashid! What power there can be in a name." The King clearly wished his name sounded so fine. "He wishes to visit our court during the early winter. He promises me some exotic birds for the park in Aachen. I cannot wait to see them. The tales describe huge creatures with tails of luminous blue and green. It is said they make a blood-curdling call. Have you seen such birds, Alcuin?" He didn't wait for Alcuin's response but hurried on. "We must welcome his visit. Let us send envoys to his court with gifts and greetings!"

King Charlemagne was fascinated with foreign cultures and delighted in the contacts he received from the Arab world. Both Alcuin and, later, Paul the Deacon provided useful information for such contacts and were of great help to him in maintaining connections to that exotic world. The King had, also, noted the economic success of the Moslem world. He hoped to learn the secrets of commerce from them in order to enhance his own realm's economic base.

As the King began to speak, a guardsman appeared at the door of the library. "Forgive me for disturbing you, Sire. There's a courier seeking audience, says that he's been riding the entire night, Sire. His horse went lame some days back which caused a lengthy delay before he could secure another. He wished to get this to you as soon as possible. It's from your sister, your Majesty," the guardsman added as he handed Charlemagne the sealed parchment.

"How splendid," the King's face filled with delight. "Receiving a letter from Gisela always brightens my day. She never sends me ill news." But as he read the letter, the King no longer smiled. His forehead wrinkled as he read her words. She wrote that she was coming for a visit and asked for his itinerary, the better to find the court's location.

Dear Brother,

"I have a very serious concern to speak about with you, Brother," she wrote. "This must be done face-to-face.

Please do not relocate the court until you have received me. I do not object to moving as the court moves. It may well be that I need two or three days of your time...and your serious attention as we work to resolve this worry."

Your loving sister,

Gisela

With this last statement, Gisela ended her letter. "Gisela has made but one other unsummoned trip to me," the King muttered. "And that was her warning about my second marriage, the one to Desiderata of Lombard. If only I had listened to her good sense then, all of us would have been spared a world of pain and destruction." He looked out of the tent door. "I look forward to her visit; but her concern sounds dire, indeed."

***

The next morning, Charlemagne awoke, dreading the news his sister would bring. He played with his morning meal and sent for Rinaldo, determined to get some governing work done. But, alas, the King found it difficult to sit through Rinaldo's state-of-the-realm report. This weekly appraisal of events in the kingdom was always dull and uninteresting. But because this Peer knew all that was happening throughout the realm, Rinaldo was a very effective adviser. So, Charlemagne curbed his impatience and tried to listen. Rinaldo confirmed the attendance of several lords at the upcoming annual assembly, a gathering for the expressed purpose of choosing the summer's battles. The King looked forward to the upcoming annual assembly. It was always rich in the comradeship of soldiers and old friends. For the good of the realm, organizational issues, rewards and punishments, plans and changes were announced. Of a certainty, battles and military maneuvers for the summer fighting season would be evaluated and chosen. Hearing this ill news about rebellion, the king was more than ready to begin his trip to Franconia for this year's gathering.

"Excuse me, Sire," Rinaldo paused. "I seem to have lost your attention. Mayhap, we should consider a different topic. I go to bring Lord Theo to present our next issue." Rinaldo's subtle update on a rumored rebellion made Charlemagne more than ready to   meet with his supporters in the annual assembly. Mayhap, he would consider beginning their march to Franconia earlier than planned.

"Good morn to you, Sire. I trust that the night was kind to you." Theo motioned for the guardsmen to vacate the tent and turned his attention back to the King. "We'll just wait for Rinaldo to return. He's sending for bread and cheese to break our fast."

"What? He's what?" the King asked impatiently. "I've no time to eat. You know, Theo; I eat little in the early morn. I must check on our readiness to move the court." The King frowned. "Rinaldo does overstep himself." The King rose, heading toward the door of the tent.

"Don't be hasty, Sire. There is much to speak of. Rinaldo is following my request. We have a pressing threat which we must address, today, this very morn." Theo spread his hands, asking the King to resume his seat as Rinaldo came into the tent with Alcuin.

"Food will be here directly, Sire," he announced. Glancing at Theo who nodded imperceptibly, Rinaldo approached the King. "Might I ask, Sir, that you hear my report before commenting? Lord Theo may have information to add to mine. You will want to deliver a swift response, I know." Lord Theo and Alcuin sat together on a bench facing the King. Theo nodded and gestured that Rinaldo begin.

"I don't wish to alarm you, King Charlemagne," Rinaldo began. "But we have discovered a plot against you. The majority of the nobility in Franconia and Thuringia intend to arrest you when all gather for the upcoming assembly. The leader of this treachery is Count Hardrad." Rinaldo raised his hand as Charlemagne jumped to his feet. "Please, Sire; there's more."

"There is a continuing debate among them: should they kill you shortly after you arrive or hold you for ransom. That action hasn't yet been decided. We must assume they would demand your abdication before striking you down. Several of our spies have identified both the men and the place of attack." Charlemagne opened his mouth but Alcuin shook his head.

"Wait a moment, Sire," Alcuin said. Rinaldo continued.

"Since many of the traitors are well-known to you, Theo and I agree that you should decide their punishments." Theo nodded. "It's our opinion, Sire, that all should be put to death. And this we would do! Aye, we know that the king must be merciful..." Rinaldo added as Charlemagne put out his hand. "But, in this instance, security must outweigh mercy. This is not an ill-conceived plot by a small rebel faction, Sire. Nay, it is a direct affront from nobles who benefit greatly from your rule." Rinaldo turned to Theo.

"I have nothing further to add, Sire," Lord Theo

responded. "My spies have confirmed this plot against you. They have, also, identified the conspirators. Nay, there is no doubt that this plan, unholy as it is, has already been set in motion. Yesterday, their scouts began hiding along the road…to chart the court's progress toward Franconia. What would you have us do with these traitors? I would end this as soon as possible. Both Rinaldo and I have men in place to overcome them, to take them all by force. We wait only your command." With these words Lord Theo unsheathed his sword, ready for action.

Charlemagne felt his heart catch. He was hurt but not surprised at the news. Previous attacks on himself and even on his children had required that he be alert to constant threat — the hidden as well as the obvious ones.

"They oppose me at their own peril, friends." The King said. "They are unable to accept that God Himself directs my steps. Mayhap, these particular men are dissatisfied with the limits on their power. This region has always been ruled by hot-heads so I must act quickly, with no hesitation. Underhanded plots behind my back do the Frankish realm no good."

"Take them," the King commanded. "In the name of mercy, I will exile the leaders, rather than kill them. Capture them and take them to the monastery in Rouen. It shall be their prison. We shall distribute their lands and holdings to our more loyal commanders. Offer their wives and children protection as they vacate the manors and escort them where ever they want to go." He turned to the scholar.

"Alcuin, consult with Count Janus to identify those to be rewarded." Charlemagne turned back to Theo. "Kill all their supporters. Dead men hatch no plans." The King felt energized by his ability to respond to the threat. He thanked his advisers profusely and, also, provided rewards for their success in rooting out the plot. Though gratified by the discovery of this betrayal, King Charlemagne worried about the nobles who would be even more opposed to him, especially when the perpetrators' punishments were announced. *Any conspiracy, successful or not, invariably produces another one,* the King thought to himself. "I do hope Gisela does not come, bringing word of anything like this. The nuns may easily have overheard careless men talking and relayed their words to her."

***

To the King's surprise, his sister arrived at the court the next day, just after mid-day. He was taking Bertha and little Gizzie to the mid-day meal when his sister's escort drew up. The little girls threw themselves into their aunt's arms, laughing and crying so much that no one could determine who was happiest to see whom, Gisela or the girls.

Soon, half the court had come to welcome his sister home. All loved her dearly, even as outspoken as she was. "Nuns," the people would say — nobles and peasants alike -- "serve the Great Ruler. HE gives them leave to chastise us all. Even the King must be moved by his sister's direction."

"Charley," Gisela began later, as she and the King sat in the library. "I've not wished to alarm you; but something must be done for your children. I have received letters from each of them: Charles, Rotrud, Bertha, even a cry of "help" written by Gizzie in one of Rotrud's letters. And most worrisome of all are the requests from Louis in Aquitaine and Pepin in Lombardy. They beg that I do something to improve their sisters' circumstances here in your court. Each of them complains of never seeing you, of being caught between their previous habits (when their mother was alive) and Queen Fastrada's expectations, of being constrained and limited in their daily pursuits."

"The appeals of their teachers and nurses seem to

carry no influence with, or even acknowledgement, from your wife. Fastrada's pregnancy appears to have made things much worse. The present state of affairs cannot continue. Even given their exaggeration of their present circumstance, your girls are truly miserable. Their distress is severe and seems to be increasing. Charles wrote to say that he, Bertha, and Gizzie begged me to let them live with me at the abbey!" She shook her finger at her brother. "Can you imagine--a prince and two princesses who wish to leave court and live among nuns? Rotrud wrote she does all she can to shield them from your wife, but is less and less successful."

"I will not leave here, Brother, until Fastrada makes some accommodation. If necessary, I will confront her myself. Changes MUST be made!" Gisela's eyes were wet with tears. Her whole being reflected her worry for her brother's children, especially the girls. Fastrada had quickly become a stern dictator to her stepchildren. She cared nothing for them, only demanded, day in and day out, that they act like 'princesses.'

"I will not allow this to continue. They are my children as well as yours; I am speaking for Hildegard. Their home cannot become a prison, nor will their buoyant spirits — finally recovering from the grief and loss of their mother — be shadowed or stomped upon." Charlemagne dropped his head, acknowledging his awareness of his children's unhappiness.

King Charlemagne nodded at his sister's words. He determined some time ago that Fastrada was not a mother to his children; she wasn't even a good acquaintance! Fool that he was, he thought she would make an effort to become friends to the younger ones. Little Gizzie was small enough to lean on her, to see her as a mother. But Fastrada was harsh with them, when she thought of them at all. Because of her own pregnancy, the king told her, very clearly, that any child she carried would be loved. But no child would replace another, nor be more important than anyone else. Even though Louis and Pepin were far away, in their own kingdoms, they were his dear wife's boys. No children could ever be as dear to him as Hildegard's. The King smiled but the smile did not hide his sorrow at losing their mother. He re-iterated that loving her children was not a choice he made; it was a fact of his life.

Fastrada made more and more unreasonable demands each day. She carried the "Queen" title far beyond normal bounds! Charlemagne's frown, his stare off into space, his mouth's downward turn all reflected the frustration and sadness coming from this wife. He spread his hands in appeal to his sister.

"I've had no success in controlling her, but I do understand and share your concern for Hildegard's children. I turned my back and did not deal with this wife – her selfishness, her resentment of my daughters, her effort to control anyone she can. I apologize for the trouble, that you needed to make this long journey." He clasped his sister's hands in his own massive ones. "I must control my wife. I love my children and will no longer allow Fastrada to ruin their daily lives nor to compromise their relationships with me."

"Ohh, my dear Hildegard, how much I miss her! She understood my hope for the Frankish people and did all she could to assist me." His eyes filled with tears which he slowly wiped away. "If I had only dealt with Fastrada earlier. I should have seen that no man can be lucky with each woman he marries. Our parents' distressing union should have warned me." He stared at the firepit. "I even had a warning with my second marriage, that disastrous union with Desiderata. It seems I learn very little in the marriage arena." He smiled ruefully at Gisela.

"I'm such a fool, Gisela, such a fool," the King shook

his head.

The last thing Gisela wanted to do was bring trouble into her brother's life. But something had to be done about Frastrada's undermining, hurtful influence on his children, especially the girls. The happiness, responsibility, and sense of belonging that Hildegard was so able to create must not be taken from these children. Their place in the court would last much longer than this troublesome wife. Knowing her, Gisela had little to no concern for her or her needs. Gisela dropped her head. As a nun she should be benevolent to all of them; she knew. But her nephews and nieces were her first concern.

"Give me some order, Charley. Tell me what you wish me to do!" Gisela begged. "I will do anything you ask to restore some peace to my nephews and nieces."

"Let me think upon it, as I should have done long ago, Gisela," the King requested. "Mayhap, I can find a quiet solution which directs Fastrada's energy away from my children. I must not embarrass her. She will be able to take revenge against any of them without my knowledge. And the girls say little...for fear of reprisal. Please give me some time tomorrow, after the mid-day meal. We shall talk again then."

Chapter 3

CHILDREN'S NEEDS

The King begged leave of Alcuin and postponed their meeting to the morrow. He hurried to the stables, hoping that physical activity would help provide a solution for his children's problem.

"Ready my horse," he directed the stable lad, "and find Foxer, my dog. Where can she be? I thought you kept the dogs close by, especially when they're being trained." The King grumbled. "I've neglected her. Knowing that the kennel master is training the pups each day, I should have been spending more time with little Foxer. Else, she will not recognize me as her master. Straug, how does she with the kennel master?"

"Oh, Sire, she do be biddable," the boy exclaimed. "The kennel master praises her right often. She does have her own mind. Ha! But she listens to his directions and obeys as well. She and Master Peppin's bitch keep company. Each likes and protects the other, a little strange in that they both are females. The kennel master took them for a run the day before this one, to practice giving commands and improve their obeying, as he calls it." Charlemagne tried to speak but realized that the young stable hand delighted in recounting his dog's exploits.

He continued with his praise, extolling "Little Foxer's obedience. She did, he offered, bark at the other dogs, either fussing or encouraging them. None of the stable hands were sure of her meaning. She was a 'feisty little thing,' always standing up for a weak pup and for herself. But she didn't make much noise, only occasionally barking at her litter mates. Otherwise, she was unusually quiet.

"I think she would take much punishment, if anyone should so use her. But she do be a loving animal, Sire... always eager for a pat or a rub. She does favor her stomach's being stroked, though. I learned that right quick. She turns on her back before I can blink, gets that stomach up-sided, so to say." Straug was enthusiastic about this pup.

Charlemagne smiled. He'd not anticipated a litany of Foxer's strong qualities, but he was thankful for the observations of the stable lad. The lad's enthusiastic praise shed much light on his little pup, all of it painting her very favorably. *I hope she is characterized truthfully here,* the King thought. *This lad apparently is much fond of my little 'Fox'.*

"I'm pleased she is responding to the kennel master's training, lad," the King answered. "She is a smart, as well as a pretty little thing - all the better if she becomes responsive to commands and knows her place in the pack. She and I will have fine times together. Will you seek her out for me? I want to see if she'll ride on my horse."

The stable lad's eyebrows rose inquiringly at the King's last comment; but, finishing his saddling of the King's mount, he went off whistling and calling the little Foxer's name. He returned in a heartbeat, carrying the pup and stroking her back. King Charlemagne was in his saddle. He reached for the pup. But the lad was not there. He first took Foxer and stood in front of the King's horse, holding her so the two animals could see each other. The horse took a step toward the boy whereupon Foxer licked the horse's nose. The horse snorted but brought his nose around to nudge the little pup.

"Lord, have mercy!" the stable boy cried. "Did you see that, Sire? Seems they be friends already." He grinned with delight and brought the half-grown pup back to the

King. "You know, your pup sleeps in the stables wherever she likes. Mayhap, she and your mount share a bed. That would explain their loving ways to each other. I know this mount not be Samson, your Majesty. Samson, Sire, he was one of a kind! But this one here, he's a strong, biddable horse, ever ready to do his best for you. I have a mind to tell you the story of his training when...."

***

"Nay, my lad," the King interrupted him, chuckling, "not now, if you will spare me. I really must get to the far hills as soon as possible." With that, King Charlemagne turned his reins and left the stables, little Foxer lying across his thighs, the King's hand on her neck. The King rode the morning away, searching for a solution to his children's unhappiness.

As the sun moved below midpoint in the sky, the King whistled for Foxer, gathered her up and remounted his horse. He had come upon the very place where he and his first-born son, Peppin, years ago had discussed Oliver's value. Although saddened by his memory of Oliver, Charlemagne--in remembering his steadiness-- felt more able to deal with Fastrada--truly not a fit queen but his wife, nonetheless.

***

"I've formed only one plan, Gisela," the King whispered to his sister as they began the evening meal. "Let me put it into action and report the results to you. Come to the library tent before you retire this night."

***

"Fastrada," the King called his wife's name, as he entered her room that evening. "I know you believe

44

my children, especially the girls, are ill-mannered and uncontrolled. It's time to prepare them for future roles in the court, so I am seeking your suggestions on methods to improve their behavior."

Fastrada, clearly surprised by King Charlemagne's request, took a moment to gather her thoughts and then responded. "I'm relieved you finally see my concerns, dear," she answered. Fastrada hurried to provide her description of the perfect princess. She demanded they be demure, elegantly clad, and pictures of tranquility. She found Charlemagne's girls too boisterous and careless in their actions. Their bawdy songs challenged her sensibilities – her the queen of innuendo, blatant sexuality, and revealing dress.

My queen would never, the King surmised, *characterize her own past behavior with me as lewd. But, I termed it so then and continue in that belief.*

Fastrada continued her litany of criticism: unacceptable clothing, thanks and kindnesses to the court workers, happy interactions with everyone serving them, and, yet again, their 'sloppy, poorly-fitting clothing'. She feared that Rotrud's tunics would fall from her shoulders, there being so little cloth covering her bosom. The tunic was just a decoration, in any case. Bertha seemed even more unkempt, wearing her hair in extraordinary ways. Fastrada believed she may just not be dressing her hair. It looked like it was never been brushed, never had any long, careful attention.

"Bertha's hair," she declared, "is just like yours: fly-away, and without much substance." Fastrada didn't pause to take a breath.

"And the smaller girl, what IS her name? Oh, aye! Gizzie, she runs about with no shoes, oftentimes in old, worn tunics inherited from Rotrud. The girls' arms are always scratched, sometimes bleeding. Gizzie's hands and feet are filthy. They all have the most unusual manners at table, asking for second helpings and complimenting the cooks on the tasty dishes."

"Of a certainty, Fastrada," Charlemagne's voice hardened, "their mother encouraged them always to be kind to those who served them: maids, stable hands, cooks and servers, gardeners... even field workers."

His obvious acceptance of this did not stop Fastrada's complaints. She damned the children for eating far too many 'delights' and fruits. Their knowledge of the scriptures was miniscule. She admitted that the girls were well-schooled in comportment and manners but mocked their positions by their behavior. None of them reflected Christian behavior, though they were excessively kind to peasants and grateful to stable hands. Fastrada complained of their dashing about on secret errands, always with conspiratorial smiles. Glancing at the king, the Queen's words trailed off. His anger was readily apparent in the red face, puckered lips, and balled fists. She stopped speaking and sketched the girls in torn clothing, hair in disarray, with streaks of dirt on their faces. She could neither read nor write so she sketched. Fastrada knew she had tested Charlemagne's patience. She only hoped her silence would defuse his reaction. The king glared at her and spoke with great care.

"Such descriptions are unnecessary, Fastrada. I will not have my children so misjudged and, then, condemned by your lack of understanding. I have heard enough! Their behavior may not meet your...high...standards; but they are neither as unkempt nor as headstrong as you suggest. I will hear no more of this – not from you are from the lips of other women in this court! I order you: curb your tongue!" Getting his temper under control, King Charlemagne continued.

"As you rightly suggest, my first concern for all my

children rests in the development of Christian values. In addition to instruction in Christian behavior, I now realize they need a model to emulate. And so, I give the task to you."

Fastrada frowned...before her eyes rose in surprise. She didn't want to watch their every move. She deserved freedom from these children. She would **not** be their teacher! It was ludicrous. Charlemagne added that Fastrada should be worthy of their emulation, in her day-to-day activities and in her unworldliness. She must be demure, wear pleasing but undecorated clothes, and style her hair plainly. He added that he also expected her to instruct Charles and Rotrud in Christian virtues in the early hours of the day and do the same for Bertha and Gisela after their mid-day meal. He emphasized that she would need two different approaches for each group. Then, the king apologized for the amount of work all this would entail.

"You will be very busy; I am quite certain." He emphasized, clenching his jaws to keep from smiling as he imagined Fastrada's absence at the noble women's morning gossip sessions. "But, you will agree, this is the most important task you shall ever have. I feel sure the children will be diligent, as well as responsive to your efforts. Please designate others to oversee all other aspects of their lives." He directed. "You will be much too involved in this to waste your time on their daily needs. After your own babe is born, delegate the care of that infant to a Countess. Any of them will be amenable to your directions. All other decisions will be my province," the King declared.

He was much gratified to observe Fastrada's look of horror. He had caught her in her own web and he knew she understood. Queen Fastrada, her face frowning and pale, nodded in agreement as the King left the tent.

***

Fastrada responded immediately to King Charlemagne's command. Her first action was to remove herself from any physical responsibilities for the children. She no longer gave orders for their meals, even the few they took away from the banquet hall. She didn't check on the washing and drying of their garments, didn't concern herself with clothing for royal activities, and never again entered their bedchambers, either in the tents or in the manors as the court stopped. She, who previously demanded their hair be washed every ten days, no longer gave a thought to any cleanliness standard. She abdicated all responsibility for their physical or emotional needs.

Of course, years before Queen Hildegard had instituted daily routines to provide care and support for her children. The individuals responsible for them continued their duties so nothing was amiss. Life went on very much as before but without the criticism or complaints of the queen.

Castle servants washed their clothing in river or stream and spread it across bushes to dry; the ladies of the court sewed and embroidered long and 'short' tunics, used as blouses. Cobblers fashioned shoes from animal hides. And, rarely, the King traded a horse or a pregnant bitch for a piece of gold jewelry. He favored rings for his daughters but, more than once, declared their exchange too dear for his treasury. As if to counteract the lack of jewels, the herbalists often brought amulets containing sweet herbs or dried flowers.

***

On the morrow, after his talk with Queen Fastrada, King Charlemagne sent for Rotrud. As Alcuin left the King, Rotrud turned the corner in the corridor and entered her father's chambers.

"Good morrow, Poppa," she greeted as she walked into the room. "I am responding to your summons." Rotrud sat on a bench covered with an embroidered linen which she knew was her mother's handiwork. She rubbed it softly, remembering Hildegard's love and positive spirit. King Charlemagne saw his daughter's abstracted, sad expression, as well as her hand gently rubbing the stiches.

"You still miss her a great deal, don't you, my girl?" he asked, the sadness reflected in his quiet inquiry. "It is not justice--for children to lose their mother; but it does seem the way of the Frankish world. You had her such a short while; but poor Gizzie hardly knew her. And Fastrada offers no mothering, I know. I did put a grievous burden on you, my child. I beg your forgiveness." Rotrud sat motionless. Never did her father speak of his wife to her...or to any other of his children.

"From Gisela's recent talk with me, I now understand I relied on you to keep your sisters and Charles intact. Such a burden is not a light one, daughter. But now I have a plan--one to relieve you of Fastrada's passion for decorum and one which, I hope, will lighten your interactions with her. I cannot prevent her continuing to command you; but I do relieve you from responding to those commands."

Rotrud looked up quickly at her father's words. The emotions flickering across her face as Charlemagne talked confirmed her difficult interactions with her stepmother. Rotrud guessed that carrying a baby inside you demanded lots of strength, but she thought the queen more and more hateful to them all. She also understood Fastrada's proud, tyrannical nature. She was a mean, selfish woman who managed to get what she wanted, no matter who was hurt. Her Poppa's awareness of Fastrada's resentment surprised Rotrud. But, then, she remembered that her Aunt Gisela had come. She would open his eyes. Her father watched the canopy of emotions play on her face: the disgust, the weariness, the confusion. At his words, Rotrud's head lifted; her eyes brightened; her mouth trembled as the weariness drained from her face. She opened her mouth to respond; but the King continued.

"Aye, to answer your unasked question, my girl. Your Aunt Gisela brought some of her own concerns to my attention. My request to you is this. Henceforth, if you see unfairness from Fastrada toward your siblings, please let me know. It's clear I must oversee everyone in this court and such diligence, of a certainty, must include the Queen - her most of all."

He looked at Rotrud steadily, hoping she saw the frustration and regret he garnered from Fastrada's behavior. Except for Rotrud's embarrassment about his marriage, she was always gentle and accepting of the constraints of rule. His oldest daughter was the only child with whom he could readily share his thoughts and concerns. Rotrud nodded her assent to the king's words, too taken aback to say anything. She excused herself and left.

***

Although Rotrud knew not to take the Queen's displeasure to heart, she still found the 'Christian lessons' painful. In addition to highlighting many 'thou shalt nots,' the Queen emphasized her feelings with shouts of displeasure and sarcastic criticism. But, even those ended soon thereafter. Upon the birth of her own daughter, Fastrada declared she must devote all her energy to her newborn. She no longer had time for the Christianizing of her stepchildren. Charlemagne's children were delighted. The King welcomed her withdrawal from this so-called 'instruction' and passed the duty to Alcuin.

The only child for whom Queen Fastrada appeared to have any concern was Peppin the Hunchback, the King's firstborn, the son of Himiltrude. Years ago, he returned to the court to learn from his father and the Peers. But, because of his back's deformity, all knew he could never rule Frankland - not a single acre of it. Mayhap, Queen Fastrada's concern for Peppin originated because Queen Hildegard was not his mother, but, no matter. She devoted some bit of time to Peppin: championing his swordsmanship by cheering and clapping at his practice, providing richly embroidered tunics on special occasions, and gifting him with a beautiful sorrel horse on his birthday. This attention, directed to the one child, made the King uneasy. But Charlemagne acknowledged his own neglect of Peppin, so he said nothing. Thus, Peppin got a small measure of the Queen's time and her new babe consumed the rest.

***

Just as the court was ready to leave for the Assembly, Peppin's mother, Himiltrude, wrote to ask if Peppin might be allowed to visit her. He left her house more than four years before, with only one visit back in all those months. She yearned, she wrote, to see the lad who was but a boy when he left her home.

Charlemagne was eager for Himiltrude to see their son. In those four, short years, Peppin had grown into a fine young man, well-respected for his courage and perseverance. It was lonely at the court for him, especially after Olivers left; but Angilbert, Alcuin's adopted son, befriended him, as did a few others. Charlemagne was well content. Other men, mostly the Peers, gave Peppin guidance and concern and helped expand his education, his military skills, and his maturation.

"Peppin is a lucky lad," the King remarked, attempting to lessen his own guilt. Now, with Fastrada out of his children's daily activities, Charlemagne felt everyone's general happiness improved. He need have no worry about any of his offspring.

***

Eager to fight his battles before fodder for the horses and oxen died in the fields, Charlemagne began his march to Franconia. There would be many conversations, disagreements, and questions before the army actually began its work, but he must march and fight while there was food to support his animals. For safety, he often left the women and children of his court some distance from the battlefields. There were soldiers to protect them, of a certainty; but they need not be too close to the fighting. The cooks and bakers prepared food which could be delivered by cart and, also, stayed away from the fighting.

Copying his father before him, King Charlemagne had a core contingent of professional soldiers who formed the sturdy center of his fighting strength. No matter how willing, farmers, horsemen, tinkers, and stone masons were generally ineffective – if not disastrous - fighters. Their peaceful life-style did not render them deliberate, trained fighting men. The cavalrymen were expected to be marksman with the bow and, as such, lead the army's direct attacks.

In most confrontations, several groups of foot-soldiers attacked the enemy from many sides, applying Charlemagne's famous 'pincer movement.' In it, he placed the bulk of his men on one side of the enemy. On all the other sides, he sent small contingents of soldiers to attack and, thereby, divert attention from the main assault. And, then, each of his groups would move slowly toward the side opposite them. Effectively, the enemy would slowly be pushed together, making them easier targets for the advancing Frankish soldiers. Bows and spears were the main weapons used by Charlemange's soldiers. The horsemen used swords, as well, but not the foot soldiers.

By the time the Frankish army arrived in Franconia, Rinaldo and Theo had already arrested and imprisoned the men plotting to de-throne the king. There was much murmuring about the squashed rebellion and considerable sympathy for its perpetrators after they were banished to various monasteries. But, eventually, the criticism died down. Nobles and Frankish advisers argued over specific, upcoming battles and planned the military's most effective methods for fighting. Such wars were a yearly occurrence so considerable skill and awareness underlay the fighting techniques, and the pace of the fighting. Once, again, the Frankish army won battles, took prisoners, and expanded the realm a little more.

The rewards of the battle season, in addition to spoils given to each soldier, culminated in the hunt which followed the annual battles. Forest animals were hunted for sport, of a certainty, and for food. None of the men would venture to guess which was the more important reason. The cooks and, even, the stockmasters gave directions to as many men as could be accommodated in the preserving of meat for the cold winter which lay ahead. As in the battles, each person had some responsibility for curing and drying meat and getting it back to villages and manors safely. The strength of the farmers in the spring rested on the foodstuffs they consumed in those bitter, winter months.

***

At last, the hunt was over. Some of the meat, preserved and stored, was for the King's own table; but fighters returning home after this battle season were, also, carrying meat back to their own farms or home villages. The dark chill of winter crept steadily through the days; finally, Christmastide and rest were near. In this winter of 786, Charlemagne's court left for the Aachen manor as most of the soldiers set out for home. The king's plans called for spending an entire fortnight inside the rock-hewn walls surrounding Aachen. Because the manor provided great, warm firepits, a nearby chapel, and spacious bedchambers, many court members hoped Charlemagne would extend their stay. The King especially looked forward to the baths fed by the mountain's warm springs. The Christian injunction for cleanliness was a challenge during the bitter cold days of Frankish winters; the thermal springs made the challenge as nothing in Aachen.

There was a babble of voices as the court arrived in Aachen. People began to unpack their personal belongings and delighted in rediscovering sturdy furniture; large, immovable storage bins; and bedchambers with fireplaces, not pads on the floor of a tent. Each person in the court had some favorite activity, related to Aachen alone. After settling in, each one of them gravitated toward the hot springs and, then, visited with old friends, cleaned and prepared animal furs for clothing and bedding, planned livestock breeding programs for the spring, and rested.

***

For little Gizzie, King Charlemagne's youngest daughter, discovering secret places in the castle was great fun, especially if she came face-to-face with animals. She really didn't prefer one animal above another: rats from the walls, bats from the attic, stray kittens running from everyone. All of them piqued her interest.

And now, trying once more to catch an elusive kitten, Gizzie herself felt a prisoner. Louis, her older brother visiting from his court in Lombardy, found her loitering on the kitchen steps, trying to catch a gray-striped tabby kitten. She did so want a kitten of her very own, one which belonged only to her. But Louis, ever the upright, 'do-as-you-should' brother, took her hand and led her to the day's first lesson.

Gizzie actually didn't need to be encouraged to attend her lessons. She loved her studies. Master Alcuin started the court academy just about the time she was born. *I started learning right off!* Gizzie thought to herself. *Charles, Rotrud and Bertha had to work more than me. They learned the Bible stories; Abbot Fulrad knew all of them. But, numbers are easy for me and they say they can't 'member them.* Of a certainty, Louis and Charles learned in their own courts; but they had no one like Master Alcuin to teach them.

"But no matter how hard I try," Gizzie whispered, "I can't catch one sweet, little kitten!" She tried to pull her arms from Louis' grasp. "Leave me alone, Louie!" she shouted. "Let go. Let me go, I tell you!"

"I will be certain you get there, Gizzie," Louis answered, his mouth turned down, the frown deep between his eyebrows. "You are already late, messing with a horrid, filthy cat. Why can't you act like a king's daughter and behave yourself?" Louis demanded. "Look at your arms. You have scratches all up and down them. Your arms are a mess, just like Mirandie's and she gathers eggs the chickens and geese lay in the brambles! You are a princess. Why can't you stay clean?"

"Clean? Clean and do nothing, just like you? You, you... you're *a dastardly n'er do well.*" Gizzie answered, trying out the cook's description of the butcher. "You act so good the captain of the guard calls you 'Ram Rod Louie.' I don't want a name like that. I want people to like me." Gizzie pulled away quickly and ran to the classroom, leaving Louis with his arm stretched out to grab her again

"It's the truth," Gizzie muttered. "I don't like Louis. All he can say is "do the right thing." In her experience, doing the right thing was almost never any fun; and, oftentimes, other people didn't like you very much. Louis was, also, the court expert in quoting the Bible to anyone who would listen. Sometimes, the quotes didn't make much sense to her. She knew Louis quoted the Bible to get others to be good. But she never paid much attention. She seemed always to be in trouble; but, the truth was, she enjoyed her little scrapes. Poppa didn't mind if she explored, got dirty and hid when people called her. She just had to answer him! Gizzie knew he wanted her to be happy...and she tried to do just that.

All of a sudden, she glimpsed the edge of Rotrud's mantle down the corridor. Louis flew out of her mind. *Oh, there's Rotrud! Wonder if she'll let me ride with her?*

Gizzie opened her mouth to shout to her sister to wait while she got her pony. But her lips snapped shut as she got a close look at Rotrud's face. *She's still sick,* Gizzie thought. *I heard her crying and vomiting her supper in the night. She's sad over that sweet man. He's leaving the court. She likes him sooooo much... but his father is sending him away. I heard her tell Bertha she wants to marry him. Maybe, his father doesn't want a wedding. I know Poppa doesn't...not for us. He says we can't marry. He says we must stay with him forever. That suits me.*

Gizzie opened the schoolroom door, went to her seat and found the daily copying assignment on her desk. *Time to practice my letters again,* she thought as she settled down to work.

"Today we are going to learn something new." Master Alcuin announced to Gizzie's class. "You are going to write a poem. I hope you learn to appreciate all kinds of poetry. I don't expect you to become poets; but I do hope you develop a love for poems. One of the younger teachers is going to talk to you about it. Rembember? We have talked about parables, about tales, and about rhyming stories. Correct? The truth is, you know about poetry already. You've been singing poems...in all your children's games. In addition to having words which sound like each other —

words that rhyme--poems use words in special ways. Let's see what you think of them. Master Angilbert will share some of his poetry with you."

Gizzie loved Master Alcuin. He was always patient with her mistakes, kind, eager to listen to her most recent adventure, and full of praise for her copying ability. If he believed Master Angilbert knew about poetry, it must be true. Gizzie wiped her mind clean of the kitten, of Louis' overbearing personality, of Rotrud's bruised heart and gave her full attention to the study of poetry.

Charlemagne walked by the Aachen classroom and stopped in his stride as he heard laughter coming from the classroom. He opened the door, just a crack. Looking directly inside, he could see Gizzie grinning from ear to ear, clapping her hands in merriment.

"I believe you all would agree that's funny," he heard Alcuin speak loudly, getting the students' attention. "The reading we just heard is, also, a poem. Can anyone tell me how I know this was a poem?"

"...because the words sound the same: 'blow' and 'low', 'side' and 'ride,'" one of the children answered.

"Because the words are fun," another replied.

"Because you said we were going to learn about poetry...and a piece of poetry is a poem," shrieked one very excited young lady.

"All of you are exactly correct," Alcuin praised them. "Now, Master Angilbert is going to read you some poetry about the Christ Child, so we can remember His birth in yet another glorious way. Pay heed now and listen. I wish you good morrow and a wonderful Christmastide. We shall meet again in eight days' time." Alcuin moved toward the door, as the room erupted in cheers and whistles.

"Ahhh, Sire," he acknowledged the King as he slipped out of the classroom. "Would you like to join the poetry class?" His eyes glinted at the King, knowing how much the King admired poets. He even knew King Charlemagne attempted to write a poem or two but was reluctant to let Alcuin see his efforts.

"Not now, Alcuin," the King smiled. "I need your counsel on some other business. Please refresh yourself and join me in the library. We need to talk of the clergy, if you're free before the evening meal."

"Aye, I shall join you there directly, Sire," the Master teacher answered. "I'll change my tunic for the evening so we may talk until time to enter the banquet hall." And he took his leave of the King.

***

Before coming to the library, Charlemagne sent his guardsman for refreshments for Alcuin and himself. It was just after mid-day so he had several hours to confer with Alcuin in the library. The rapid progress which Alcuin made in implementing their educational plans astounded and pleased the King. He was excited about the changes in subjects the students were undertaking, as well as the enthusiasm most of them reflected.

"If this excitement can arise in such a short time among young people," he said – just the evening before - to his sister, "I can hope adults will listen to a few new ideas." His eyes glistened with hope. "I must help Alcuin extend his ideas throughout the realm. And, still, the best unit for reaching the entire kingdom is the clergy. My efforts to have the few learned monks teach the rest are only marginally successful. Progress is much too slow! Mayhap, Alcuin has some methods for applying his educational methods to the holy brothers as well." He grabbed a handful of toasted nuts as he considered other possible teachers. Deep in thought he munched on pecans and walnuts as Alcuin entered the library.

"If those nuts are half again as tasty as your munching

suggests, I must have some, Sire," Alcuin greeted the King. Charlemagne smiled and extended his dish.

Alcuin accepted a handful of nuts and sat down. He thanked King Charlemagne for the court's Christmastide visit to Aachen. He readily saw the happiness and excitement the Frankish court members showed in returning to their favorite manor. The court's traveling schedule was monotonous, moving from abbey to a noble's house, then to a monastery, and next to a count's holding. Aye, each traveler had his favorite destination. For the King, Aachen headed the list.

Alcuin's heart beat the same as his King's; both were committed to educating the people of the realm. To the King's inquiry about his progress in establishing academies, he responded that plans were moving ahead. But, he admitted that he did have one worry.

Charlemagne nodded, indicating Alcuin should voice his concern. "These children vary in their enthusiasm for study, as you would think. It's true; the older ones are being rigorously challenged, I believe. But I do hope, Sire, these demanding days do not eradicate their individual interest in learning. When one is pressured to rethink his past lessons, apply lessons in a different way, and confront misunderstood information, the tendency is to discontinue the process. Most people do give up, Sire, when confronted with their own deficiencies." Alcuin explained.

"I fear for the realm's children. Their lack of learning is not their fault. Throughout your kingdom, there is no fault to be found, just the necessity to provide basic educational experiences." Alcuin expressed his concern. "Alert me to displeasure among the young of the court, would you please?" he begged the King. Alcuin knew all too well the human tendency to deny one's inability to understand or to figure out a problem. In the past, he observed the human's natural reluctance to appear stupid to his acquaintances, be they fellow students, parents, or friends. In order not to be judged, many people would not learn. They would forego knowledge entirely. The Anglo-Saxon scholar continued.

"There is much ignorance among your court population, Sire, and much smugness around ranks of nobility, places held in the court, and relationships with the King. All these values, spouted from parental mouths, make it more difficult to emphasize the joys of learning to my students. Please let me know when the criticisms, reactions and impatience begin. They will surely surface, if they have not already."

"You do over-react, Alcuin," King Charlemagne hastened to reassure Alcuin. He did not want him disquieted. "I told these youngsters to give you their full attention. They will become scholars yet. You shall see their devotion. I have so ordered it!" The King spoke explicitly. The King genuinely believed his orders were all that were needed to motivate the young of his court.

"My son," Alcuin smiled to temper his next words, "It's not possible to order a person to learn. You may establish an expectation, aye. You may provide bribes and rewards to encourage obedience. You may praise those who appear to be following your commands. But, none of those acts will truly lead to learning. I need you to understand, Charles. Not all these students, nor even your adult nobility, will embrace learning willingly! Some of them will resist so strongly they will be unable to learn; they are stubborn and very short-sighted. Many will dismiss you and the value of knowledge; they are fools. But, in the end, there is nothing to be done about such choices. I can only teach those who want learning."

It's so simple, Alcuin thought. *How can he not understand?* And, then, Alcuin had a moment of clarity. *He does not see. He cannot understand because he loves to learn. He is unable to imagine another choice.* Alcuin gave a small prayer of thanks for this king and vowed to support his dream as much as possible. He turned to King Charlemagne. "Aye, as you point out, Sire, there are methods to be applied, techniques to be explained, and content to be presented. But the love of learning comes from the students' hearts. From among the many, there will be a small number who respond in the way you hope. You must not despair of the others. They will work, serve, live their lives as they are able. The learners' lives will change in ways the non-learners can never understand...nor value. But learning is a choice they will make, that only each individual can make. It can never be demanded." Alcuin looked keenly into the King's face.

"You must not expect miracles from these academies. An educated populace could not exist during this king's lifetime; it was impossible. There were not enough days nor enough educated men and women to instruct, to ready the realm. "We can offer reading, writing, mathematical understanding to everyone. But philosophy, the theoretical bases of science and literature, the theological doctrine which you so love to debate, these will not be in the province of our students. Only those who yearn to become scholars will have the strength and the interest to continue to pursue knowledge. And that pursuit is a lifetime quest. Such 'learners' always represent a handful of the people! But their influence, certainly, is far more substantial than their numbers."

"Hell, Alcuin! I dream of discussions, debates, lectures given by invigorated and informed thinkers!" the King shouted. "I wish my people to understand, to act from conviction and evaluation, to become truly knowledgeable. Where will the philosophers go to seek answers to their questions; who will be their comrades; who will appreciate their lives—the life of the mind?"

"Exactly, Sire," Alcuin shook his head. "I am telling you this. The level of education obtained by your people will be determined by your people, one by one. Your preference, your hope, your wishes have power only in offering a choice and in providing teachers. Some will choose to become scholars and reflect all these capabilities you value. Some of the people will be happy with reading, writing, and understanding the basics of numbers. Some will reject all of it. You must understand. It is not your choice! You will live within a realm of people who reflect many different levels of learning, the level each one chooses for himself. Do you see my distinction? You and I may live to give the realm the opportunity for learning. But all will not seize the opportunity; some will not even understand it."

King Charlemagne nodded his head. "So be it, Alcuin," the King declared but he could influence, he could pressure people to improve their learning. He would impose certain expectations on the clergy.

He could do that as king. As the head of the Church in this realm, he would set standards for those who serve the Church. He would no longer accept unlettered holy men. The lads must come to the monasteries, the girls to the abbeys, and educate themselves at a basic level. Only if they obtained this minimal level would they be welcomed as monks or nuns. "I can do that, Alcuin, correct?" He asked.

The King demanded a response from Alcuin whom, he hoped, would guarantee literacy throughout his kingdom. As Alcuin spoke, King Charlemagne realized acquiring knowledge was an individual choice. He expected to impose a base of learning. Now, he saw this was impossible. But he would demand it where he could.

"Let a brother try to head a scriptorium, if he cannot recognize fine literature." King Charlemagne threatened.

"Let a soldier attempt to rise in the ranks, if he cannot sum and divide. Think you a Count able to command a contingent if he does not understand subtlety and tactics? It may be as you say, Alcuin, it may be. But such men will not be a part of my court, my clergy, or the affairs of my realm!" The King was adamant. Charlemagne sighed and breathed deeply, his heart breaking with disappointment. He changed the direction of their discussion.

"On a different subject, Alcuin, I wish you to read my completed 'Capitulare de Litteris Colendis.' I am much interested in your reaction," the King declared.

"Of a certainty, my King," Alcuin beamed. "I did not realize you were writing capitularies for education, as well as for church protocol! Sire, how long have you labored on this?" Alcuin was surprised. *Where did the King find the time to undertake such a study?* He wondered.

"There is great need for directions on teaching the study of letters. I do anticipate this reading, Sire." Alcuin grinned in enthusiasm. Here was another side of his King!

Alcuin inclined his head toward the King, giving his praise in a quiet, impressive manner. He has good instincts, the scholar thought, but it is not possible to force people to learn. *Knowledge he has always respected but that's not true among the peoples of his realm or, even, among the people of his court. I daresay he has only two thinkers among his children--Rotrud and Bertha-- and three others in the entire court: Angilbert, Theo, and Rinaldo. If the scholars I seek come to Aachen, our influence will be great and, mayhap, we can create a community of learners. How excellent…if only Aachen can become a beacon of light in this illiterate world!* Alcuin stopped in his musing. *If Aachen becomes this beacon of light, piercing the sea of ignorance, what will our king be?* His eyes settled on the far horizon, outside the window, as he thought about the question.

He is the foundation of our beacon, emanating conviction

and hope, Alcuin decided. *He is the only ruler, the only ruler who burns –sometimes in fits and starts, sometimes steadily. ... such a beacon in these dark times, burning to light the way to knowledge and life for all!*

Alcuin could see the King's mind close on his educational concern for the young and revert to his mission of educating the clergy. His vast organizational ability allowed him to compartmentalize every issue. *I suppose he must do that in order to maintain the clarity of decisions,* Alcuin mused. *And he is a master of decision-maybe because others' feelings are of no concern to him. I would not have his duty for all the books world-wide.* Alcuin shocked himself with this unbidden thought but knew it was true.

"You were not here, Alcuin," King Charlemagne began, "when we reorganized the administration of the realm. I propose we apply the same principles to the Church in our Frankish realm. We must initiate significant change. I know there will be resistance, powerful resistance. I have visited each Bishop within the last four years. There is the explanation for some of our Christmastide locations. Ha!"

He laughed, recounting the grumbles of his court. They hated the remote locations he chose, thought the king was punishing them. In fact, he was examining the priests' literacy, determining the educational offerings available to novitiates and brothers alike, and evaluating each church's ability to offer education to the populace. He found that all the Bishops were able to read and write. In most of the churches, whether there be a monastery or an abbey attached to it, the Bishop was the *only* churchman who had even basic skills. Many of them tried to teach their followers within the Church; but a great number did nothing.

"I replaced some of these Bishops but have not the number of replacements I need. After remedial instruction, I hope some brothers may be promoted to these unfilled places and others may replace the nonreaders holding them. Oh, aye, I know it will be painful." The King held his hands out.

Then, he changed the subject and asked Alcuin to create a coinage system for the realm. To use in place of bartering but the people had to have something of value to buy and sell. He knew the bartering system would not disappear but the exchange of coins for products would help Frankland's economy along. In his enthusiasm, the king waved his hand about, his voice rising with hope.

He assured Alcuin that the Church would benefit most of all. When people had food and shelter, that peace of mind would enable them to consider holy thoughts.

"Education must flow into the population. I demand it! I will have it so!" Charlemagne bellowed. Seeing Alcuin's attention, he lowered his voice. "I know it will be unsettling. Churchmen will be displaced. Many will feel unfairly judged. But so be it!" The King's face was red, his eyes wide, his arms waving about again.

He continued with his sermon as Alcuin smiled in spite of himself. He looked down at the floor to cover his response. The King continued to expound on his dream… to the one man who already understood and approved of it. Mourning the people's holding to their old priorities, Charlemagne wanted power and influence, obtained from birth parents, replaced by thought and knowledge. There was no time to lose, he insisted. Changes were coming, whether from the enemies he defeated and, then, welcomed into his realm or from neighboring tribes who moved into Frankland for protection. People must help themselves. And in accomplishing this, his government must prepare them…teaching them to read, write, and think. If present clergy cannot learn to read basic scriptures in two to four years of study, we must school clergymen who can. The way must be open for those who are able!

"I do not mean to be a despot, Alcuin. But I see no other course."

Alcuin nodded and described Lord Theo's description of the reorganization begun to govern the realm. The Scholar complimented the King on the revised court system and his improvements. He praised the now reliable reports which constantly updated awareness of events throughout Frankland: relocation of tribes, newly established efforts to breed horses, train more blacksmiths, organize families into groups of farmers, etc. With up-to-date information, the king would be better able to provide oversight for new endeavors. All of this would, of course, be a boon for the Church as well.

But, Alcuin hastened to add a warning. The King must prepare himself for resistance — mayhap, outright defiance. Alcuin paused for Charlemagne to absorb his warning.

"You are the King and defender of the Church so your will shall prevail. But we need to examine this reorganization model methodically step-by-step. That way, no one can accuse us of indiscriminate or haphazard application. Both promotions and demotions must follow established procedures or the process itself will have no validity, certainly not for the clergy who are replaced."

"Aye, Aye, I know that!" the King acknowledged impatiently. "It will be as you say, Alcuin."

But Alcuin knew otherwise. He, also, heard Theo's lament over the exceptions made among the lords and nobles chosen during the administrative reorganization. Nobles said a shared interest with the King in hunting guaranteed one a dukedom. A standing contingent of soldiers in the army promised land rewards; even a gift of horses or herd of cattle would likely earn a title at court. *If I might be spared the politics and keep to my educating,* Alcuin dreamed, *my efforts would be far more fruitful.*

Chapter 4

PEPPIN'S HOME

This conversation between the King and Alcuin took place just as Peppin - the King's first-born, hunchback son - prepared for his journey back to his mother's house. He was eager to return home; he had not visited once since coming to the court.

Peppin believed his mother would be pleased with his physical growth, as well as his ability to conduct himself around others. *I was so shy growing up,* Peppin thought. *Much of it had to do with the deformity, of course; but I had so few men from whom I could learn. Mother will think I am modeling myself on Poppa; but she does not know the influence Lord Oliver had on me. He is the one who formed me...with his gentle, courageous ways. His leaving the court was my greatest loss. None of them know the regard I have for him, though Poppa suspects...not that he likes it. I know Angilbert would have valued him, if he had only been in the court while Lord Oliver was here. Oh, the world is a story of lost friends and lonely undertakings, is it not?*

***

As Peppin cinched his saddle, Charles, the King's second-born son and his heir, walked into the stables. He clapped Peppin on the shoulder and handed him a leather bag.

"Just a diversion for your journey, Peppin," Charles began. "I wish you God-speed and a wonderful reunion. It must be fine to return home, more grown-up and confident than when you left." Charles smiled to show he was sincere in his good wishes. His hand on Peppin's shoulder tightened. "I shall surely miss you, Peppin. Take good care of yourself...and be alert on the road. Oh, I know you go with an escort. But so-called 'outings' and 'pleasure trips' cause soldiers to grow careless; they will not be at their best. I do not fear for you; but, all the same, wariness is a virtue I would that you adopt."

Peppin swallowed the lump in his throat. Charles' good wishes were totally unexpected, especially coming to the stables to send him on his way. It was a characteristic gesture of his young half-brother, the sibling who was the most kind to him. Striking a cocky pose, Peppin asked.

"Charles, what's in the bag... an oats ball for my mount, here? You have been very thoughtful...to bid me a safe journey." Peppin sobered as Charles untied the bag and nodded for him to open it.

There in the bag was a rolled parchment, entitled Philosophy of the Masters, and a cunning boot knife resting in an embroidered cover. "Oh, Charles," Peppin murmured as Charles looked on good-naturedly.

Charles could see Peppin's surprise and delight and, beneath both, a real, unfeigned thankfulness. Both of the lads felt surprise as they realized their genuine concern, each for the other. But they hid these emotions from each other.

"Thank you for these, both the parchment and the knife! What a perfect combination of gifts. Thanks for your thoughtfulness, Charles." Peppin glowed at his brother. "You have made this leave-taking joyous, indeed!"

"Never doubt it, Peppin. I wish you well." Charles responded, gratified that Pepin liked the gifts. "Be on your way before the day is old. Stay safe." He slapped the rump of Peppin's mount as Peppin settled in his saddle, nodded at the head of the escort, and waved Peppin on. Peppin turned to Charles, waved heartily, and began his journey home.

***

The journey to his mother's manor was uneventful. Although Peppin stayed alert, as Charles directed, there were no threats along the way. Even the weather cooperated, being mild and rain-free for the entire journey.

Traveling was a pleasure. The green expanse of spring stretched as far as the eye could see. The buds of daffodils, crocuses, and wild flowers were just before bursting. And those early robin returnees busily pecked the ground for worms and insect larvae. There was a bit of frost one morning, their third one on the road; but it was more brisk and invigorating than troublesome.

Peppin and his escort camped in the open, shared in hunting for their evening meal, and exchanged guard duty during the night. At court, Peppin often trained with several of the men in the group. They quickly fell into the comradeship of patrolling soldiers and enjoyed the relief from more strenuous duties. Within four days' time, the small party was less than a day's travel from Himiltrude's home.

His mother's small but prosperous manor, sat near the foothills of a mountain, surrounded by forests and plowed fields. Peppin knew it was too soon to see the house but he strained his eyes at the horizon, none-the-less. As the early morning mist lifted, a sunny day dawned. Peppin and his escort set out. After a mid-day break to rest the horses and enjoy a cold meal, Peppin rode quickly ahead to greet his mother.

***

Tears ran down Himiltrude's cheeks even before Peppin left his escort behind and cantered toward her. It's been so long without my son, she thought, though I know his being at court was necessary. *I even asked for it. God help me! I just hope I don't have to lose him again too soon, that he does not have to return quickly. I know he's well-off there; he has a place nothing here can match. But I do so yearn to hear his voice, to anticipate his footfall coming toward my chamber. My dear boy, thank the dear Lord God! You are finally home!* Restraining her delight, Himiltrude stood quietly as Peppin rode the last one-half furlough home.

"He looks so tall in his saddle," she commented to his old nurse. "He is a man, now,Yevette. And how like my brother he rides!"

Peppin was off his horse, running to hoist his dear mother into the air and plant kisses all over her face. "Mother, Mother," he cried. "How fine it is to see you, once again. It's been far too long." His mother wept through her smiles and repeatedly gave him hugs, too overcome to speak through her tears.

"There's no need for weeping, Mother; I am come to stay awhile." Beyond his excitement and love of his mother was a growing concern. Was she always so thin? He asked himself. Peppin thought, maybe he had forgotten how little his mother was. He hoped she wasn't ill. She felt so light a wind might blow her away. He reached out to hug her again, holding her close. The remembered scent of her hair waylaid his fears.

"Oh, Mother, I am so happy to be home, at last." He whispered.

"Come, come, my son. Let's go inside and share news of our lives since we parted," Himiltrude said. "But, first, there are people who have waited impatiently for your return." She opened her arms as the members of the household hurried up to her son. The cook, the baker, the stablehands, and the farmers all rushed over to him, hugging and exclaiming 'how much you've grown!" The youngest maid assured him that the household, as soon as they got King Charlemagne's message, undertook an orgy of cleaning, cooking, polishing, gathering and cooking some more!" Himiltrude smiled at everyone, even as the tears pooled in her eyes and, then, ran down her cheeks.

They squeezed his shoulders, kissed his cheek, asked after his health. Peppin beamed at them all; he was in the bosom of his true family. His mother and her household members anticipated his every need, for — truth be told — his wants were very few. All that could be done to welcome him was complete. He looked happily at all his friends, smiled with great enthusiasm, and gave as many kisses and well-wishes as he received. The cook began to recite the foods waiting for him--most especially the 'delights'. The kitchen workers each asked if there were any particular dish which would tempt his palate.

"I must get out and ride, perhaps I shall run alongside my horse," Peppin joked with his mother. "All this attention, especially to my belly, will expand it until you all urge me *not* to eat." He laughed. "I am so delighted to be home; can't fathom why I didn't come sooner," he added as he gave his mother yet another kiss.

"My dear," his mother began, "you can't know the excitement here. We yearned so for you, even grieved a bit, I daresay. But you are here now. And I must tell you something. In a few days' time, we shall receive a visitor. This visit, planned for months, was set just as I received your father's letter. I hope you won't feel slighted. The visit will be only three days' duration; a mere moment in your time here. You are not displeased, my dear, are you?" she worried.

"Nay, nay, Mother," Peppin replied. "I will be delighted

to receive anyone who is your acquaintance. Don't worry. As you say, this will be a small break for us all. After the visitor's departure, we shall return to our homecoming, refreshed for the break from it. Who will be our visitor? Do I know the person?"

"Although it does seem strange," Himlitrude began, "we will be seeing Adelchis again. He heard of your return home and yearned to see you for himself." She shook her head sadly. "Since you left, we seldom visit Septimania. What wonderful days we all shared there!" She saw Peppin's confusion. "He returned to Byzantium about the time you settled in your father's court. He visits as often as he can but plans often keep him in Constaninople." Peppin's face lit up.

Adelchis was more a father to him than any other man. Throughout Peppin's childhood, he and his mother spent many weeks with Adelchis, sometimes at his little-known manor in Septimania and sometimes at his mother's manor. These two were his true parents.

"Adelchis?" Peppin exclaimed. "But is it not dangerous for him to be in Frankland? I'm sure Poppa would be incensed, if he knew he were anywhere in the realm. Mother, we must not become careless. Adelchis is taking a great risk. Don't you think so?" Peppin asked in great alarm.

Peppin knew forgiveness was not in his father's character. Adelchis' father, Desiderius, the Duke of Lombardy, openly fought to take the Frankish realm from Charlemagne. All in the court damned Adelchis, though the King appeared not to share their opinion. Only once did Peppin hear the King speak of Adelchis and, then, Charlemagne was kind in his praise of the prince.

"Poppa does love him; of that I am sure, Mother." Peppin offered. "But after Poppa's defeat of Desiderius and Adelchis' flight out of Lombardy, Poppa deemed him a traitor. You know, I even asked Poppa if he were sure Adelchis fought in the battle; but he would never answer - just said: 'like father, like son.' I don't know the full story, of a certainty."

"As always, Adelchis comes in stealth." Himilitrude confirmed. "He has visited here several times since his return to Byzantium. He is always vigilant and comes disguised." Noting Peppin's confusion, she added: "He will explain it all to you. Our friendship is long-standing, remember the fun we all used to have together?"

Peppin, noting the color in her face and her shy pronunciation of Adelchis' name, looked at her closely. Naturally, I know that. Peppin thought. He knew his mother cared deeply for the former prince of Lombardy; they both did. He just didn't want her or Adelchis hurt by the foibles of the King!

"A courier brought a letter three days ago. Adelchis wrote he was leaving Constaninople and would be arriving within seven or eight days. But he will not linger; he never stays more than three evenings - playing it safe, he says." At Peppin's frown, she added. "He cannot, dear. The danger is too great."

"Except for you, Mother, he's the person I most wish to see. Adelchis is a wonderful part of my life—the part that represents love, security, and concern. He ever watched over me. I do love him for making this journey...though its danger is worrying." Peppin accepted yet another cup of herbal tea from Marsta, the young woman who had been his childhood friend. He smiled into her happy face and mouthed his thanks.

"Somehow, all the people of this manor...including Adelchis...made me feel special and cherished. It was not until I entered the Frankish court that my humpback preceded me everywhere. Oh, don't worry, Mother! I'm a big boy now. It is of no consequence—what others say and do. I grew a very tough exterior." He raised his cup to all in the room and beamed, emphasizing his happiness at being back among them. Peppin said this with no pain and no apology. Of necessity, he dealt with realities and things as they were. If not, by now, he would be quite mad.

"Adelchis did not want to interrupt your homecoming; but I knew you would be glad to see him, dear." Himiltrude said. "We often talk of you and our old times together. He tells me of the blessing you are in his life...and in mine, of course. And he is completely correct." With that, Himiltrude closed the discussion. Peppin did not mention Adelchis again. He watched his mother, trying to evaluate her health. The more time he spent with her, the greater he worried. She seemed so fragile!

***

The following morning Peppin walked up the narrow path into the mountains, delighting in the new leaves of the oak and birch trees. He remembered when he measured his own growth by seeing how far around the largest oak his arms could stretch. The canopy of leaves, the sunshine filtering through in patches, reminded Peppin of his childhood. He heard a gurgling nearby, pushed aside a bush tangled with vines, and found a small stream tinkling toward the river. He stopped to get his bearings, looked closely at the trail and suddenly saw the entrance into Jason's cave. He was the only herbalist for many furloughs.

The herbalist, spreading roots to dry on a blanket, looked much older than Peppin remembered. He appeared to be inventorying his herbal stores: classifying his herbs and placing them in what seemed to be a new storage case. The case, full of little pouches with ties, lay on the table, all the ties loosened. Most of the pouches were empty.

"Good morn, Jaston," Peppin greeted him. "I hope you

remember me fondly, if possible."

"Ahhhh, Peppin, of course. Welcome home, son! Everyone in your mother's manor came to tell me of your visit. The happiness from that house soothed us all for weeks. My boy, what a fine man you've become! You look like your mother, of a certainty; but I can see a bit of Charlemagne in you now. You have his hair color and a bit of his gait, seems more pronounced than when you were a lad. You appear healthy and fit, my boy. How are you...truly?" the old man inquired. He radiated the pungent smell of dried herbs. He dried and stored them in the spacious cave behind the stream and lived there as well. Peppin smelled his ever-warming peppermint tea and noted the small piles of newly picked herbs.

"I'm fine and happy to see you still at your work. You lessened many an illness for me. I remember your quiet kindness and your fresh smell — always of rosemary, sage, and dill. An odd combination, mayhap, but reminiscent of you." Peppin replied.

Jaston bowed his head at Peppin's words. It was good to be remembered in such positive ways. He thanked Peppin for his kind words and squeezed his arm. Pepin got right to the point.

"Jaston, what's wrong with my mother?" He asked with poorly-concealed concern. "She is so thin; I can feel her ribs with my fingers. Her face is much the same, some older, I daresay, though I'll never mention that to her. But her color...she is so very pale! Her eyes no longer sparkle; her hair is dry to the touch. Tell me that this is not a grave illness. Jaston looked over Peppin's shoulder, his forehead furrowed. "Let me be clear; she has said nothing to me, though the opportunity presented itself. Did she seek advice from you? It is too soon for her special tonic, isn't it? Have you seen her recently?"

The herbalist looked directly into Peppin's eyes. Noting

his serious concern, he answered. "Sit down, Peppin. Let's have a drink and some fruit. Then, I shall answer your questions." Peppin felt his stomach drop. The grave look Jaston gave him confirmed his worse fears for his mother. The healer brought an herbal drink and a wooden platter heaped with dried pears, peaches, and tart grapes. When they ate their fill, Jaston set aside their flagons.

"And, now, for your questions, lad. Aye, your mother is ill. She is quite seriously ill, Peppin. She knows her health is not as it was; but the gravity of it, she does not understand." Tears rushed into Peppin's eyes; he hunched over, trying not to weep aloud. Jaston acknowledged that he had not spoken with Himiltrude about the illness, not knowing the best advice to give her should she ask him what to do. He admitted he could give Peppin no advice either. The truth was, he declared, there was little to be done to halt the illness. His mother's illness was a 'wasting' disease, inside her stomach or breathing cavity. His herbs would ease her pain; but such pain often appeared near the end of the illness, possibly only in the last few days. The herbalist rose to get more drink for Peppin. He laced the liquid with chamomile and a little milk of the poppy. Such grave news was difficult to accept. He hoped the drink would dull the shock.

Peppin did not stir, his mind busy with unanswerable questions. My *mother is dying? Why did I stay away so long? Did my being away hasten her illness? What will Poppa think, or feel, when he hears the news? What do I do? What's going to happen?*

Jaston handed Peppin the flagon, indicating he should drink. Peppin dutifully did exactly as was expected of him. In fact, he took three huge gulps of the liquid. Jaston nodded his head in encouragement.

"Drink as much as you can, lad. This is disturbing news, I know. First, let me be clear. I only just discovered the illness, two weeks ago. There was a sharp turn in the wet weather we've been having, three dry days with promise of more to come. I took the opportunity to visit your mother's small manor. Every year I check on each one in the house, prescribing tonics, evaluating health, that sort of thing. Some people, you know, need an herbal brew to boost them out of the winter mindset. They feel dull and disinterested in their surroundings. One of my herbal concoctions gives them a 'zing,' helps them move on into reawakening, just as spring reawakens the earth."

"Anyway, I spoke with your mother, just like all the rest. She said she slept poorly, that the trouble began in late winter and was with her yet. She admitted to being very tired. After noting the paleness of her face, I gave her a spring tonic. She told me her weight plummeted during the winter and she complained about the dryness of her hair. She suspects some body rhythm is out of balance." He placed his hand on the young man's shoulder and gave it a squeeze. He repeated that the illness was grave and even though her distress was pronounced, it was not yet debilitating.

He assured Peppin there was nothing anyone could have done to delay or to prevent this illness. It struck old and young alike and he was unable to find a reason for its attack on one person but not on another.

Jaston gave Peppin all the information he had. The illness appeared to strike more women than men and; because of that, there might be some connection to child-bearing. But he could not be certain. Men, also, succumbed to it. If there were any positive thing to say about it, he could attest there was very little pain. And the pain appeared only in the final days of the disease's progression. He fell silent to allow Pepin time to absorb the news. Then, he asked if there were anyone Peppin wished to let know. This was a grievous burden, more so as he just returned home.

"Nay, Jaston, nay." Peppin responded. "Mother and I, there's always been just the two of us and Adelchis, of a certainty. I thought she seemed very weak, weak and slight—almost like a newborn bird. Her limbs appear just as thin and unsubstantial as a chick."

"I can't predict the course of her illness," Jaston responded. "Sometimes, a person is hearty and engaged until just days before the end. Other people so afflicted decrease slowly by inches, barely seeming themselves as the end draws near. I do so wish I could anticipate the next months, my son; but I cannot. If it be possible, perhaps you could stay near...at least until we see how the illness is progressing."

"Of a certainty!" Peppin replied. "I could never leave her, not now." He was not needed at King Charlemagne's court, in any case. He could be here indefinitely and so he said to Jaston.

"Dear God, what will I do? Should I tell her?" Peppin thanked Jaston for his time and his forthrightness. And asked for Jaston's help as the illness progressed. He, then, asked Jaston to define his mother's needs clearly, as they walked this path together. Peppin briefly held the old herbalist's hand in his. Jaston put his arms around Peppin and gave him a brief hug.

"I'm here for you and for her." Jaston responded. "Be brave, for your mother's sake. Though the words sound trite now, I must remind you; life is transitory, filled with good and evil. You've enriched your mother's life fourfold. As far as I see, she has no regrets about her choices, absolutely none about you. She doesn't even regret the time you were in the King's court. That, she said, was necessary...for both of you."

"Be gentle with her, my boy; but, also, with yourself. Your presence will soften her path. Know this from your old healer."

"I thank you, Jaston, not only for your care but for your comfort." Peppin replied as he left the herbalist's cave and turned toward home.

***

Drawing close to the manor, Peppin's heart sank. There in the distance was a small dust cloud, clear warning that a small party headed toward his mother's home. "Now, who can that be?" Peppin wondered. "We received no word of plans for visitors." He knew the group must be headed toward Himiltrude's manor; there was no other habitation for several miles.

"Oh, yes," Peppin remembered. "This must be Adelchis!" He nudged his mount, anxious to get home; change his clothing; and prepare to welcome his true father. Adelchis' being here would help him deal with this deep sadness, though he feared his tears would leak out... at the most inappropriate time. To home, then, and to a short break from this sorrow.

By riding quickly across the fields, Peppin reached the house; raced to his chamber; changed his tunic; and, then, entered the courtyard - just before a small group reined in their mounts. His mother stayed inside, giving him the honor of welcoming their guests. Peppin suspected today's nip in the air was too much for her and readily agreed to the duty.

***

Peppin stepped forward to greet the tall, stately man on the beautiful roan stallion. "Were you an enemy to this house, Sire, I would still welcome the owner of such an animal," Peppin stated. He surprised himself with this statement and hurriedly continued. "Oh, forgive me, Sir!

You're indeed welcome...even without your horse. I extend the hospitality of this house to you and to your escort. They may find places in the rooms attached to the stable, to the right, Sire." Peppin feared his words embarrassed his mother. He did not want Adelchis to think him lacking in courtesy.

"I've never seen such a magnificent animal," he said by way of apology. "He caused me to lose my senses." So saying, he tore his eyes from the stallion and, once again, looked at his guest.

Lord Adelchis nodded solemnly and spoke. "I welcome the hospitality of your house, Peppin and your presence, at last. Though we may now be strangers to each other, I remember our previous contacts with pleasure. As a young boy, you did delight my heart. I expect no less of the man. How excellent it is to see you once more, after all these years!" Adelchis beamed at Peppin, weighing and attending to his behavior, as well as his words.

He is as gracious as I remember. Adelchis thought. *It seems my mount overwhelms the lad. At least, the boy knows a good horse, knowledge which he did not attain here.*

"I trust your mother is well," he added, concerned that Himiltrude did not appear to welcome him. *This is very unlike her.*

"Please dismount, Sire, and be welcome," Peppin responded. "Mother eagerly awaits your appearance in the hall. Because of the demanding weather, she wishes to provide refreshments as soon as you enter. We have several hours before the evening meal. Come in and refresh yourself. It's wonderful to see you." He stepped to hold Prince Adelchis's reins as he dismounted. The horse reached over to nip at his sleeve, surprising Peppin with his gentle touch.

"I think he dislikes my holding his reins, Sire," Peppin laughed, "but he's greeting me, it seems." He released the reins and rubbed the horse behind the ears. Then, he turned to hug Adelchis. "I am so happy to see you!"

"He is wise in identifying those who like horses, Peppin," Adelchis answered. "I have yet to see him misjudge a man." Adelchis laughed. This was one of his methods of evaluating men, letting his horse close enough to touch them. If his horse did not move close to the man, Adelchis was very wary of him. Smiling, Adelchis dismissed his men and entered the cool manor entrance with Peppin.

Himlitrude greeted Adelchis in the doorway, thinking 'to hell with it,' and hugging him herself. "I'm so glad you've come! It's been much too long since your last visit. Please, come into the library. Let's have some juice and fruit. You must have need of a drink, riding in this heat."

"Thank you, my dear," Adelchis answered, "I feel I, too, am home – much like Peppin, of a certainty." Adelchis maintained his always gracious composure but Peppin saw the shock on his face as the older man looked at Himiltrude. "Have you been well?" Adelchis immediately realized his question. "You're more beautiful than ever. How can you retain such charm as I age before my eyes every day?" He beamed at Himiltrude, still holding her hands in his. In that moment, Peppin knew these two held very deep feelings for each other. The looks they exchanged and the oneness about them testified to their regard one for the other. They moved toward the library, talking quietly to each other, completely oblivious to anything else.

Peppin interrupted their conversation and apologized. He must, he explained, change his footwear for it was pinching his toes. He promised to return immediately.

Peppin sat on the bed in his chamber, suddenly realizing that his mother and Adelchis had loved each other for years. He had only to think back to his childhood and their idyllic days together. They deserved a bit of time alone.

Their need of it was obvious, even to his untutored eyes.

***

Peppin lingered until he feared his mother would reprimand his rudeness. Then, he returned to the library. Himiltrude and Adelchis sat across from each other, drinking tea and chatting quietly. Peppin could see the worry for his mother in Adelchis' eyes, as he looked quickly into Peppin's face. Peppin shook his head very slightly and went to give his mother a kiss.

"Isn't she remarkable, Prince Adelchis? I've been away for almost four years and she's as beautiful today as the day I left. She's the world's most beautiful and loving woman," he added. "Of a certainty, some would say all sons believe that of their mothers. I know this is not true. But she is my miracle, in any case." He searched Adelchis' face.

"She is a wonder; I agree with you, Peppin," Adelchis answered, his conviction echoing in his response. "But, then, I consider both of you remarkable. You blossomed under very trying circumstances. Your mother moved with you to an unknown place, nourished you, delighted in your growing skills, and provided a supportive environment for your development." He quietly kissed Himiltrude's hands. "You, in turn, became an attractive, courteous (here Prince Adelchis smiled), and compassionate young man. You're both to be commended."

"I've always felt blessed to call your mother my friend; and, now, I hope to have the same honor from you." Prince Adelchis continued. "I appreciate your discretion in allowing us to reminisce for a bit, as well." Adelchis added, his eyes twinkling, his lips curving into a rueful smile.

Chapter 5

RESCUE WITH LOVE

Himiltrude gave a hand to each man, one on each side of her, and said: "And, now, it's your time to re-establish your acquaintance. I wish to check with the cook to verify preparations for our evening meal. I'm getting hungry! If you want more fruit, let me know. Talk. Have some wine, if you like." She turned to Peppin. "You know where the mead is, Peppin. When our evening meal is served, Dorva will summon you. The servers will ring four bells to alert you. Please excuse me." She left the library. In a moment, her head popped back inside the door.

"Adelchis," she said, "Peppin will have many questions. Feel free to answer them, any of them, as you will," she directed and disappeared. Adelchis frowned, a little loss and unsure of Himiltrude's intent. As he turned, Peppin began speaking.

"Prince Adelchis, please know. You're under no obligation to explain any of your actions to me. You are my mother's friend and were always a father to me. I am fortunate that you're here. I can't thank you enough for coming." Peppin struggled to hold his tears; his mother's delight in their visitor tore at his heart. "My wish is always to see her face and heart as carefree as they are at this moment. You are much welcome."

Peppin had no intention of saying these words; he surprised himself. But he didn't regret a single word he uttered. His mother's happiness was now his single concern. He hoped delight during the last days of her life would counter some of the very difficult days she had both with and without his father. She told him long ago their marriage dissolved because the King loss interest in her. He found her boring, she recounted. But Peppin knew his own hunch-back was a great tragedy for the ambitious prince and, eventually, a liability. It alone was reason enough to put his mother away. Peppin recognized his mother's selflessness in her support of him and, also, knew this characteristic wasn't applicable to all mothers.

Look at Queen Fastrada, he thought; she will willingly sacrifice anyone for her own rising. "Her dislike of Poppa's children is obvious to anyone with eyes. She even spoke to me of an exalted position when her secret rebellion succeeds. Because she seems to know so much, I believe she had something to do with the plan to imprison Poppa, the one he discovered led by Count Hadrad in Franconia. But, if Poppa suspects her, no one knows it." He muttered under his breath. Adelchis was examining the new parchments on the library shelves. Peppin drew his thoughts away and turned to the prince.

"You saw Mother and me, Adelchis, back when I was young. Being in court, you can imagine the life I would have had there…as the damaged son of a warrior father. Our banishment was a reaction to my humpback, not to any deficiencies in her. Truly, I owe my mother for a life without bitterness. She loved and fought for me every day, never denying or bewailing my hunch back. Her joyous approach to life defined my childhood and encouraged me to value myself. And," he told Adelchis, "she deserves some happiness in return for her sacrifices." Adelchis nodded very slowly and stared at the floor.

"She is very ill, is she not?" Adelchis asked, tears standing in his eyes. "She has shed two or more stone's weight since I saw her last. And that beautiful, lush hair is gone. What's wrong, Peppin? Do you have any idea? I know you've just arrived here yourself." Prince Adelchis sat heavily, holding his head in his hands, trying to shield his anguish from Peppin.

"Aye, she is very ill." Peppin replied slowly. "I spoke with the herbalist today, just before you arrived. You've already guessed the serious nature of her condition. Mother is dying. Forgive me, Sire, for being so blunt." Peppin put his hand on the Prince's shoulder, squeezing it gently. "There's nothing to be done," he continued. "Jaston believes the illness, a 'wasting disease' he called it, began some time ago. We're only now seeing its results. I'm relieved you are here, Sir, for completely selfish reasons. I don't know what to do; what to say to her — if anything. I cannot think of the best course."

Pepin didn't know how to explain his not returning to the court to his mother. If he didn't tell her of her illness, she would insist he return quickly. If he did tell her, she would still insist he continue with his new life and not stay here. He admitted to Adelchis that he was overcome with guilt and worry." Peppin spread his hands in confusion.

Adelchis grabbed the young man's hands and pulled him close. "We both love your mother, Peppin," he began. "We'll decide together what is to be done. Don't despair; you're not alone. I yearn for us to be reacquainted, to feed and grow our friendship. But that's secondary to taking care of Himiltrude." He declared they would support each other. They needed to make plans, determine the best things they could do for Himiltrude. "She has given her life for you and, in some very meaningful ways, for me. Let's make some plans and determine the best methods to help your mother. We mustn't bring her any unnecessary worry or pain."

Adelchis and Peppin talked until time for the evening meal. Later, after Himlitrude went to bed, they talked into the morning hours, attempting to concoct a plan that would survive the scrutiny of everyone, but, especially, of Charlemagne.

"Let me sum up our thoughts, Peppin. See if this makes sense to you," Adelchis suggested almost as the sun rose in the east. He was adamant that they would do anything they could to bring comfort to Himiltrude. Since her life was ending and staying at the manor would require they inform her people of her illness, he suggested that Peppin and he take Himiltrude on a trip. They would choose a far-away destination because they wanted no visits from anyone else. And they needed to implement their plan quickly to prevent others from learning about Himiltrude's condition. She would hate being 'cared for,' and such attention might very well hasten her death.

First, Adelchis proposed that they journey toward Byzantium. Adelchis could not linger here; he had only three days left to visit. He was banished by Charlemagne and forbidden entrance to Frankish lands. If he were found in the realm, he'd be imprisoned and, then, executed. Adelchis was adamant that Peppin could not take care of Himiltrude alone. They had already discussed those reasons. He also proposed that they not tell her of the serious nature of her health and offer her an exciting journey.

Despite Peppin's doubts, Adelchis wanted to consult two doctors in Byzantium who might offer a more hopeful prognosis. Prince Adelchis ticked off the additional reasons for implementing their journey now. This was the most favorable time for travel. The days would be mild, the nights cool, the weather dry. Following obscure roads and avoiding well-traveled ones, they could move as quickly or as slowly as conditions demanded. Traveling disguised as peasants, they wouldn't be stopped nor questioned by the King's soldiers. And, if need be, they could lose themselves in the outlying regions of the kingdom.

Another reason for a trip, he declared, was the protection it offered. If Peppin and his mother announced a trip to Rome, which neither had ever visited, no one would suspect they were leaving for good. And the manor would be left in the hands of those who always served it.

"Does that outline our plan then, Peppin?" Adelchis asked.

"It's logical to me, Adelchis, logical and reasonable. My only concern is Mother's reaction to all this traveling. Won't she become even more exhausted than if we waited here for the end?" Peppin hated to speak of his mother's death; but that, again, was the reality they faced.

"Aye, she may be more exhausted. But, it's worth the risk. And she will have both of us to rely upon. I'm hoping that the excitement of a trip with her 'two best men' will keep her spirits up and camouflage her waning health. If she suspects the state of her health, she will worry for you and me. This way, we're all journeying together, forming the unit she and I always dreamed of. But no one will identify us or report on us." Remembering the men accompanying him, Prince Adelchis explained that the men in his escort were long-standing friends and always accompanied him on visits to Himiltrude. They would never betray him. It was fortunate Peppin had already sent his escort back to Charlemagne's court. No one would question their plans. Adelchis reviewed the plan over and over. He felt it a sound one. He did not believe Himiltrude would survive the journey; but, even that, he considered a positive.

"We can bury her away from this land of pain and treachery," he told Peppin. "She will rest in a land with clear skies, warm weather, a land where no one knows her, cannot betray her". Adelchis felt his eyes fill with tears. He was weeping at the most inappropriate times. But he didn't hold the tears back. *Let anyone, even Peppin, think what he may; I mourn the love of my life.*

Adelchis' description of their journey intrigued Himiltrude. He regaled her with stories of gypsies living on the road, having great adventures; and described the tents, carts, and amenities they guaranteed. Laughing, she embraced their offering wholeheartedly. With most of the plan in place, Adelchis and Peppin packed everything within a day; and, on the third day of Adelchis' visit, they left Himiltrude's house with three extra horses, a traveling cart piled with stuffed, sleeping linens, foodstuffs, and more wine than they could ever hope to drink. Himiltrude was in high spirits, much excited about the trip and the presence of her two, dear traveling companions.

Peppin sent a courier to Charlemagne's court, explaining his mother wished to visit her niece in Lombardy. He noted he neglected to visit this family before he'd been summoned to King Charlemagne's court and thought this the time to make amends. He would accompany his mother. To the King he sent a personal missive, indicating his mother felt unlike her usual self and suggested a visit to family members would restore her spirits. Peppin, again, enumerated his neglect of the family and told the King he planned to return to court just after the next Christmastide.

***

He and Adelchis began their journey with Himiltrude. In order not to weary her, they made a lark of the first day: stopping at streams to wash their feet, raiding early blooming orchards for apple and peach blossoms, and poking along lonely, wandering sheep trails. That night they camped amid the smells of the earth's reawakening: freshly plowed farmlands, pear blossoms, and the earthy miasma of newly growing plants. Himiltrude slept early and deeply, waking with an anticipation she thought gone from her life. And her two men - asking her wishes for breakfast; serving her cups of fresh, mint tea; and pointing out any bird or baby animal they saw - accompanied her on the last great adventure of her life.

Peppin and Adelchis spent several hours around the campfire at night. Himiltrude, not noticeably weaker for their travels but tiring easily, usually retired right after the last meal of the day. To give her additional rest, the two stopped long before the sun set and finished the evening meal shortly after. Then, they spent the evening together. They talked about many subjects, not the least of which was King Charlemagne's court, his vision and successes, and, on occasion, his lack of success in implementing his ideas. Before their talks, Peppin had not realized that Adelchis spent time at his father's court. And so he was surprised at the regard for the King in Adelchis's voice.

"I was very content there, Peppin." Adelchis said more than once. "The King was eager for me to polish my fighting skills, valued my presence in court society, and trusted me to lead small scouting parties. We often hunted together; he always bagged the largest buck, of a certainty."

He told Peppin that his sister, Desiderata, was very eager to marry Charlemagne, but she had none of the gifts of a queen. She and the king were never well-matched in any case. "And, despite Father's hope to somehow get the Frankish kingdom away from the King, I'm certain Desiderata grew tired of being an afterthought to Charlemagne." Prince Adelchis' mouth turned up, a hint of a smile crossed his lips. Desiderata was a hard woman to like, her brother admitted. She always was simple-minded, concerned with balls and clothing, with compliments about her beauty. She never showed the kindness which should characterize a Queen and lacked any concern for people." So, her present position, a lord's wife, is perfect for her."

"Did you know of my betrothal to Gisela, the King's sister?" Prince Adelchis asked Peppin. At Peppin's look of surprise, Adelchis nodded his head. He explained that there was never any hope of a marriage! His father hated Charlemagne too much to bring his sister into the Lombardy court. Prince Adelchis chuckled. "But my father and her mother betrothed us. I have heard she is an abbess now. She was surely strong enough for such a role, even when I knew her!" Adelchis laughed at his memories, lost in a time when his life and future were new and unspoilt.

"But, how do you know..." Peppin's voice trailed off; he didn't know how to ask about Adelchis' relationship with his mother. Was it not more than a little strange that Adelchis and his mother even knew each other? When he was younger, Peppin had not thought of their relationship but, now, he wondered. It was clear, they were dedicated one to the other.

Adelchis smiled at Peppin. "I wondered how long it would take for you to ask me about your mother. But I owe you that, for the love I bear you both." He begged Peppin not to deem his love for Himiltrude sordid and began to explain those events so many years ago.

When Adelchis arrived at the Frankish court, Charlemagne's mother, the Queen Bertrada, had already sent Himiltrude away, banished both her and Peppin. The Queen Mother, always a manipulator, wanted her son to marry Desiderata of Lombardy, thinking to unite the two realms. "What a mess are the lives of royalty, huh?" Prince Adelchis held a stick and doodled in the dirt.

"Some months after the marriage, Desiderata left King Charlemagne. My father was humiliated that your father rejected Desiderata. But Father was determined to put the best face on it for her sake so that he could marry her off to a high-born lord. He sent me to escort my sister home, spreading the rumor that Charlemagne had wanted Desiderata to engage in 'abnormal sexual play." I met my sister's escort and traveled with Desiderata toward home. We moved swiftly as we returned to Lombardy."

Adelchis described the serious injury he sustained a day later. Running swiftly, his mount stumbled and knocked him into the rider beside him. He fell to the ground and one of the horses shied. In trying not to trample Adelchis, the animal lost its footing and tumbled on his left leg. The pain was so severe he lost consciousness. Hours later, he revived. Desiderata was frantic with fear that her brother would die. Understanding that he could speak and make decisions, she took Adelchis's pleas to heart when he begged her to continue to their father's court, to set out for home. Adelchis was twice relieved, knowing he couldn't listen to her shrieks and cries and, then, her complaints for the rest of the journey.

Although reluctant, Desiderata left two men with Adelchis and rode for her father's house. Adelchis and his men camped in a near-by cave, hoping to travel within a few days. But that was not to be. The wound in Adelchis' leg seeped with foul-smelling liquid and began to drain. Trying to decrease the heat of his leg, Adelchis placed a wet cloth on it. The pain was so great he quickly removed the cloth, accidentally hitting the wound. Great globs of white liquid leaked out. Seeing that, one of his soldiers left to seek help. The soldier rode to your mother's manor and begged for aid. Himiltrude recognized the serious nature of the wound, sent one of her men back to the manor for a horse cart, and moved Adelchis to her house. She nursed him for weeks and, eventually, saved his life. Finally, his fever dropped and the Prince began to recover.

"Ever will she be an angel to me, Peppin, and not just because she saved my life." Adelchis wiped his eyes. "Your mother is kind, funny, and filled with enthusiasm—unlike any other woman I ever knew. I wanted her to accompany me then; I hoped to marry her along the way; but she would have none of it."

"'Nay,' she said to me, 'I married above myself once. Never will I make such a mistake again. It brought me heartache and banishment and penalized my little son. I'll not choose that road a second time.' I returned to see her, Peppin; I vowed my undying love; but she chose to remain in her own home, among 'her people,' as she described it." Prince Adelchis fingered the cross around his neck, a gift long ago from Himiltrude.

"She's my lover, aye; but she's my heart-mate as well, the angel of my life." Adelchis stared into Peppin's face, begging for understanding.

Peppin clasped him around the chest and answered. "You've my gratitude, my understanding, and my approval---whatever they're worth to you." Peppin answered. "Thank God, my mother has a great love. As a young boy, I could sense her loneliness and puzzled out she was terribly betrayed. But she never mentioned a single one of Poppa's faults to me. Having been at the court, I now understand some of the difficulties of the man. I value your friendship for myself, your love for my mother, and our shared mission in this difficult time. We shall continue, you and I, through the ages to come. Of that alone am I certain."

The two men talked of tomorrow's route and, then, took to their sleeping blankets. As Peppin looked at the stars later that night, he felt a calming peace unlike anything he had experienced before. A shooting star raced across the sky and Peppin, all of a sudden, understood the King's love of astronomy.

If only, he could devote himself to his children as he does to his interests, what a better world he would create. Peppin thought. He felt regret creeping into his heart until his mind shouted. "Forget Poppa!! All will be well on this journey." That thought brought him comfort.

***

The fifth day of their journey, Himiltrude came to Adelchis in the early hours of the morning.

"Adelchis," she spoke quietly. "Is there any necessity that we leave at day's light? I am having difficulty sleeping and would postpone our start 'til after mid-day, if that not be an inconvenience." She whispered softly.

"Nay, that's a good choice, Himli," Adelchis assured her. "I told Peppin last night we should fish in this river for today's breakfast. Would a fat trout not make your mouth water? This is a pleasure trip, after all. We must take our pleasure in slow moving, in outside meals, and in ease. Yes?" He took Himli back to her tent, kissed her soundly, and arranged her linens.

Adelchis passed the word to Peppin and the escort. They would remain in camp for the remainder of the day; perhaps, for even longer. Himli's face looked almost transparent; and, even though she walked back to her tent with no difficulty, she seemed weaker than at the previous mid-day meal. The end is near, Adelchis thought. "I shall be left in this world alone, cut off from the one who really matters to me." And so it was.

Peppin and Adelchis buried Himiltrude beneath a giant oak tree, that its branches might cool her and soften the rain as it fell. They each said their brief goodbyes and mounted, dry-eyed to continue their journey. They both knew she was happily at peace, gratified her heart's love and her son renewed their friendship and, now, were united in their love for her and for each other. Peppin decided to accompany Adelchis to Constaninople, taking comfort from Adelchis' presence and their shared love for his mother.

Along the way, Peppin identified a courier returning to the Frankish court and sent another missive to King Charlemagne.

Poppa,

I have just buried mother. Her health, not as hearty as we had presumed, failed and she was taken to God last evening. I'm not ready to return to court, Poppa. This loss of mother has come upon me too sudden; I must have time to grieve for her and to reflect. This seems a good time to visit Rome, to expand my experiences through travel, even to search for Oliver. I was ever told that he journeyed in this direction when he left Frankland.

Do not concern yourself with my welfare. I am broadening my education with travel; please pass this on to Master Alcuin and bid Charles a fond farewell from me.

Your faithful servant,

Peppin

***

When he received Peppin's missive, Charlemagne was in the library. His face grave, he read the short letter and asked the courier if he had any additional information to provide. The courier replied that Peppin himself placed the message in his hand. He had no knowledge of the funeral or the location of the burial. The King's guilt, his mother's mistreatment of Himli, tore at his heart.

"Can it be that all women, except for Queen Bertrada, die young?" he asked himself. "I can make no peace with this passing. How much I hurt this woman; how much pain I gave the mother of my son!" The king, again, remembered the laughing, perky girl he married; and, then, he mourned her death.

He thought of the women he had most loved, Himiltrude and Hildegard. Both were women of deep feelings, loyal to a fault, and the best of mothers. Considering his own dictatorial mother, her selfishness, her eagerness to rise and get her way – no matter who was hurt – he should have loved these two wives much more. Nay, he took them...and their goodness for granted. And they were true mothers as well, always choosing the best for their children, no matter the sacrifices demanded of them. And, then, God help him, he thought of his children. He failed them one and all by not taking enough care of them, of their very souls. He discounted Peppin early on, because he would never be a warrior. Now, in his attempts at government, he needed statesmen, negotiators, fair-minded, thinking men – not martial fighters as much as thoughtful, innovative minds. Any of his sons might have become such...if he had established a true relationship with them. Ahh, and his daughters? Each in her own way had much to contribute to his realm but he valued them even less...except for Rotrud, of course. And she he had almost alienated completely.

Hildegard warned him, time and again. He could not expect his daughters to forego a life of their own...a life with a husband and family. It was not normal; it was not sane, she had repeated over and over. Looking back, he could see so many mistakes he'd made with them. But he would not have them be taken advantage of! They would not be under the thumb of a husband...like he had been so long under the thumb of his mother. He wanted them free... free from manipulation, free from social pressures, free from the court's expectations! He would not condemn them to that sad state – a marriageable princess. He would not have it!

***

"It seems like death follows death, Rinaldo." Charlemagne spoke the following week, looking across the battlefield. "Some of it comes in the night, almost gently as the sunrise. That is the good death. Some of it, like this, comes in destruction, in panic, in horror. And it seems this horrific passing comes much more often than the first. What possesses men to value this violent death and not the quiet, gentle one?

Rinaldo did not even glance at the field. He was nauseous already. He could not focus his eyes on the blood and guts. This attack on the Avars sickened his soul. King Charlemagne, following his father's lead, was close to annihilating these people. Even with such a large number of dead, Charlemagne ravaged the Avar land - homes burned, cattle's throats slit, fields set afire. Rinaldo could not explain the need for such destruction. Instead, he looked toward the sky, away from the carnage, and responded to the King's question.

"Master Alcuin says the explanation of that, Sire, is in men's heads. We discussed it last week, when you were out riding the high field." Rinaldo added, by way of explanation. "In fact, he reflected almost your same thoughts."

"Master Alcuin said the preference for a fighting death comes from our need to believe we are in control, in control of our lives and our destinies. A death in combat reflects a life of purpose, a fight which is worth one's life, a freedom or a loyalty or a value worth dying for. That purpose, the reward — if you will — doesn't exist when one dies in his bed. But it does seem sad, Sire, that the final moments of life are deemed so valuable? It seems all life before the battle is nothing, lost on the wind. Master Alcuin commented that such a need arises because we are so fearful of death, not understanding that it is, yet, another beginning."

King Charlemagne stared at Rinaldo. Despite all the Church teachings he embraced, the reward of heaven was one the King could not imagine or expect. "Mayhap, Rinaldo, mayhap. But what do you think of death?"

"It is a waste, Sire, unless the body cannot go on. What do we lose with the deaths of all these men? Our future, perhaps? Our humanity is surely compromised by war's very existence. I have no answers, Sire, but hundreds of questions."

"We should discuss this very issue at the next 'philosophy' discussion. I'd like to hear others' thoughts on this topic." Charlemagne suggested. Rinaldo shrugged.

It cannot be that physical death is a 'beginning,' the King thought. *How might any of us earn a new beginning with a past filled by killing and strife? Mayhap, I take the responsibility for the ordering of these battles and, thus, my followers are absolved of the guilt. Then, they may, indeed, earn a new beginning. But, not me, and not Pope Hadrian... for we know our disobedience of God's laws. We know.*

"We shall camp a few furloughs from this place, Rinaldo," the King announced. "Our presence in these lands, newly returned to our realm, will hold this Avar pestilence at bay. The court will remain here. I daresay we shall not venture forth again 'til time for the spring assembly. Please pass the word to the commanders and so inform my Queen."

Chapter 6

CONFRONTATION

As the sounds of battle died away, the King spoke to his exhausted soldiers. The upcoming evening meal was to be a feast, complete with many meats and sweet 'delights.' After that, the spoils of war would be divided among all the soldiers. So, he urged every man not to drink too much ale in order to protect his additional goods.

"Rest; refresh yourselves from this battle," he told his troops. "By necessity we remain in these lands to protect our interests. The Avars will be stirring in the spring; I've no doubt. Rather than march from a long distance to quell them, we shall camp close and strike early and strategically. We will be finished with them before the next assembly, probably in Ingelheim once again. Prepare yourselves for victory after victory! We shall win all our battles. You fought hard and long. Booty will be distributed and honors given after our feast. God bless you. Long live Frankland! May HE continue to give us victory!" The King left the battlefield, heading for the river to wash the remnants of this gory battle away. Later, dressing for the feast, he spoke to the Queen.

"Fastrada," King Charlemagne looked at his wife. "What say you to our daughters' having their evening meal in their tents? Many of the nobility have been imbibing ale all afternoon, celebrating our military victory. Oh, I do not wish to curtail their celebrations; their service to me this day were exemplary. But I don't wish my daughters, yours and mine, to see this drunkenness. And Rotrud demanded that this young man, in whom she apparently delights, sit beside her at table." At Fastrada's irritated movement, Charlemagne's temper raged.

"Never fear! I told her it was not possible. I will never acknowledge her heart interests. She seems just to mishear my words or to ignore them. It will be best to serve my girls this night away from the banquet hall. Please so inform them." But the King forgot, for a moment, the will of his eldest daughter.

***

At the courier's announcement, Rotrud turned her head, looked back at her sister, gathered her shawl around her shoulders and began to stand. "I will have dinner in the hall; I don't care what the king commands. He may ruin my life but he will not starve me! Because he laughs at my heart's needs does not mean I will not eat!"

"Were I you," Bertha replied as she held her sister in place, combing her hair. "I would make an *entrance*, not meekly crawl to my seat. Were I you, I would attract the eye of every male in the hall. Were I you, I would flirt with my lover's father. See what our Poppa will say to that." She smirked at Rotrud with an air of challenge in her eyes.

Rotrud jumped up and stared at her sister in astonishment. "How can you think such things? You are younger than I! This is what comes from your visits to Lord Cranston's manor. You girls! You plot and plan behind angels' faces." She stopped, understanding Bertha's words. "Do you think I can manipulate Poppa this way? Do you?" She asked breathlessly.

At Bertha's positive nod, Rotrud exclaimed: "What a brilliant suggestion! How marvelous....and Poppa can say nothing because the hall will be full of guests. What fun! Maybe this will end his eternal meddling."

As Rotrud turned back to the clothes closet, Bertha shook her head sadly. "Nay, Poppa will never reconsider," she assured Rotrud. *Only I understand; he will never let any of us go.* Bertha thought to herself. *We are his daughters--to be kept away from temptation and away from unwanted alliances. The king will never compromise, never align us with another. He does not need any alliances such marriages might bring him. He will not permit his daughters to cement his kingdom. He can do all that for himself... and his sons can produce heirs. He doesn't want heirs from any of us.*

Bertha rose from her chair, gathered her hair ornaments, brushes and combs and went to dress her own fair curls.

***

In the front courtyard, a small contingent of soldiers, led by a nobleman's son, was mounting to ride out.

"Go directly home, Janus. No stopping for hunting or wenching; do you hear me?" Lord Janlur stood straight and tall, held himself erect and commanding. His face was stern and unreadable. Janus nodded solemnly, his face a mask of stern control, though his hurt was not lost on his father.

"As you say, my lord...straight home. I would as lief have you send me on a mission, some quest for which you do not have time, perhaps?" Janus almost begged.

"Nay, I have no such need. I will join you at home within the week." His father answered. Janus nodded curtly, his eyes asking one final time if all were lost. "This thing is not to be," his father confirmed softly for Janus' ears alone.

As Janus led his men homeward, Count Janlur spoke to the other contingent waiting patiently for his orders. "Places for this night's sleep and that of tomorrow are prepared for you. We delay here for no more than two days; I must speak with the King. No boisterous drinking and wenching. Let us be courteous this night; we are in a

Christian court."

Count Janlur dismounted, handed his reins to his captain and turned toward the chamber where the commanders gathered. "We shall speak on the morrow," he added as he dismissed his captain.

***

The Count walked quickly toward the assembly room, distracted from current concerns by Janus' pain. *My poor boy.* Count Janlur mourned. *You have come face-to-face with reality, the reality of a determined ruler.* Count Janlur disliked this development. His son's indiscretion in wooing the king's oldest daughter could bring disaster upon his family. Everyone knew the manner in which the king confined and controlled his children, particularly his daughters. He often heard Charlemagne declare his daughters would never marry. He wanted them always with him. And Charlemagne was powerful enough to do this. He did not need alliances through his children's spouses; he was the king of the Frankish empire and permanently positioned. He had three healthy male heirs and needed no additional competition from sons-in-law. The Count shook his head, unsure what he could do to help his son.

Putting Janus' problems in a back side of his brain, he watched for this so-called 'assembly chamber.' The King tried to convince his commanders that a special room, one dedicated to the annual assembly of nobles and churchmen, advisers and hangers-on, would increase respect for the assembly, for the choices and decisions the men made. I would ask him to consider more humane choices for his daughters, the Count thought. "They are each and all beautiful girls. How can he deny them husbands and children? Where is his Christian heart, I wonder?"

Spotting the crossed swords on a chamber door, Janlur turned the knob, ready to go inside. "Where is everyone?

Oh, Lord!" he whispered. "I was supposed to go to the banquet hall." He turned in the opposite direction, still preoccupied by his son's suffering face. Count Janlur walked resolutely to the banquet hall, still analyzing the King's strange expectations. I wonder by what manner a king can so deny his daughters? Janlur thought. "Surely, with his own colorful, marital history, he does not consider himself a model of propriety," he murmured. "Rotrud is a daughter of his third wife, one for whom he had much affection. At least, he put away a wife for this girl's mother. Does that not suggest love and caring...or, on the other hand, maybe it was titillation and lust? Who knows the whole of it?"

Whatever the King's concern, Janus would be a long time in recovering. His heart was clearly in Rotrud's hands. "Janus had already spoken to me of marriage." Count Janlur muttered as he entered the banquet hall.

***

The banquet hall was hot and stifling. The seats at the main table were for the king's military commanders. But rows upon rows of additional men at arms, visiting clergy, gentle men and their ladies, posturing young lords and all manner of dogs moved among the tables. The dogs grabbed for scraps before they hit the floor. Guests reached for food or for more potent liquid refreshment. The rushes muffled much of the noise produced by so large a company, though many at the peripheral tables appeared to have been drinking their meals.

"My lord, my lord, Janus!" the King's son, Charles, called. "Your place is at the main table, three places to the right of Poppa."

Count Janlur signaled his acknowledgment of this direction and turned his feet toward the main table. He could not, for the life of him, see any space at all in the designated area but knew space would magically appear as he drew nearer. And, indeed, there was a space next to one of the King's young daughters as Count Janlur approached. Just as he reached his place, the young girl stood up, smiled shyly at him, and ran from the hall.

"Welcome! Welcome, Count Janlur." King Charlemagne gestured for him to sit. "Please let us know if you have need of items you do not see. Eat. Drink. Refresh yourself. We would have you well taken care of before convening tomorrow. I trust your accommodations are adequate? Oh, you have not yet seen them? Well, let me know if they do not suit. Sit, join our company!" the king offered.

Count Janlur took his seat, asked for meat and ale, and drank a large mouthful of vintage Rhinish wine (with an excellent bouquet) when complete silence rolled through the hall. A little disoriented by the absence of noise, he did not immediately identify the figure moving toward the table. As he began to focus, a sigh echoed through the masses and, then, a shout of approval rose to the rafters.

Aye, now he could see. It was one of the King's daughters, surely the oldest one. Janus once described Rotrud to his father. Lord Janlur disbelieved his son's poetic description but then realized he saw the young woman some several months ago. On seeing her move forward into the banquet hall, he realized she was surely no longer a child.

She flowed into the banquet hall – elegant, graceful, and smiling. Her shining, dark curls were artfully woven with sparkling gems, colors which reflected the great hall's fires. The cut of her clothes – the deep neck of her tunic, a seam which emphasized her small waist, a flare which moved the eyes to her hips – emphasized her womanly charms. Her creamy skin reflected pinpoints of light. As she approached the table and the King, her eyes flashed with life, identifying and acknowledging the many admiring, male eyes. She appeared as light as air, floating down the aisle, curtseying to anyone who responded to her. *Ahhh...but she is stunning! Dear Lord, has she grown up!* Lord Janus sat in stunned silence.

A moment later, Rotrud took the seat beside him, the one just vacated by her young sister. As she sat, she, accidentally, brushed her thigh against his. He startled at the pleasant tingle such contact brought and immediately put out his hand to steady her... or himself; he really was not sure which. Rotrud laughed deeply in her throat, looked directly into his eyes and, then, toward his mouth.

"Ahhh, Count Janlur, it's a pleasure to welcome you to my father's court. He often wishes you were here to discuss maneuvers. We do hope you will do us the honor of an *extended* visit," she purred.

Count Janlur saw the eyes of jealous men spread out below him. *Why does she sit beside me?* He wondered. *And what is the tantalizing fragrance wafting around her?*

"I am honored to have the pleasure of such a beautiful woman beside me, my dear," he answered. "Every man in the room does envy me this place." Rotrud's eyes widened at the compliment. She smiled and slowly licked her lower lip. She pursed her lips, showing her dimple, covered his hand with her own, held his eyes, and murmured:

"An honor, perhaps; but pleasure, I hope, for both of us."

Count Janlur felt, more than saw, Charlemagne rise to his feet. In a distinctly frosty tone, the King proposed a toast to welcome his 'dear friend.' Next, he bade his daughter to make the count feel at home. Lord Janlur thought the suggestion might be a decided mistake. He acknowledged the toast and turned to the beautiful young woman at his side.

"I did not anticipate the pleasure of your company or I would have hurried to my place much sooner. Your entrance into the hall gladdened the heart of every male in the room," he declared, playing on this young woman's vanity.

"Oh, I doubt that," Rotrud replied. "After all, many of them see me on a daily basis. I'm not cloistered away, you know. I ride, hawk, even fish on occasion. And, of a certainty, many of us study in the palace school together. Oh, we do not all study the same thing!" she exclaimed, seeing his confusion. "But I do listen to the fencing master so I am familiar with all types of thrusts, feints and other movements." Rotrud had an expressive face so her straightforward words did not match her knowing, conspiratorial expression. "Do you fence, Count Janlur?" she purred. "...for pleasure, I mean?"

Count Janlur was fascinated: watching the light play across her daringly exposed breasts, the shining wealth of her hair, the sultry promise of those startling eyes. He had no memory of the foods he consumed or of the great amount of wine he drank. His description of her charms to her father, the King, as he left the banquet hall was effusive; he felt captivated by her — the love of his son's life! Shortly after Janlur's departure, the King spoke to his wife.

***

"Fastrada, can you do nothing with my daughter? Rotrud must be controlled in some way; she is absolutely defiant against the world. Did you see her at the evening meal...flouncing into the hall, mesmerizing poor Janlur, and laughing all the while — gathering the attentions of every man in attendance! What IS the matter with her? She knows this is no way for a young woman to behave." Charlemagne slapped his wife's desk in frustration, unable to fathom his oldest daughter's behavior.

"She is impulsive, I agree," Fastrada answered. "But she is eager to marry Janus; your refusal to discuss the possibility has angered her. Surely you can understand that. Remember the fuss YOU caused when you wanted to marry me. There were those who did not believe your reputation could survive it. She is hurt and bewildered, Charles."

"I don't understand the reason. I make this decision for her own good. I know how easily marriage traps young people. Look at me. If Desiderata and I had not been of like mind, we could easily have been trapped in that hopeless marriage for eternity. I would never have known you, my dear, and what a loss that would be. Nay! Nay! Nay! I do not care what defiance my girls show; I will not countenance marriage for any of them. It is my duty to spread Christianity throughout this realm; it has a good structure in which a people may grow and prosper. It provides order out of chaos. It defines a purpose for man's existence. But the movement to compel men and women to remain married for a lifetime is barbaric!" Charlemagne was adamant.

"I cannot help but compare the miserable nine months of my second marriage to the first nine months of my first. What a horror, my dear. What sadness for both man and woman when the understanding they both wish does not develop, when there is no knowledge or concern for each other. Nay! Such lifetime bondage is not for my daughters. It asks too much, this Church!"

King Charlemagne often discussed this same topic with others. He thought the barbarians' orientation to marriage the best one: if either partner wished to sever the relationship, it was done. "That way, each one – man or woman – is protected, has a choice." No one – his wives, Alcuin, Abbot Fulrad, his Peers – ever made an argument which deterred Charlemagne from his steadfast refusal to allow his daughters to marry. He simply must protect his girls from the possibility of a deteriorating relationship; he would not have them bound for life.

"You know there will be repercussions from this." Fastrada stated. "Young women will not lead monastic lives; everyone wants...and needs love, Charlemagne. You know this. You may well be embarrassed."

"I will deal with whatever or whomever comes." Charlemange replied with a slight smile. "Give me grandchildren conceived in love, not by the constraints of society, and I will honor them. Love, freely given, should be sought. If it does not sustain itself, then the pairing was not to be. I can live with temporary or, even, long term embarrassment...but not with misery for my daughters."

The King's experience with sexual and permanent liaisons was heavily influenced by his society. Germanic women were allowed some freedom in their sexual activities; societal culture did not require a marriage. It accepted mutual pairings but did not require permanent allegiance by either party. So, in addition to fear for his daughters' being locked into an unhappy marriage, Charlemagne reflected the Germanic attitude toward sexual liaisons in general. In the Christian church, marriage was an iron-bound commitment, not easily altered, and, therefore, for King Charlemagne a situation to avoid.

***

The next morning Count Janlur broke his fast early so he might search for Rotrud. He could not wait to see her again. He enjoyed the beauties of the garden, ambled into the stables, observed the training exercises for the youngest soldiers, but could not find the raven-haired beauty of last night. Just as his captain of the guards crossed the courtyard to discuss training exercises, Rotrud sped by on a black stallion. Her laughter floated across the yard, producing smiles from young and old soldiers alike.

"Good morning, Count Janlur." his captain greeted him. "I have had the men begin physical training exercises this morning, to be followed by fencing and assault techniques. Is that satisfactory?" the captain inquired.

"Aye, that sounds like a good regimen. Good that they're up, Captain, after the food and drink of last night. They are well-disciplined, Captain, thanks to your tutelage." Count Janlur replied.

"Shall we prepare to start for home on the morrow, sir?" the captain asked. "I heard last eve that the border next to Count Resirer demands daily patrols. That is a little too close to our own lands for me to feel easy. We should leave for home on the morrow...or today, if it pleases you."

Count Janlur was startled. Aye, he planned to leave King Charlemagne's court quite soon. Leaving today would be wise. Count Resirer spoke with him before his departure a week ago, the trip made to retrieve his foolish son from court. Resirer had confirmed Lombard invaders were looking for easy lands to subdue.

"Let me see how the morning goes, Captain; we will speak again after the mid-day meal." Count Janlur answered.

"Very good, sir. I am concerned that our small contingent at home not be vulnerable. I know Janus is a good soldier but he is not a tactician like yourself. His talents are in negotiation, compromise and flexibility — well-suited for court service. I expect those gifts work well with the ladies as well."

"Yes, I expect they do," Count Janlur agreed. *They had surely seemed to work in winning Rotrud's interest.... What am I doing?* Count Janlur asked himself. ...*Competing with my own son to entice Rotrud?*

"Captain, "Count Janlur decided. "Cancel the morning's activities; we start for home within the hour."

"Very good, sir; the men are ready," the Captain responded, moving to implement the order.

Chapter 7

EDUCATION, THE KEY

Count Janlur's choice to return home effectively presaged the winter season. Battles were over for yet another year; most of the harvesting was complete; and dull, dishwater skies foretold the coming snows. The King did not realize, of course, the reason for Janlur's quick exit. But he knew the battles had been exhausting and the manors, small villages, and settlings needed to gather wood, repair homes, and preserve food before the coming winter snow and ice. The next few months, including the days of Christmastide, would be a time for rest and recuperation. Court members, not far from the Christmastide location, were eager for the comforts of a manor whose walls were stone and wood.

But the King was not content. He still yearned to expand his kingdom and hold sway over all the lands that he knew. The lack of respect granted him by the nobles of Bavaria, in particular, irritated him. Reports of incursions into Frankish realms rankled the King. Count Tassilo, in the far reaches of Bavaria, had increased his power, believing himself protected by the Bavarian Alps. He declared he intended to remain independent of Charlemagne. He announced that a threat from King Charlemagne, a demand to swear fealty, would force him to make an alliance with the Avars. Gerold, Hildegard's brother, appeared before Charlemagne and eloquently described Tassilo's intentions..

"Tassilo is determined, Sire," Gerold repeated yet again. "He has amassed war materials and soldiers; he is well-protected behind those vast mountains. I tell you true. The land over which he holds sway is the same as mine, only more remote and more difficult to travel. Tassilo will preserve his people's freedom at any cost; he will not bow to your authority. Leave him be and all may yet turn out well." Gerold had the support of the other commanders. Even Audulf, the King's own seneschal, discouraged King Charlemagne from a provocation of Tassilo.

"This past battle season against the Saxons has been difficult, Sire, and has exhausted us all," Audulf reiterated to the King. "Though there was some late harvesting, much of the grain and roughage was lost before it could be taken from the fields. There is want across the land ....now, even before the worst of the snows. Men cannot sacrifice their families' lives any longer. They must be home to gather nuts for winter meals, to repair weather-damaged dwellings, to hunt and fish, to dry and store provisions. They must go home, Sire! Before we know it, spring will be here again, along with yet another season of battles. This is not the time to confront Tassilo or anyone else."

Despite Audulf's plea and Gerold's evaluations, King Charlemagne continued to move his army. Invigorated by his recent defeat of the Saxons and determined to increase his lands to increase the influence of his Christian nation, King Charlemagne undertook a winter march. He left his wife, children and court at Ingelheim, feeling freer to march unhindered. Because many fighters in army returned to their homes for the winter, he called on those soldiers whom he knew would respond to his summons--his most faithful East Franks. He promised them, too, there would be no winter battles, assured them he was but positioning his troops for the spring. After the soldiers joined his own forces, he turned toward Italy. He also called other soldiers, including conquered Saxons and Thuringians, to meet him in the upcoming summer at the Bavarian frontier.

As he marched through Italy toward Rome, the King was reminded of Rotrud's betrothal to Constantine, the king of Byzantium. The agreement was years old and was no longer of much value.

"There is no reason to continue this mockery," he muttered to himself. "I shall let none of my daughters marry. I have three fine sons to inherit the kingdom. And, in fact, three are enough. The girls must not have husbands who might compete with my sons and, certainly, not grandsons to be considered as well. I love my daughters as I do my sons; but they cannot inherit my realm. And I will take no land from my boys for dowries. Never! I divide my realm only among Hildegard's sons. Considering that, I shall dissolve this betrothal."

"As headstrong as Rotrud is, she might yet embarrass me with unacceptable behavior. Better for there to be no betrothal than for her to provoke further outrage if she is indiscreet. The Byzantium Church would make much of a careless liaison. Her fascination with Count Janlur's Janus proves her unreliability. I'll not be humiliated by an injudicious marriage, not my own and not one of my daughter's choosing. I have learnt the lesson of hasty joinings well. Rotrud must be spared such knowledge."

***

Unable to ask his army to march against Tassilo in the winter and knowing Pope Hadrian would aid him, Charlemagne directed Tassilo to come to Ingelheim to answer charges of treason. Tassilo, receiving the summons from a courier, was reluctant to open it.

"It is, of course, a reprimand," he said to his followers. Supporting Tassilo for his independent streak and hoping for him as their ruler, rather than Charlemagne, the nobles were anxious to hear any news from the King. To a man, they each had sworn their loyalty to Charlemagne and feared his knowing they now supported Tassilo. "Never fear," Duke Tassilo told them. "King Charlemagne will be unaware of my incursions until it is too late for him! The Alps are our ally!" Duke Tassilo was confident he could elude the King for years...in the wilds of Bavaria. "If I appear at Ingelheim, he will arrest me that very moment. I'll reply that the snow is already deep, and I cannot dig my way to Ingelheim before the spring."

Tassilo decided to appeal to Pope Hadrian. Surely, the Pope would remember Lombard's early support of Rome and his own loyalty in that support. The nobles listened closely. Charlemagne knew the Pope believed his support for the Church and Hadrian's interests appropriate. He swore he would support the nobles' interest, even if Gerold of Bavaria would not agree with him. But, all of them could overcome Gerold's absence! The King was certain of it. He asked, again, for them to give their support. All agreed, all but Dreyfus.

"You are hoping for a miracle, Tassilo," Dreyfus said. "King Charlemagne has ever had Pope Hadrian in his pocket. You must make a decision, not at this moment, mayhap, but before the spring thaws begin. The King will surmount the mountains. As is his habit, he will attack from two or three different directions. His army numbers thousands; they will not be naysaid. You must prepare to die, to be banished or you must make some peace with the King. His sons are already fighting beside him. Aye, they are young yet; but how long can you resist? As you age, they become better trained, more confident, and, God help us, more able! Think on a truce, Tassilo, or lose everything! I am warning you!"

Tassilo inclined his head to Dreyfus. Despite not

providing the encouragement I wish to hear, Tassilo thought, Dreyfus has got the truth of it. *My 'tit-tat' games with Charlemagne are at an end. He has become too strong in his armies for me to defeat. He has severed my friends from my side; and he's readying to invade my land. What might be the result for my family? They will live in shame and want forever, for this King's memory is long indeed.* Tassilo answered his own thought.

"I shall appeal to Pope Hadrian, nonetheless, Dreyfus. And make my decision after his reply reaches me," Tassilo repeated. "Fear not. I shall keep your interests in mind and announce my intentions to all of you. I thank you for your encouragement, in our shared hope for our country."

Pope Hadrian refused to intervene on Tassilo's behalf, and the King increased his war plans, constantly building his army's ability to overcome Tassilo. Just as Dreyfus had predicted, armies began arriving from three directions, the 'pincer' movement having served the King well in the past. Seeing no quarter, Tassilo surrendered to King Charlemagne. To guarantee his compliance, Charlemagne demanded hostages; one of them was Tassilo's own son. He and his son were held as prisoners until the spring assembly of 788. There, they would be on trial for treason.

The confrontation with Tassilo had been more difficult and more exhausting than Charlemagne expected. He had been away from Frankland for many months, traveling, but with little actual fighting. His wife and family had not come on the journey. He missed them mightily and was eager to return home. As a reward to himself, Charlemagne decreed that Christmastide was to be spent at the court in Aachen, the court which provided healing in the warm, thermal waters of the River Grannus. The Aachen castle was the King's favorite home; all he valued was there.

***

It was at this Christmastide that Alcuin begged the King to establish the Palace School permanently in Aachen. "I cannot train teachers, Sire," Alcuin began, "if I am not near them on a daily basis. The attic rooms here would be more than adequate for students who have been sent for an education. The rooms over the stables would provide housing for other students--those who work for their lessons, the sons of tradesmen who value education for their offspring. Sire, the School cannot build a reputation, cannot even be effective, if it is mobile. I cannot offer positions to scholars if there not be rooms, meals, and appropriate manuscripts. This beautiful country is conducive to rigorous study. Here, the young people of the land can learn, think, and grow—all the better prepared to assist you in the continuing demands of an expanding realm. The library I have acquired must have a stable home. The manuscripts, the parchments are both undermined by the packing and repacking, the traveling—even in their cases—in all types of weather. If we are to provide manuscripts for the people to read, there must be a scriptorium, manned by many copyists. With no permanent location, your educational plans must be curtailed. It is not possible to train or educate successfully in a mobile court."

Alcuin didn't dare breathe. He risked incurring great displeasure from the King, for Charlemagne followed his own time-table in implementing plans. *If we do not have a permanent school,* Alcuin promised himself, *I must return to Tours. I must have other minds around me, others with whom to converse, master teachers who can implement effective instruction, space for students at different knowledge levels. Without a physical location, we cannot attract scholars who teach.* The king stared into Alcuin's face, seeing the hopeful dread in the master's eyes.

"Do you have anything to add to this request, Alcuin?" King Charlemagne asked. "Any argument which you feel would influence my decision?"

"Nay, Sire," Alcuin sighed. "You've heard all my arguments, repeated more than once, since last Christmastide. I can only emphasize that the situation is more dire as we speak than it was last year at this time. Oh, I do have master teachers expressing an interest in coming here. They are waiting for information about the employment contracts, Sire. I cannot delay much longer." He let his hands fall to his sides and sat on a near-by bench. "I have nothing to add."

At that moment, the King's second-born daughter, Bertha, came into the library. Not seeing her father in the shadowed corner, she walked to Alcuin, curtseyed and spoke.

"Master Alcuin," Bertha began, "where are the other students? I need help with my reading and hoped someone would be here in the library. The best students often study here. Everyone cannot be returning home this soon." Her voice fell away at the impossible thought. "Christmastide is more than ten days hence. I would not ask you to help me, Master Alcuin. My needs are too small. But is there no other student about?"

"Nay, Bertha, I believe not," was Alcuin's answer. "All are packing, clothing and gifts for family and friends. Those with the court for Christmas are helping cook with nut shelling for the promised 'delights.' It occurs to me you might read to your friends shelling nuts, entertain them as they work. Then, if you have trouble, there will be someone there to help." Alcuin's eyes twinkled at Bertha. He knew all too well that she was shy of reading aloud, even to the older sister who often tutored her.

"Do you think they would not laugh, Master?" Bertha inquired. "The older students always laugh at us younger ones. Sometimes we don't even know the reason." She dropped her eyes, afraid she had given away some secret.

"I have a solution." Alcuin patted her shoulder.. "I shall come with you to the cooking hearth and introduce you as the 'recreation reader.' How about that?"

"If you say so, Master Alcuin," she replied. "But I don't know what '*rek ree'a shun read r*' means. Will I be doing that?" She looked at him with a tinge of fear.

"You will, indeed, my girl," Alcuin replied. "You will be reading and, thereby, entertaining your friends. Come with me and let us begin this fun, this recreation." He smiled as he took Bertha's hand and headed toward the cook hearth.

***

"If I did not know Bertha, I would guess Alcuin planned this little scene," the King said as he emerged from the shadows. "Even if he did, things must change! My own child cannot find anyone available to listen to her read. Dear God! We must correct this situation immediately. Alcuin will have his school, here in this castle before the court begins its new year's journey! I will see to it." Charlemagne spent Christmas week talking with Gisela, expounding on his views of education.

His voice rising, the King assured his sister, Gisela, that his proposed academies would be glorious. Different students would enjoy educational experiences tailored for each of them. Captains would study maintenance of arms, the rudiments of troop deployment, basic mathematics, etc. Clerks would learn basic math, polish their courtesies, and keep accurate records. Those who transported goods for the court would benefit from a knowledge of packing methods in carts, on horseback, and in boats. And so on for each worker.

"Charlie," Gisela interrupted his description. "This all

sounds excellent and laudatory. Have you teachers whom I don't know? Who is able to educate, even just the young lads who come for soldiering? Father Beachus cannot read; he just recites portions of the testament. Didn't you say, some time ago, that few of the clergy were capable of reading? Isn't this the reason Alcuin joined the court, to teach priests?" She noticed the complacent look on her brother's face. She caught her breath and whispered.

"Has Alcuin agreed to start a school, one which others can use as a model? Oh, Charley, this can be true progress! Is Alcuin teaching the students himself? Will he teach the monks? How can he do all that? He is no longer a young man. The sisters in my abbey are all teachers, so has it been for ages past. But many of the monks do not have the same knowledge. I have seen only one or two monks who could read the catechisms and perform holy rituals from written directions. Even in the scriptoria, a few priests read passages so that the illuminators may illustrate or decorate the manuscripts. Who is to do the teaching?" Gisela asked her brother again.

"Damn it, Gisela! I had such high hopes," the King admitted. "I labored for years…to encourage a literate clergy. Alcuin sees the challenge. The bishops look at me blankly when I demand the clergymen must learn to read and write. Aye, Alcuin is here, firstly, to start a Palace School — one which will educate my children and those of the court. But schools must be established, spread throughout the realm. I want each person, each Christian, to read the Holy Scriptures on his own. It seems such dreams will take decades to materialize."

Charlemagne's face turned pasty; his eyes lost their sparkle. His lips turned down at the corners. He was stricken by Gisela's words. He looked at her in horror, one hand attempting to push her words away.

"How could I believe men would not value knowledge

or be reluctant to learn and share that learning? I imagined Alcuin assisting those in the court; but his skill must influence learning throughout the realm. And he needs help. I had proof of that, just this day. Can you believe Bertha could find no one to listen to her read, listen and help her? At this moment, we have only two or three teachers for this entire court! Think how much worse the situation is in the rest of the realm." The King rubbed his forehead, trying not to lose heart.

"You are correct still. Despite my best effort and my loudest exhortations, very few of the Bishops and fewer still of the Abbots encourage learning. In appointing uneducated men to the clergy, rewarding unlettered men for their service I am weakening my churches and denying the Frankish people education." The king's previously animated face crumpled in dejection, as the excitement of his educational vision tarnished in the reality of his kingdom.

Gisela's heart beat faster; she found it difficult to breathe. Watching her brother, she understood his anguish. Her own learning began late. Her tutor, although under the supervision of Abbot Fulrad, was grossly inadequate. When King Pepin discovered the man's limitations, he was furious. He hired another tutor immediately but Gisela's learning, ever after, was filled with miserable, unrelenting effort.

"You must, somehow, find a way, dear dreamer," she said quietly to the King. "You must find the world's best teachers and bring them to our people."

***

Conferring with Alcuin, Charlemagne set his plans in motion within a fortnight. He sent a handful of bishops, along with Rinaldo, and Theodulf, to Italy, Spain, and England, urging them to recruit teachers for his palace school. He told them not to return without scholars. With Alcuin's help, he identified the most renowned scholars, Peter of Pisa and Paul the Deacon, and attracted them to Aachen.

Ever was the King grateful to King Offa of Merci. Years before, he learned of Alcuin's work in Tours and encouraged his first meeting with Charlemagne. The King's persistence brought Alcuin to him. Now, he reapplied that persistence to breathe new life into his ideas for educating the children of the realm. Alcuin turned a military training school for the nobility into a liberal arts-based school for boys and girls alike. And this 'academie' would be replicated all over the Frankish realm.

"If I go to school, so must you!' Charlemagne admonished everyone within his court. He even encouraged his wife and demanded his daughters attend the palace school with him.

***

Even before the Palace School attracted students and instructors, the King and Alcuin talked late and often about literature, language, theology, and philosophy. Alcuin was, of course, the master of learning but was encouraged and, occasionally impressed, by King Charlemagne's depth of thought and questing mind. They each began to invite others to join their discussions. Rinaldo often came to learn, he said, but contributed much through his questions. Angilbert had, despite Alcuin's reservations long ago, become a fine and prolific poet. He was a significant member of the 'philosophy group,' adding to the intellectual discussions on Latin and Greek literature. Theodulf made his way to Charlemagne's court and produced, possibly, the best poetry of anyone there. The group became such supportive company for each other they even took 'new' names for themselves. The

119

King was called 'King David' and, on occasion, 'Solomon.' Angilbert's code-name was 'Homer'; Gisela, now the Abbess of Chelles and welcomed by all, was called 'Lucia.' Rotrud, the King's eldest daughter, was called 'Columba.' Even the famous historian, Einhard, was given another name—'Bezeleel.' In such a barbaric land, these learned discussions were only possible because the king was dedicated to learning and supportive of anyone who wished to read, debate, learn, and share knowledge.

Charlemagne's politics and control of his kingdom, while reflecting near to dictatorial power, were founded on his personal dedication to helping his people, on his belief that knowledge was power and should be available to everyone – a decidedly unusual stance for an eighth-century barbarian king ruling during the Dark Ages of continental Europe.

In an effort to record the history of his times, Charlemagne sought Alcuin's direction. "Who should write the history of my reign, Alcuin?" he asked. "I want my grandchildren to understand my efforts. Sometimes it seems my sons don't share my view, don't even understand my vision. Mayhap, my grandchildren will value it."

"Sire, you are far too demanding of yourself. Listen to me. You are much beloved and admired. Thousands of men have served you over the years. Aye, many thousands have died for you! There can be no dishonor in their dedication. You have brought Christianity to scores of people! You are bringing reading, writing, even thinking to Frankish nobles and peasants alike. We in your Philosophy Club call you 'the candle in the darkness.' You must not denigrate your accomplishments." Alcuin spoke with feeling and enthusiasm.

"Mayhap, mayhap," Charlemagne replied, pleased at the scholar's reassurance. Over the years, he and Alcuin had become friends. That friendship had served him well; it was one of his greatest strengths. But he had a legacy which he wanted recorded. Alcuin saw his king's furrowed brow, saw the concern that King Charlemagne placed in this endeavor, and replied.

"As for a scribe, I'd recommend Einhard, Sire. He is thorough, fair, and adept with the pen. He was educated at Fulda, an exemplary school. He would truthfully record your accomplishments. I'm certain of it. You'd be pleased with his writing and his intellectual metal."

"But is his writing exemplary, Alcuin?" Charlemagne smiled sheepishly. His love of words made it important that his life and accomplishments sing from the parchment. He wanted style and eloquence reflected in the story of his life. "I'll be led by your recommendation, Alcuin," Charlemagne responded. "Please send an inquiry to determine how quickly he might join our court."

Einhard responded almost immediately to Alcuin's missive, asking questions which Alcuin hadn't addressed. Einhard admitted he was flattered to be asked to join King Charlemagne's court. Its intellectual energy was well-known and many eminent scholars were answering the King's invitations. After the spring thaw of 792, Einhard presented himself to the Carolingian King.

"Sire, I'm honored," he acknowledged, overcome that he was to have the privilege of describing Charlemagne's life and accomplishments. "I've so anticipated the rigorous scholarship of your court and prayed that I, by some small measure, might participate in the educational oasis you are creating here."

Charlemagne beamed at the praise and rejoiced that Einhard would consider recording the Frankish court's accomplishments. He welcomed Einhard, thanked Alcuin for his recruitment, and scheduled a meeting to describe his court's successes to the chronicler. He was, he said, eager for Einhard to determine if the two of them could share an effective, collaborative relationship. He wanted to provide some background for his early decisions and give him a little history of the court.

The king hoped that readers, hearing his own plans and dreams for the realm, would judge him fairly. He knew that other versions from nobles, military commanders, even his queen would provide altogether different interpretations. But he, also, wished to speak for himself, as long as he was able.

"I promise not to brag or overstate my accomplishments," Charlemagne vowed.

"I shall write as you speak, my King," Einhard responded. Charlemagne nodded his agreement and began.

Charlemagne explained that he vowed long ago to conquer and Chrisianize the heathen anywhere they dwelt within his realm. He believed this great work his destiny. And he wanted to teach all men to read so they might interpret the scriptures for themselves.

"For civic advancement and legal control, many of my conquered peoples follow their traditional ways. But for a Christian nation, all must adhere to the laws in a common manner. I have strengthened the Church's doctrines and have demanded—aye, I have forced-- people to accept Christian precepts. A ruler must often be harsh to command obedience," he said. "The Saxons have especially tried my patience, so much so that people were killed who refused to fast as directed. Any who broke the strictures which I enumerated paid for that evil choice with their lives. All men must know I took these actions to enhance their relationships with God the Father. All of Frankland will be Christian. I must save my people's souls," the King declared.

"But what an obtuse idea," Einhard muttered, examining the King's words as he quickly wrote them down verbatim.

"What is that?" King Charlemagne asked. "What did you say?"

"Excuse me, Sire. I do have a habit of muttering to myself. I was puzzled at your statement: that people were killed who refused to fast? How can that be? If you kill them, they surely cannot be deemed Christians then. You would kill them to save their souls?" Einhard looked directly into the King's face, wondering at the obsession in these words.

"Death has come to some--to many--of them, Sir," the King responded. "An example must be made of those who don't show obedience. God is displeased." Charlemagne ceased speaking. His eyes stared unseeing at his library, the walls holding parchment rolls.

Einhard hoped he had not made a misjudgment in coming to Aachen and replied. "Proceed with your first memory, Sire; I'm ready to begin."

King Charlemagne seemed not to have heard the scribe. "If I could only forgive myself, my slaughter of those Saxons. Have you heard about the 782 campaign? I murdered 4500 souls! In a fit of anger which I have never been able to explain, I had hundreds of soldiers killed. Dear God! Even were HE to forgive me, I can never enter Heaven!" He bowed his head, fighting his memory of that terrible day. "I can never forgive myself. There can be no forgiveness for such deliberate killing, no forgiveness at all."

Einhard sat completely still, struck by the King's remorse and by his willingness to show his regret. He knew nothing to reply.

"It's true that I've done some good," Charlemagne continued. He counted off those successes on his fingers. He defended the Pope and bestowed great wealth on the church. He gave no quarter to heathens; to stay in his realm, he demanded they become Christians. He even moved them from their homes to new sites, sometimes hundreds of miles apart, to control them. And, aye, he admitted some of them had been put to death. He cleaned the Church, lessened the corruption-- both to resurrect its ancient, holy mission and to rehabilitate its clergy. But none of these efforts would remove his murder of those Saxons. "How could I face my God?" The King seemed to forget Einhard was in the room. He appeared frozen in his memories, haunted by the wholesale slaughter which he ordered.

Long minutes later, the King looked at Einhard. "Some good I have done, Einhard," he said, "but this cruelty, of my own making, will haunt me forever." He rubbed his eyes and motioned Einhard to leave. "We will stop for today." Einhard left the chamber.

The session with Einhard took all of King Charlemagne's energy. "I must get my mind away from that unholy massacre," he scolded himself. "This does no good, this constant re-visiting of that horrible day. I must try to forget! I must think of a pleasant memory." The King looked around.

Of course! He smiled. *I am in Aachen; all praise and thankfulness must be given for that happy event. How dearly I love this place!* King Charlemagne thought to himself. But, once again, even Aachen could not shut out the cares of this realm. There was a knock on the library door; Alcuin entered with a grim face.

King Charlemagne shook his head and glared at Alcuin. Slamming his hands against the table, he shuddered, knowing from Alcuin's look that trouble had come. Alcuin led a courier into the library. The courier stumbled with exhaustion, his tunic torn and muddy. Weary from hard riding, he delivered his missive, informing the King of yet another Saxon revolt. The King prepared to march, calling for help from the Slavs.

***

The Slavs army joined with the great Frankish army. Together, they confronted the Saxons. The fighting raged for two long years. This renewed fight with the rebellious Saxons began just as another peoples, the Avars, threatened the Frankish kingdom as well.

Many years before, the Avars, a nomadic people from Eurasia, were forced from their traditional homelands. In their flight, they drew close to the Frankish realm. Eventually they settled in the Pannonian Plain, a vast land caught between several mountain ranges: the Carpathian, the Alps, the Dinaric Alps and the Balkans. The natural defense of the mountains protected them and allowed them to recoup their battle worthiness.

In the few weeks just passed, they began plundering. Seeking new lands, the Avars left the Pannonian Plain and moved into the Frankish empire. Using 'burn and flee' tactics, they never directly attacked King Charlemagne's great army. But they undermined the peace, as well as the prosperity, of the land-- destroying crops, animals, and homes as they ranged ahead of Charlemagne's troops.

It was now late autumn. Charlemagne knew the weariness of his troops; they had been in the field since early spring. Needing to 'live off the land,' as his army moved, the King was dismayed to find the Avars had stripped the land of berries, fodder, and animals. Even the wild greens and nuts were gone. Having little provisions and an exhausted army, he headed for home.

He must try to defeat the Avars once and for all, not have them constantly revolting as was the case with the Saxons. Hoping for a quick and complete victory, he decided to use surprise and the quick movement of his troops to overcome the enemy. The most expeditious way to do this was transport the army by water.

The King began constructing bridges across the rapidly-flowing rivers along his route. Planning to use these waterways to increase the speed of his attacks against the Avars, he searched for likely crossings along the banks. But his efforts failed. The swiftness of the rivers made it impossible to construct sturdy bridges. The water invariably washed them away. With no ability to move his army rapidly enough to surprise the Avars, the Carolingian King was unwilling to confront the enemy troops.

Chapter 8

CHILDREN – SUCH SURPRISES

The difficulty of an attack and his few military choices led to much frustration for the king. He became restive over these limited choices and that led to introspection. In a desperate frame of mind, he began to enumerate his failings to his family. His greatest one, he believed, was to his dearly loved wife, Hildegard who died in childbirth. Over the course of his marriages, the King's first three wives, as well as nobles of the court, begged him to choose a permanent home. Hildegard, birthing children almost yearly, had yearned for a place to 'settle,' as she called it. Only a few weeks after his marriage to Fastrada, his fourth wife, too, asked him to discontinue his trips through the kingdom. Everyone in the court longed for a permanent home. Fastrada's words rang in Charlemagne's mind. 'Any place that doesn't move,' she said. *Fastrada asked when she knew I was still bedazzled by her...or by her gifts in the bedchamber,* the King thought. Reviewing his memories of the early days of his fourth marriage, the King now thought of himself as a voyeur.

Even so, his grief at Hildegard's death was almost beyond his ability to endure. He disconnected from his own body. And so, he watched his behavior as though he were another person. *Never had I allowed myself to fear for Hildegard's life,* the King thought. *...not Hildegard, she had already birthed eight healthy babes. The ones who did not survive were lost months after their birthings. How could I* *think this little one would prove deadly?*

Fron this perception of his failure, Charlemagne's thoughts veered to another stupid choice. "Without a doubt, when I changed my second son's name from Carl to Pepin, I broke my first Peppin's heart. Of a certainty, it appeared to my first-born that I denied his very existence, that I dismissed him from my life...because of his hump-back. How can a father be so stupid? I wonder when he found out about it?" He searched for some way to reassure himself.

Mayhap, I worry needlessly. Each of my sons with Hildegard has a part of the Frankish realm. It was propitious to replace Carl's birth name to Pepin when he was named King of Lombardy; it was his grandfather's name. On that same day, Louis was made king of Aquitaine. Charles, my first son with Hildegard, has one-third of the realm left to me. Surely, these three sons are enough to guarantee the strength of the empire. But in giving the Hunchback's name, Peppin, to another son, I have rejected him yet again!

"Why do I make such poor decisions about my children?" He wailed to himself. Then, the king was immobile. He sat down, the better to think deeply. His thoughts only plunged him into deeper misery. He admitted that he did not know his children very well. As they grew up, he spent little time with them...only to re-iterate his expectations to them, the boys and the girls. Rotrud always did challenge him, if only by asking "Why, Poppa?" He left their growing, their learning, their very beings to Hildegard. And she was wonderful! But she died when Charles was eleven and Rotrud was barely eight years. No wonder they all felt rudderless!" The king moaned his lost opportunities and prayed that those teaching and caring for Carl and Louis were up to the job. Still, he must do better with those here in the court. It was certain Fastrada would do nothing for them. He must work them into his days; it was his most important duty.

Heavenly Father, this is my day for sorrow, for backward looks and for huge regrets. "But, if I do poorly by my own offspring, I am providing education for the children of the kingdom." The King reminded himself. "I must remember to ask Alcuin to check on the monasteries. I've directed the Bishops to seek out working men's sons, even peasant children, to attend the church schools. The nobility won't be the only educated people in my sons' realms." The King's thoughts jumped from one idea to another.

"Alcuin's palace school is proceeding well. Children are happily coming to classes." *I have even attended classes with them. What a joy it was, to see both the quickness of Gizzie's mind and the great depth of Rotrud's. My girls don't disappoint me. Thank God for their presence; each one reminds me of her dear mother!* "The proof of the good of this school is in my own children," the King noted.

"Charles and Bertha, though previously schooled by monks, find the learning difficult. Charles is uninterested in the philosophical discussions which I so love. But Rotrud has surprised us all. For someone so dedicated to society, she has a remarkably flexible mind. Louis, reared far away in Aquitaine, is religious enough for us all, and, when visiting, seldom enters into any of the court discussions which are so common during the evening meals. Bertha doesn't read well, though her voice has been well-trained and is melodious. Needless to say, the monks have taken no credit for the popular, sometimes bawdy, songs which the girls sing with such great enthusiasm. Ha! I need only look at my daughters and my heart is lifted."

***

Bertha was the only daughter who shared her father's coloring. Like him, her hair was light brown, her skin fair and easily prey to blistering. Because she spent much of

129

the temperate days in the gardens and orchards, her skin was a light honey-brown well into the late autumn and set off her sun-streaked hair. Not nearly as tall as her father, she never-the-less was tall for a woman, stately and full-figured. Had she not kept a tight rein on her sweet tooth, she would have mirrored her father's figure, though his girth was from love of meat, not sweets.

***

Poppa so enjoys life! Bertha often envied him. *No matter what dire news comes: rebellious tribes, attacks on cloisters and monasteries, even the loss of his beloved soldiers, Poppa is unfailing positive.* "Mayhap the gift comes only to kings.... or to men." Bertha wondered aloud.

Bertha was proud of her hard-earned abilities. She read poorly but could both write and speak Latin and Greek. She would sometimes quote the scriptures. And she labored to understand the hierarchy of the Church. Nonetheless, she wished to ride her horse well beyond the castle lands, to swim unhindered in a forest stream, to make a journey without a retinue of servants.

"It must be fine to be a man," she often said, "to go as one pleases, not to sit waiting for an invitation from a simpering, foolish count's daughter who wants only to talk of eligible men." Bertha sighed, remembering Rotrud's hurts.

Sensitive and withdrawn, Bertha worried about her sister. Rotrud would not accept the king's dictum that his girls would never marry. He would not allow it. No one, even Master Alcuin, knew where this order came from. It mattered not; Charlemagne's words were law. Despite this, various counts proposed marriage to Rotrud. Their father seemed to welcome the proposals, played with the counts and lords a day or two and, then, refused the proposal. The court thought his mind changed when he betrothed Rotrud to Constantine, prince of the Byzantine Empire. But nothing had ever come of that.

"Rotrud was a baby, only six years old, in 781 when that betrothal was announced. Even later, I never expected Rotrud to spend time in Constantine's court...and she did not. Today, Rotrud is heartbroken yet another time."

Bertha recalled her father's march into his daughters' sitting room. As cold as possible, he looked around and announced that Rotrud's dalliance with Count Norico would cease. Rotrud was horrified, then embarrassed. Several counts's daughters were there with us, discussing clothing for the upcoming ball. Their presence did nothing to stop the king. He added that he would not have her consorting with a man of so limited circumstance.

"Hah! What a joke! Poppa doesn't care who Rotrud 'dallies' with. He just wants no permanent liaisons and, certainly, no love matches. Rotrud is devastated; she does truly love Norico and wishes to make a life with him."

Bertha envied Rotrud her emotional distress; she could find no young man who remotely interested her. *Just as well*, she mused, *Poppa would allow nothing but friendships in any case.*

***

Bertha was just opening the door to go to the orchards when her stepmother, Fastrada, came into the room. "Oh, my dear; I'm so glad you're here. Can you suggest anything we can do to help poor Rotrud; she's ruining her voice with shouting and her face with weeping."

"No, Queen Fastrada. There's nothing we can do because she is inconsolable. I won't tell her a lie, that she'll have other chances with more wealthy suitors. You and I both know Poppa won't allow her to marry, not anyone. There's no consolation to give, no advice to help her – not if we speak the truth."

Bertha spoke very frankly to her stepmother, having understood long ago that Fastrada was a scheming wife who would never openly confront her husband nor stand up for any of them. She had little imagination and no persuasive powers Bertha could identify. She guessed Fastrada pampered the king in private and, as a result, got very close to all she wanted. Despite her father's praise of this wife, Bertha saw Fastrada's contempt for her and her siblings. *Fastrada is a cross in our lives, a cross we must bear. She surely has no influence with Poppa on the question of our marrying.*

Thinking of her mother's short life, Bertha sometimes believed being husbandless might not be a tragedy. At least, she wouldn't bear a child every single year. And she wasn't sure if she could bear them and lose them. Children in the court seemed to die as quickly as they were conceived. Again, she wished her mother were alive, to share her secrets about pregnancy and child-rearing. Queen Hildegard was respected throughout the realm for her gracious spirit and concern for everyone, no matter their station.

"I'm defeated by your father's attitude." Fastrada's voice brought Bertha back to reality. "He doesn't imagine your lives when he's gone." She smiled sadly, as she dropped a note on Rotrud's pillow.

***

On hearing Queen Fastrada sought her and left her a note in her sleeping quarters, Rotrud turned away from her bedchamber as quickly as she could. *I surely don't wish to be here if the Queen returns*, she thought to herself. *I can only be pleasant in her presence if I don't have to talk to her and if we are not long together.* Rotrud was unapologetic for her thoughts. *Fastrada is a cold, selfish, mean woman who thinks only of advancing her own interests. She dresses*

*her own daughter like a queen with expensive jewels and rich
clothing; but she gives her little personal concern. Theoderada
must remain quiet, be demure, and show as little personality as
possible.*

Heading for the stables, Rotrud passed the schoolroom
where Gizzie was laboring at arithmetic. Rotrud was
surprised to see Gizzie coming out the chamber door.

"Is there a problem, Gizzie?" Rotrud asked. "Shouldn't
you be inside with the other scholars?"

"Scholars, Rotrud? You're joking, right? We are far from
scholars!" and Gizzie laughed. "But Master Angilbert told
us, just before you came, that we're 'dill-u-gent.' Is that a
good thing? I wasn't sure." She added as Rotrud nodded
in the affirmative.

"That means all of you are trying, Gizzie...trying
hard." Rotrud clarified. "But why are you coming out of
the classroom?"

"Oh, the teacher for the 'little ones' isn't here. I was
going to find Bertha to see if she could help them with
their singing. They do that best, you know. The letters and,
even, numbers are difficult for them." Gizzie related with
all the wisdom of her nine years and the speech patterns
of her language teacher.

"I saw her tunic going out the door," Rotrud laughed.
"I'll send her back, just give me time to bolt after her." And
with that, she ran down the hall. Gizzie looked back and
forth down the corridor, afraid Fastrada would appear to
scold. The Queen had no good words for Rotrud, Bertha,
or Gizzie, just demanded they control their laughter or
walk more like 'ladies of the court.' Gizzie often ridiculed
Fastrada's walk, bringing knowing looks and embarrassed
laughter from all the children. Gizzie returned to the
teaching chamber, knowing Rotrud would send Bertha as
soon as she caught her.

Bertha was delighted at Rotrud's message. She spent hours with the 'little ones' of the Palace School – singing, playing games, and washing faces and hands. Many of them, hardly three years old, demanded to come to school because their older brothers and sisters attended. Rather than discourage the young students, Alcuin had shorter classes for them. He taught them counting rhymes or songs that identified colors, and fruits, and animals. "Never discourage a student," was Alcuin's directive to all the teachers, especially when someone struggled to learn and understand.

Bertha removed her over-tunic as she entered the teaching room and waved to her small charges. There was a small uproar as each 'little one' rushed to greet Bertha with a kiss, sticky though they turned out to be. There had just been a break for jam and crusts which had been a great success, judging by the red jam smeared over everyone's clothing.

"Bertha, Bertha!" the 'little ones' shouted. "Sing us a song! Tell us a story! Sing so we can walk fast – like soldiers!"

"Wait, Wait," Bertha laughed. "Everyone needs first to wash hands; dry them on the linen, and, then, sit at your places. We need some quiet now. Everyone should get ready to sing." She smiled as the little 'students' splattered water all over the stones and fought with each other to dry their hands. Some even tried to wash their mouths which were covered with remnants of jam and bread crumbs.

"I'm going to sing about the little, green frog." Bertha announced to the eager children. A shout of approval rose from the group and, then a burst of giggles as a loud 'Hrump' pierced the air. The most eager children began to clap, a beat ahead of Bertha's sweet voice.

The little, green frog slept on a log and failed to eat his

bread.

The little, green frog fell off his log and and bruised his little head.

The little, green frog ran toward his bog and jumped right in, you see

The little, green frog hopped from his bog and ran to you and me.

Bertha sang the little song three times. "Now," she said to the 'little ones,' "let's see how well you can sing it. Keep together now and clap so the rhythm is right." The children began screeching, delighted with the opportunity to sing. After the third time, they were able to keep the song moving along, helped by the rhyming pattern.

"Another time, another time," the little ones called; so Bertha led them into another round. Just as the song was being completed for the second time, she heard the door open and looked up as a man stepped into the teaching room. Bertha's breath rushed out of her mouth. She heard someone whisper: "Breathe, Princess Bertha, take a big breath." She looked down to see little Jeremy patting her hand. She was frozen, as if a mage had put a spell on her. One of the small girls stamped Bertha's foot; and, then, she did take a deep breath. All the 'little ones' erupted in laughter, patting Bertha's hands, hugging her waist, and cavorting around the room. Bertha pulled her eyes away from the door and looked at her charges in confusion.

"Let's quieten down now," she said, "I believe you all like that one! Now, who will lead the next song for us...or would you rather recite a rhyme?"

"Let's do the 'farm song'," one of the boys shouted. "You start us, Princess. We can sing if you'll start us."

"Then, listen and stop talking so you can hear the song," Bertha cautioned. And she sang.

Master Royston had a farm, ee-I, ee-I, Ohhh! And on

that farm he had a cow,

Eee-I, ee-I, Ohhh!"

Bertha stopped singing to give directions. "Ratchet, get at the head of the line and begin the march. Call out the name of the animals when the time comes. Can you do that?"

"I can," Ratchet answered as he began marching around the teaching chamber, looking over his shoulder to pace his legs to those of the smallest followers.

At last, Bertha could look up...toward the chamber door. The man was still standing there, his hand holding the door half-open. He looked directly at her. Bertha looked down quickly; she had almost lost her breath again. Breathing slowly in and out, she returned her eyes and, there he was, standing in the same place. Smiling tentatively, Bertha spoke.

"Hello," she said, curtseying just a little. "This is the 'little ones' room. The next older classroom is one down and the rooms beyond are for the oldest students. Are you looking for someone particular?"

"I didn't know until this moment; I was looking for you," the man's quiet, intent voice replied. Noticing the farm march was winding down, the visitor smiled at Bertha. "My name is Angilbert. I've come to see if the 'little ones' have any poems for me. Last week, we talked about poems and rhymes. I promised to come back to hear the poems they can remember. Is the farm march the last activity for today?"

As the children heard the man's voice, they broke ranks and ran to the door. Jumping up and down around him, each began trying to tell him their poem.

"Wait, Wait," he laughed at them. "Sit down over near the firepit in a circle. That way, each one can hear the other one's poem." He turned to Bertha.

"Would you join us, Princess?" he asked. "By the way,

I work with Master Alcuin in the school and am a writer."
He smiled at her, letting a little girl lead him by the hand.

Somehow, Bertha made her body obey her commands,
even though she was unaware of making them. She sat
on one of the benches against the wall as the 'little ones'
repeated poems to their teacher. He praised each of them
and, in some few cases, suggested a word which better fit
the rhyme the child was trying to make.

Angilbert praised the children's 'poems,' telling them
he was proud of each and every one. As he beamed at the
children, he somehow included Bertha in that warmth.
He promised to tell their parents that the court would be
overrun with poets in a few years. One of the boys protested
that he would not be one of those poets. The children
laughed, as if instinctively putting themselves in his
prediction. Flattered by his friends' reaction, he admitted
that no one would understand his poetry. He could make
the sounds, he said, but the words for those sounds were
hard to find. He looked to Angilbert, challenging him.

"The meaning is in the heart of the one who reads the
poem, Jason." Angilbert replied. "But let me say this. You
are all developing poets! You've accomplished more than
I can believe," Angilbert praised them again. He stood to
remind them that there was a celebration just beginning
over in the banquet hall. When he passed by almost an
hour ago, he saw tables filled with 'delights,' just waiting
for hungry children!" Laughing as the children cheered,
Angilbert ushered them out into the corridor and urged
them to hurry to their Christmas party.

Bertha stood up to leave with the children but stopped
as Angilbert put out his hand. "Might you stay and talk a
little?" he asked. "I've been at the court for months and,
yet, I don't see you near enough. How is that possible?
Your glow is so golden, so steady I should have noted it
from afar." His smile, growing slowly, lit up his eyes and

softened his serious mouth.

Bertha was enchanted. *They say there are no longer any gods,* she thought, *but here is one. Ahh, his hair is the color of a jonquil, his hands slender and tapering – the hands of an artist...or of a poet,* she amended.

"I'm happy to know you," Bertha replied. "I believe I've seen you from some distance, walking down a corridor, mayhap. Are you the 'little ones' regular teacher now?" She asked, searching for something to say. "They are beautiful children, each and every one. I hope Master Alcuin is satisfied with the 'schooling' we give them. But seeing you interacting with them delights me...a poet who teaches little ones!" Bertha struggled on. "We older students see many scholars in our studies but the only poet has been Master Alcuin. ...not that he's a bad poet." She stopped speaking, flustered. She hardly knew the words she said. *This man is being so kind. He must think I've wool stuffed in my head.*

"I'm the one delighted to meet you." Angilbert responded. "I must go to this Christmas celebration. Will you come? Mayhap we may share a cup of drink and a 'delight' or two." Bertha found her voice and herself.

"Aye," she replied. "Let's go to the hall. I will be well-served if you will share 'delights' with me." She emphasized the word *share.* "I've a huge weakness for any of them." She laughed at herself and preceded Angilbert out of the teaching chamber, walking with him to the banquet room. Bertha expected her father already to be at the celebration but heard he'd been delayed and would be there soon.

***

The same moment, in another part of the court Queen Fastrada was speaking with King Charlemagne, clearly delighting in her ability to surprise him once again.

"I've had a missive from Peppin," Queen Fastrada bragged. "Of course, he is saddened, overwhelmed by his mother's early death. He begs us to excuse him a while longer, 'ere he returns to court," she dropped her eyes to the floor, as if in a moment of sadness. "I told him all here are begging you to extend this stay in Aachen and that, mayhap, we shall still be here when he's ready to return."

"I feel such sorrow for him. I had Alcuin send a letter. Oh, I sent your condolences, also, Charlemagne, knowing you would wish it so." Fastrada gave the hint of a smile, seemingly delighted with her action and the subterfuge of it as well.

"How kind of you, Fastrada," the King replied dryly. "I know Peppin was appreciative of your kind words. He wrote me that several of the court sent missives. I, knowing your perfect courtesy, assumed you were in that group." Charlemagne swallowed the bile in his throat. He knew Fastrada was touched only if she profited directly from a behavior. "The lad sounds dejected. But he's resilient and will, I know, find his balance once again." He shook his head.

"I know the difficulty of losing a parent. But I cannot imagine losing a mother at his age! This is dreadful for Peppin. They were almost a unit, Himlitrude and her son. What a grievous blow! She was ever a loving, supportive mother, dedicated to Peppin's welfare." The King's voice faded with those words. He face was preoccupied, his eyes far away. He was alone with his memories.

"I do wonder the length of time he'll neglect us," the King continued. "Of a certainty, he has no great responsibilities here. He helped train a group of young lads with the bow. And Alcuin praises his grasp of geography, saying Peppin added considerable knowledge to the maps we have for regions around Auch and Toulouse. He told Alcuin of a long, summer trip in that region, seems he enjoyed an excursion with one of his mother's nephews there." Charlemagne added mournfully. The King ran his fingers through his hair, absently.

"You know, I've no idea of the life the boy led. I've discounted or minimalized events and persons who've influenced him. But, no matter, he knows I am proud of his maturity and self-discipline. I wonder if I might find a small estate for him." the King murmured to himself. "He'll want to marry and establish himself. I must alert Rinaldo to this need. Mayhap, he and Count Janlur can identify a likely manor."

"Don't be so quick to offer estates, my Lord," Fastrada bitingly replied. "You do have daughters who need dowries...before your love child should have provision. I'm startled to hear this great concern for Peppin. You should seek alliances and marry your daughters! Rotrud and Bertha, you realize, are well beyond their freshest bloom." Fastrada immediately knew she had overstepped her station. The King turned to look directly into her face, his lips curled in distaste, his eyes boring into hers.

"Leave off, Fastrada!" he shouted. "Your ambitions do embolden your tongue. I direct your own daughter's fortune, just as soundly as I direct the interest of my other children. Any girls you have, for their own good, shall also not marry. Be thankful. If you believe my two eldest daughters would now have difficulty finding suitors, you should regard your young daughter a bit more critically. She has neither the complexion, the hair, nor the vitality of either Rotrud or Bertha. Do mind your words! They kill as easily as a sword." With that, the King left the bedchamber. He held himself under rigid control, incensed at Fastrada's temerity.

Charlemagne admitted to himself that Frastrada worked at cross-purposes with him, just as his mother did with his father. He knew he had to make an effort to determine if she betrayed him, if she had been part of Hardrad's plot to arrest him. He thanked God Rinaldo and Janlur nipped that in the bud! He admitted to himself; he was dumbfounded by Fastrada's behavior and her cruel mouth. She was after something. *In no arrangement would she have more stature than as the queen of the Frankish realm.* Even a son, which I pray against every night, would grant her less influence than her place as his wife. He named his heirs long ago. Was she this hateful, her personality so grasping? "Nay, she could not be so stupid." The King refused to think any longer about his wife's ambition. She was altogether too much like his mother.

"So, dear Lord, is this your punishment to me, mayhap for my pride or my ingratitude? This Queen may be a traitor in my bed. Why is she here - to make me wary, to darken my successes, to destroy my soul?" Shaking his head, King directed his steps toward the Christmas celebration, hoping to decrease his frustration and sorrows among the cheerful throng.

***

Oblivious of the talk about him, Peppin returned to his mother's house. He needed to spend some time there, relive his memories. Then, he would be on his way back to Charlemagne's court. He enjoyed his sojourn with Adelchis but had, finally, felt he should return to the court. *Adelchis and I share many common experiences.* Peppin thought. *We were both sent from Poppa's court; we both are sons of powerful, ambitious men. We both have been isolated from others, for different reasons. And we both loved my mother. But I'm not certain that Adelchis or I, or us together, would make a better king than Poppa. That was the single conversation in Adelchis' home: the possibility of my being king of Frankland. What a thought! Adelchis says Poppa's time is gone, but he thinks I could claim Poppa's realm!* Peppin shook his head in denial. *Even if the Byzantine court would support such a thing, what debt would I owe them? What would their demand, payment for that support, be worth? Surely, I have no means to pay.*

"I'm torn in pieces!" Peppin announced to the firepit. "I've loyalties based on love and friendship to Adelchis and my mother's memory. But I, too, have loyalties to Poppa, based on blood and obedience. What kind of son am I, if I don't support my king and my father? My grandfather did usurp the kingdom from the Merovginian king, years ago. Queen Fastrada says Adelchis' father's – King Desiderius - claim on the Frankish crown was as strong as Grandfather Pepin's. But, if I support such an idea, I will betray my father. I shall do nothing." Peppin decided. "If I leave Poppa's court, that's the time to think of other choices. Right now, I'll get back to some routine in my life. I can always return to Ma-mam's manor. Oh, to my manor, I mean." And he smiled.

Peppin was surprised, a fortnight after he returned to his mother's manor, to receive a missive from Adelchis' court seneschal. Michah, ever tedious and steadfast, brought a letter from Adelchis; but, of more importance, was the escort which arrived with him. The escort's commander, after refreshing his contingent, came directly to the reason for their visit: to recruit Peppin for an overthrow of his father's rule. Adelchis' words, relayed by Michah verbally and, then by parchment placed in Peppin's hands, begged Peppin to consider the proposal, assuring him that King Charlemagne and his court would come to no harm.

"Little is required from you." He read the parchment. "All we need do is seek King Charlemagne's abdication in favor of you with Adelchis as your primary adviser."

Peppin heard this plan talked all around Adelchis' court, but hoped it came only from discontented nobles adding spice to their boring days. *Here, though, is the plea delivered directly to my hands. And it seems the escort plans to wait for my reply.*

***

As the sun climbed to mid-day next morning, a second contingent of twenty men approached Peppin's manor from the south. Peppin could only wonder at his new prominence as the captain of Queen Fastrada's guards greeted him and bowed at his feet. Less circumspect than Adelchis, Queen Fastrada had, also, sent a letter of greeting. Her second page, though, beseeched his aid in usurping the king's crown. Fastrada openly offered her service as his principal adviser.

To her letter, Peppin gave no thought at all. Fastrada's credibility was nonexistent. She was a schemer who promoted herself above any other person. Peppin had no doubt she would kill the King, if such was necessary for her own ambitions. And her hatred of Peppin's half-siblings was obvious. Isolated by his removal from court and his physical handicap, Peppin resented anyone who undervalued family. In that, Fastrada would ever be his enemy.

Fastrada's plotting he easily dismissed. But, Adelchis' request was another question entirely. *Adelchis represents the father I never knew; the father who helped define me and the man I became. Adelchis knew Peppin loved 'Splotch, his little dog beyond reason, that he delighted in training young colts, that he was an expert with the battle-ax, and that he was educating himself to supervise his mother's holding.* King Charlemagne had little understanding of Peppin or of his values And, apparently, the king had never wished to learn about his firstborn son..

Peppin paused, trying to get his thoughts in order. *You do not want to rule, yet you are not eager to stay in this manor. If you return to the Frankish court, what will you do;*

what is your place there? Or, even more crucial, do you have a place? The questions rolled around in his head, seemingly without answers.

Shortly after the Queen's detachment arrived at his manor, the social invitations began to roll in. Peppin wondered by what method the ladies and countesses of the region could know of his whereabouts. But, no matter. His presence was requested at a ball or a dinner, three nights out of four. In every gathering, he was treated as a prince, as a man's whose opinions counted, as an important personage in the life of Frankland.

Never had Peppin received such invitations, such attention from young, attractive women, such deference from high-born lords and their ladies. Some enterprising commanders even sought his opinions on military tactics, the breeding of war horses, and military training for junior officers.

"I'm overwhelmed by all this attention." Peppin confessed to his one stable boy. "But I do, at last, have some sense of place...and of importance."

"Oh, but, my Lord, you do be important," the young lad answered. "You are the first-born of King Charlemagne. Be mindful of that."

"Aye," Adelchis' captain affirmed. "Remember who you are, Sire, and what you're owed."

***

Riding off into the hills alone, Peppin reviewed his life. He was forced to admit the last several months and, particularly, the society he enjoyed upon returning home were the most satisfactory of anything he had experienced. He was no longer isolated. People didn't seem to notice his hunch- back; and, if they did, they took no heed of it. No one shied away from him as he passed people in the court or in the manors. Those of his own age--be they soldiers, nobles, landowners, or ladies--were delighted with his presence and responded eagerly to his invitations. Peppin felt he, at long last, had friends, people who delighted in his company. "To be sure," he thought to himself, "I've a changed existence. No one would know me for the boy who returned home from King Charlemagne's court, uncertain of my future and without direction. I must try to maintain this acceptance." He went that very night to talk with Adelchis's captain about a coup against the King.

***

In order to deflect attention from himself, Peppin announced he would be going into the hills to hunt. He chose his squire and Adelchis' captain to accompany him. The captain came directly from Adelchis' court, bringing luxuries and exhortations from Adelchis to return to Byzantium when plans permitted. Peppin missed Adelchis but knew his future lay in Frankish lands, not in a faraway, unknown country.

Leaving his squire to set up camp, Peppin and the captain arrived early at a small, unobtrusive chapel several leagues from his mother's home. He planned to make contact with a band of conspirators from the King's court this night. The captain assured Peppin a plan to overthrow the King was ready, planned several months before. Secreting himself in the shadows behind the chancel of the little church, Peppin waited for those who would betray the King. They arrived, eight of them, dressed in dull brown cloaks, undyed breeches, and rough, homespun tunics. They seemed in good spirits, unconcerned about safety or discovery.

"Where is Prince Peppin?" one of the conspirators asked. "We must have his blessing to legitimize our actions. None of us is worthy... not to claim ascendancy to the crown."

"I do trust he hasn't reconsidered his decision," another added. Peppin stepped out from behind the altar.

"Nay, I haven't reconsidered," he assured the eight. "I am, unlike you, hesitant to trumpet my plans to the world. Do you have no discretion? Contain yourselves; this is serious business we're about."

"Oh, ho. The prince does already give pronouncements! Nay, I would say these are orders." The first man responded.

"I expect you are waiting for just such orders, Sir," Peppin replied. He shall have less contempt for me, Peppin thought, when the next twenty-four hours are finished. *By then, I'll have his complete support of this undertaking...or I will have his life.* "Your risk is nothing, compared to mine. You will do nothing, if I do not support it! Spell out your plan. I shall deem it worthy or not." Peppin rested his hand on his sword, fingering its hilt. This man does act the fool, he thought to himself.

"Excuse us, Sir," another man spoke, mayhap the leader of this group. "Prince Adelchis, himself, has approved our plan. We come from King Charlemagne's court where others are in readiness to help us. You will be surprised, pleasantly so, at the support you have there, Sire. Overlook this braggart here. He would do well with a bigger brain and a smaller mouth; but he's a fine swordsman. If there be trouble, he'll be an advantage for us."

"You are the captain of this group, Sir?" Peppin asked. At the man's nod, Peppin continued. "Then, you're responsible for their actions. Yes, Prince Adelchis has advised me of the plan. But, if you resent my questions, I would hear of it from your own lips." Peppin replied tartly. He recognized only two of these men and was determined to remain above their idle chatter.

"Of a certainly, Prince Peppin," the leader responded with cringing deference. "But, first, introductions. I'm soon-to-be Count Oscart; my father is in failing health,

Sire. This one on my right is Count Turlis; here is Lord Mockhollen. You know Lords Sarton and Propst, I believe." Peppin nodded his acknowledgement to the four men.

Aye. *He remembered their names now. Both were landholders in the far east of his father's kingdom. They battled with King Charlemagne's forces in the last two summer engagements. He knew them for good soldiers, fair to their men and full of courage. They did not fear bodily harm; that was certain.* "Standing behind me are Count Holken, Count Carnst, and Lord Bathis. Lord Bathis' lands adjoin those of Count Janlur, just to give you an idea of the range of your support, Sir," the leader added.

Peppin tipped his head again, this time to Lord Bathis alone. Bathis he knew by reputation. Count Janlur often praised his administrative abilities but wondered at his ambition, fearing he was hungry for more land.

Had the nobles known of Peppin's evaluation of them, they would have been stupefied. Heretofore, they had given him short shrift, judging his abilities by his physical deformities. Watching him, gauging his strength, they had more confidence in their plans than was true only an hour ago.

"The plan...it's a simple one, Sire. King Charlemagne's court is on the move again, heading toward Ingelheim for the spring assembly. We plan to overtake the King in his tent, restrain him and hide in a near-by cave. Lord Bathis has a well-deserved reputation on the battlefield. As in days past, it is routine for him to arrive for the assembly and to visit the King's tent, to greet the king, after he arrives. He will, of course, have Count Holken and Count Carnst with him and, mayhap, Lord Mockhollen...unless you think three be too many, sir?"

"I would hold at three, Count Oscart. Do these three often sup together? At Oscart's affirmative nod, Peppin continued. "Any established habit or regular action should be followed. We want no warnings suspected through unusual behavior. This is a straight-forward plan, as you say, a simple one. Those are, often, the ones which are most successful. I will wait in my camp, some three furloughs distant, to hear of your success in abducting the King. Then, I shall join you...at this cave. Is that your suggestion?"

Oxcart confirmed that was the plan. He was certain that, when King Charlemagne saw Peppin, he would understand immediately. He might even determine the reasons for the plan. Peppin wasn't sure. His father had never evidenced an ounce of understanding Peppin's trials and disappoinments. These men far overestimated the king's knowledge or interest in his hunch-back son.

"One wonders what he understands, Oscart." Peppin replied. "When's this to take place? What is your time table?"

"We planned it for two days hence. The King should be near to Ingelheim by late tomorrow night. We think he will be within two hours of the castle by sunset. He'll push on to end the journey. It's a choice he has made in the past. We will act the next night, soon after the deepest dark begins to lighten."

"Aye, he and the court will be eager to get to Ingelheim. I'm sure you have anticipated their eagerness correctly. But, I'd suggest you set your plan in motion the night he arrives."

At Oscart's incredulous look, Peppin added. "He'll be weary, much less alert for threats or dangers. And the journey will be complete, no threats to the travelers' safety. The King will be in his own tent, ready for sleep. The timing will be more of a surprise, therefore, to our advantage. Also, I distrust rumors and ill luck. Your plan leaves twenty-four hours after the court is settled...for anything to happen, any rumor to circulate, any of these men to lose courage." The men's eyes widened; their arms moved toward their swords. Peppin held up his hand.

"Nay." he said. "After the court arrives in Ingelheim, the sooner you move, the more successful your efforts are likely to be." Peppin's statement broached no dissent. Oscart agreed this was most likely.

"One last reminder," Peppin added. "If there're men taken who must be killed, I shall do the killing. My grandfather always said if a man is unable to carry out his own justice, he shouldn't expect another to do it for him. He should, in fact, not order the deaths. So, I shall execute when it is needed."

Before Peppin came to meet these conspirators, he thought of his squire, Marco. "*I never want you threatened.*" Peppin remembered his words to the lad. "If this adventure turns out badly, I don't want you involved. You're to wait there in the stable; you have the farmer's agreement to pass the night there. If I don't return for you by daybreak, hurry home. Go by the back ways, no riding on the main-traveled roads."

Marco objected loudly, begged to accompany his master, and threatened to end his service to Peppin. But, in the end, Peppin left him in the stable, urging the farmer's wife to bring him cheese and bread for his late meal. Pulling his thoughts back to the present, Peppin had an odd feeling. Goose bumps popped out on his arms; he heard an owl cry in the darkness. He was doomed. *The plan has been discovered! We are thwarted!* At that moment, strong hands hoisted him onto his mount.

"Who are you?" Peppin cried. "What's the meaning of this?"

"Do not speak, son," he heard Rinaldo's voice. "We're taking you to the King. The plot has been discovered." Rinaldo's voice was filled with grief as he whispered. "Admit nothing; do you hear me? You have aligned with the very weakest in the kingdom, Peppin. Although the plot was discovered by chance, these dullards have ruined you."

"Rinaldo," Peppin screamed. "I'm innocent. Why will no one speak? I'm hunting, here on the plains alone."

"Please, my prince," Rinaldo responded. "No one is listening. We are commanded, by the King's own words, to bring you to him. It's a waste…to shout at me. My boy, make your story to the King believable. Spend this time in inventing an explanation. You are betrayed. You are betrayed."

***

Thus, Peppin began the longest journey of his life. The escort plodded non-stop toward Ingelheim's court. There was no hurry in the journey; but neither was there a halt. The soldiers, Peppin, and a group of captured men made steady progress. The second group included Lords Mockhollen, Sarton and Propst who had been camping, like Peppin, waiting to be summoned by the conspirators to the court. The prisoners kept silent. Rinaldo advised them to speak to no one, not even each other. Their defeat was clear in their bowed heads, drooping shoulders and listless bodies.

"What shall I do?" Peppin asked himself. "How has the plan come to this end? Someone must have spoken before the deed was even attempted." Yester-night's troubled questioning of the plan, the steady motion of their marching feet, the hopelessness of his plight lulled Peppin. He drifted into a fitful sleep. He awoke just as the escort stopped in front of King Charlemagne's assembly tent. Rinaldo helped Peppin from his mount and led him to the tent entrance. Giving him a brief hug, he pushed the young man inside. Quietly, Rinaldo re-entered and stood by the door.

Peppin stood calmly and nodded as Charlemagne stood. His father looked into his face with those shining, passionate – oftentimes unseeing - eyes. He looked haggard. The flesh of his face was pale, drawn toward his mouth. His mustache drooped, as if weary. But that was as nothing. From the corners of his eyes, tears began their track down his face, marking it in the feeble, wavering light of the one candle.

"Why, my son, why?" The King whispered.

At that moment, Peppin knew denial was impossible. He thought of pleading for his life, of saying he was duped, of blaming undue collusion against him. But he knew such was not possible. For the honor he owed his mother, he would not lie: not about his ambitions, not about his needs.

"Poppa." Peppin's voice rose with the finality of the word. His father winced as he heard the pain, the sadness, the hopelessness of his son's tone. "I am guilty. I conspired with men to wrest the kingdom from you. My only defense is this: I have nothing. I am the son of the continent's most powerful king and, yet, I have…I am nothing. My mother is gone, wounded and badly used by your choices. Never in those years of isolation in our little manor did you send one kind word to her. At the least, for her care of me, you should have been grateful! At the least, for her love of you, you owed her contact and communication. At the least, because I was from your loins, you might have feigned some small interest in my life! Now, that life--where I was beloved, nurtured and accepted--is gone."

"When I reluctantly came to your court, brought here without even being asked, my days reverberated with pain. I was ridiculed, by the great and the small, because of my affliction. Your queen exploited your concern for me and your guilt – singling me out for attention, pretending some small interest in my pathetic accomplishments, and snickering behind my back at my clothing, my manners, and my backwardness, as she termed it." Peppin shrugged his shoulders.

"It's true; some felt genuine sympathy for me; but few of those bothered to learn who or what I was...emulating you, I suspect. But enough of others..." Peppin squared his shoulders and looked into his father's face.

"You, yourself, have given me little, the least of which was your time. I can count on my hand the three times we rode together - three times in my long years here!" Peppin stared steadfastly into his father's face. "My sisters I hardly know. They eat at the banquet table; I eat among the dog-handlers. They dance, sing and are full of gaiety; I work in the stables, in the gardens, or in the cook tent - roasting your meat. They have entrance to your library; I borrow parchments from Rinaldo and Angilbert."

"Of my six brothers and sisters, Charles, alone, was kind to me. Are he and I encouraged to hunt together or ride? Nay. Mostly, he's off on various military maneuvers from which I am excluded. Oh, for sure, some say I am no worse off than Louis and Pepin. Not true! They are kings of their own lands and valued, I daresay, by their courts... if not by you. I have no home; I have no place; I have no value. And I have no father." Peppin turned his back to the King and waited.

King Charlemagne faltered. Peppin's words, none of which could he deny, were true. He and his court cared little for this first-born son. Only Oliver and, occasionally, Angilbert gave the boy any attention. The tears which tracked his cheeks dried and were immediately covered by yet more tears. But tears would not undo the years of his neglect, the 'out of sight, out of mind' manner in which he dealt with Peppin and his other children. How Charlemagne yearned to deny his son's accusations! But he had no defense.

Every word Peppin utters is true and I, myself, am at fault. I failed my son, never realized I treated him so poorly... because I never thought of him. Peppin is cruel in his references to Himlitrude, but my neglect of her cannot be denied. Charlemagne had no answer. He motioned for Rinaldo to take Peppin away.

***

"How did I get to this, Lord Rinaldo?" Peppin asked. Rinaldo walked by his side, refused to rebind his ankles, and steered him by the elbow. "What'll happen next?"

Rinaldo, almost overcome with tears himself, shrugged. "I don't know the protocol for this, Peppin." He answered. "The King will determine some punishment. I can't imagine he will take your life. He always shows mercy to his noble enemies, those much less valuable than you. Yet, your actions are treasonous. Early tomorrow, I suspect, you'll know your fate."

"Who betrayed us, Rinaldo? Will you name him?" Peppin asked.

"Aye. That old, dull retainer — Furson — happened to be cleaning the little church where you met the traitors. He's so slow and quiet; no one ever realizes he's about. He overheard your talk and rode himself to the King's tent. His descriptions of the conspirators' mounts — their hand tooled leather saddles, the blankets embroidered with signets, the unique drinking flagons — gave the names as surely as a parchment." Rinaldo squeezed Peppin's shoulders.

"My boy, could you not align with able men...to sacrifice yourself like this..." Rinaldo stopped to regain his composure. "The King," he continued, "had the conspirators arrested: Bathis, Holken, Carnst and Oscart. Each betrayed the other, of course; but all named you as the mind behind the plan. I know this isn't your work;

but you did agree to the effort. And so, you're as guilty as they. Who else, Peppin?" Rinaldo asked as he continued to speak.

"This is a simple plan but a sly one, too likely to succeed for these four to form it. Nay, they would have shots and battle and, perhaps, a beheading — actors that they are. This is the plan of a direct, clear-minded man. Won't you tell me? I cannot believe the kernel of the idea originated with you. I will not."

"Those who are guilty are taken, Rinaldo." Peppin answered. *Never will I betray Adelchis, nor the Thuringian nobles, who supported this plot. No one else will suffer from this calamity! God help them to try again...and be more successful next time.*

"Thank you for your kindness, Lord Rinaldo. In the morn, the King shall seal my fate." Peppin replied, entering a guarded tent and smiling sadly as Rinaldo took his leave.

***

King Charlemagne lost no time in bringing the conspirators before his court. The trial was short and methodical.

"For betrayal of the kingdom and the breaking of your loyalty oath to our king, King Charlemagne, I sentence you to death." The court's lord announced, staring at Peppin. "But, through the intervention of King Charlemagne himself, your death sentence is revoked. You're to enter the monastery at Prum for the remainder of your days."

Peppin gave a mental shrug, laughing to himself at his father's effort to be 'merciful.'

***

Charlemagne sought relief from both his guilt and his sadness around Peppin's fall in governing his still-growing

154

realm. Aye, the battles continued; but so did his efforts to bring a better life to Frankland, both through economic opportunities and a well-functioning government. The King knew he had accomplished much but knew there was yet much to be done, much for which a sound beginning must be made. He delighted in his growing family, even though he held no illusions about the selfishness and possible future betrayals of his wife, Fastrada.

***

Chapter 9

THE RUNAWAY

Alcuin quietly entered the library. The King, with an open parchment in his hand, snoozed at his work table, his face still pale and weary. Partially covered by Charlemagne's hand, Alcuin found a map of the realm, marked upon again and again. Some of the lines—they looked like boundaries—were so repeatedly marked that they cut the parchment in several places. There were notations on the parchment, symbols with the Princes' names scribbled beside them. The asterick (*) apparently represented Charles, the ampersand (&) equaled Pepin's name and the percentage (%) sat alongside Louis' name. There was a star (+) beside the hunch-back's name.

"Is King Charlemagne trying to carve out land for his first-born, for Peppin?" Alcuin asked himself. *How remarkable! I know he's angry at the Church's stance on marriage. The latest ruling – only those blessed by the Church are 'true' marriages - made him livid!* The decision consigned Charlemagne's and Himiltrude's marriage, then, to a Germanic joining only. It, by definition, made Himiltrude a concubine and Peppin illegitimate. Oh, it has angered the King! *And in such an instance, I cannot blame him. How can a marriage which was legal and holy years ago be deemed otherwise today? What mockery and what absurdity from the Pope!*

This is beyond ludicrous, Alcuin thought, slamming his hands against the wall. The Church fathers could not uphold this ruling. They'll not enforce it. It benefits only those who wish to be released from their marital responsibilities. The King could defy them all, could maintain Peppin's place, if this plot had not his name on it. Now, these recent events make this ruling on marriage unnecessary...unnecessary for the King.

Alcuin entered the door of the King's chamber. "Why does any man wish to be King? I cannot fathom the pain. How I dread to wake him to yet another problem." Alcuin lightly tapped the King's arm.

"Sire, Sire, you must waken." Alcuin whispered. "There are particulars for your ears alone. You must waken, Charlemagne." The King, opening his eyes from an exhausted sleep, took a few moments to focus on Alcuin's face.

"Did you rouse me, Scholar? Or are you just another bad dream?"

At Alcuin's hesitation, Charlemagne smiled and clapped his friend on the arm. "I hear you, man; I hear you. Give me a minute so I can right my mind." He stood, poured a flagon of water, drank deeply. Then, he splashed water onto his face, wiping it on his sleeping tunic sleeve which was much the worse for wear, anyway. "This had better be of the utmost importance, Scholar," he threatened quietly, "or I'll have your head to hold my writing tools." Alcuin flinched, doubly aware of the King's strain of the past few days, and saw the exhaustion resettle on his features.

"It is grim news, Sire," he responded, "far greater than the 'utmost importance.' I am pouring you ale. You must drink before I continue. I fear your temper will cause widespread destruction before I complete my message. Drink this and try to control your anger." Alcuin handed Charlemagne a flagon he himself brought to the chamber. It, indeed, was filled with ale, as well as with a calming portion the herbalist assured Alcuin would dull the King's reactions.

The King quaffed down most of the ale and handed the flagon back to Alcuin for a refilling. He sat once more on the bench and looked at his friend, misery hanging in his eyes.

"Anything which makes your face this grim, Alcuin, is likely to kill me. If you must, tell me quickly. I've just condemned my firstborn to life-time imprisonment. What can be more horrible than that?" He looked at Alcuin, trying to convince both of them that no news Alcuin had to relate could be worse than the events of the past two days. Alcuin came to the story quickly.

"Sire, Rotrud is missing. She has disappeared. We've searched the court tents, her tent, the cook tents, the herbalist's tent, the Queen's tent, her sisters' tent, the horse line. We cannot find her. She's not in the camp. We exhausted the possibilities. I come to you for further direction." He dropped his hands in defeat, beseeching the King for help.

"Dear God, will these crises with my children never end? Are you seriously telling me my daughter can't be found?" The King cried. "...cannot be located in the entire court? It's not possible to disappear from here! There must be three hundred souls in this court. Has no one seen her? Has she come to harm; can you tell me that?" Hearing his own question, the King stood quickly, stumbling to the door.

"Guardsman," he shouted. "Bring me the captain of the guard. Immediately! Quickly, man, quickly!"

King Charlemagne turned back to the scholar, rubbing his hands in worry. In desperation, words tumbled from the king's mouth. He told Alcuin that he and Rotrud understood each other; they spoke about the needs of the kingdom just yesterday. He shook his head as he remembered the conversation. His eyes lost their focus as he recalled the thoughts they shared about the safety of the realm.

***

"Rotrud," Charlemagne began the conversation. "You have too many brothers. Nay! That's not it! All your brothers want to be kings. Nay," he said, holding his hand up to delay her speaking, "Nay. They each wish to rule in a different way, to rule their own lands, giving no thought to the empire. I attempted to inspire them with lands and soldiers; yes, and with booty, too. I've urged them to bind their lands together — to think as one. But each protects his own, and nothing more. What can I do? They don't understand!" The King stopped speaking; his words faded away as he wearily rubbed his temples.

The King's frustration did not surprise Rotrud. He often described battle tactics to her, and identified the spoils — financial as well as political — which resulted from battles lost, nobles displaced, lands re-assigned, allegiances broken, rebels won. Over time, Rotrud became his 'sounding board.' As his sons grew and their ambitions followed, the King could not plan empire-wide strategy with them. Their own desires tempered their reactions and their advice, especially in reference to their personal realms. Finally, King Charlemagne stopped seeking their advice. He cloaked all his plans, concerns, and visions to them in terms of their own self-interests, describing specific events' probable impact on their individual kingdoms. If he needed military support to strengthen his domain, he divided the problems and sought help from each son, somehow protecting the entire empire within limited and proscribed methods.

He need not worry. His sons would always fight - fight forever - to protect their own lands, but not so to guard the holdings of each other. It reminded Charlemagne of his brother, Carloman; never did they share the same vision either. *For me, this fact is the most personally hurtful and disappointing of my failures - my sons cannot appreciate the realm I struggle to build! Nor will they commit themselves to guarding it. Charles protects my realm but prefers to leave Louis in Aquitaine and Pepin in Lombardy on their own. Those two care little for each other and less for us here in my court. None of them care about the needs of the whole realm nor realize the mutual protection it provides.*

Charlemagne's vision, his force of character, his organizational ability, his concern for his people – his sons did not value these gifts. They scarcely understood them. Charles, Louis, and Pepin cared nothing for the barbarian lands Charlemagne conquered, for the multiple peoples he linked together, for the virtual wilderness that he, if not tamed, controlled.

***

"Oh, they will fight when I tell them," Charlemagne told Rotrud. "But they see only trees; the forest escapes them entirely." With his sons controlling pieces of his vast realm, the King plotted to keep the kingdom strong and together — and greatly in his plans were his daughters.

"I respect you all, Rotrud - you, Bertha and Gisela - even though she is very young. I forbid you to marry because the kingdom must not be further divided. Three separately ruled lands are proving more than I can hold together. But I am delighted to keep you near me; your presence in my travels delights me. I want you always near. You keep the memory of your mother alive in my heart." He praised their skills, believed them beautiful and without equal. He knew their loyalty was always to him. "I know all you girls support my every undertaking." *And they admire my abilities.* Exposed to his thoughts during the evening 'entertainments' and released from the necessity of military training and drills, his daughters early became interested in their father's pursuits, often copying his behaviors.

Long ago, understanding the King's love of the hunt, each daughter in turn embroidered rabbits, squirrels, deer, boar, and guinea fowl in her needlework. As small girls, first Rotrud and, later, Gizzie spent hours in the kennels, eagerly "training" the pups of each litter. The girls absorbed tactics from Charlemagne's "hide and seek games," learned his style of planning, recognized his feints and subterfuges, and admired his physical strength. That they sometimes used this knowledge to best him bothered them not one whit. Charlemagne and his daughters were the best example of that all-encompassing statement: 'all is fair in love and war.'

Such mutual admiration produced loyal support for the King from Rotrud, Bertha, and Gizzie and steady devotion to them from their Poppa. He didn't spoil them or indulge their every wish. But in the truly important requests, he denied them little. He never countenanced marriage for them. This effort to protect them had, so far, its greatest impact on Rotrud and Bertha, for they were the two oldest. But Rotrud, much like her father in persistence and temperament, would not let him control her. King Charlemagne remembered that as Alcuin spoke.

***

His mind returned to the present, to Rotrud's disappearance. He turned to the scholar.

"In any case, find her, Alcuin. And when you do, bring her to me. Find her as quickly as you can." he reiterated.

***

Various people searched the court again: the guardsmen,

Alcuin and Angilbert, and, finally, the King himself. Charlemagne ranted and raved, striding the spaces between the tent spaces, directing everyone in various and sundry directions. But no one could find Rotrud.

King Charlemagne was brought to his knees, frightened to death that an abduction had, this time, been successful. He vividly remembered Hildegard's fright, those many years ago, when Rotrud's kidnapping had almost been successful and increased Hilde's dread of physical assault. His knees went weak with the possibility. He began to ride around the camp.

All of a sudden, the King turned his mount and rode to his daughters' tent. He hurried into the huge tent, searching the separate sleeping areas, each divided from the other by tapestry hangings.

"Bertha! Bertha!" the King cried. Neither Bertha nor Gisela was there. They, too, were out searching for their older sister. About the time Charlemagne had seen no one was in the tent, Bertha came running to his call.

"Poppa, I'm here," she responded, coming from behind to grab his shoulders.

"Oh, my precious one," the King sobbed. "Where can Rotrud be? I fear for her life. Have you seen her today? Did she tell you that she was unhappy, that she had need to scorn her father? Do you know where your sister might be? Mayhap, she's hurt or worse, lying somewhere in a furrow! I can't think of another place to search, I cannot!" He wept into Bertha's hair.

"Poppa, Poppa," she soothed. "Don't consider the worse; she may be completely safe. Calm yourself and let me think. I've been running about so much, searching and searching in likely places, that I've not considered her thoughts. Please, Poppa. Sit down. Here's some ale. You must have some of it." Bertha poured ale for her father. "I know, I know...you don't countenance spirited drink; but you do need calming." And she thrust the flagon into his hands.

Charlemagne, with tears streaming from his eyes, gulped the ale. He pounded a near-by writing desk in frustration. A guardsman stuck his head in the door, an inquiring expression on his troubled face.

"Please, Gratit," Bertha murmured, "fetch Gizzie and Charles. Poppa needs them close. Seek them at the cook tent. They were there to break their fast, when I raced this direction." Taking his hand, she led the King to a sleeping bench and sat him down. "There, there, Poppa," she whispered, "all will be solved. We cannot believe Rotrud has been harmed. She's much too wise to take some foolish chance. She's a planner, Poppa, we'll find her."

The guardsman returned with a herbalist in his wake. The herbalist immediately poured a white powder in the flagon and mixed in a little wine. He handed this to Bertha and mouthed his words: "The King, the King." Bertha handed the flagon to her father once again; he quaffed the liquid immediately, holding on to Bertha's hand, as would a dying man. Gizzie and Charles rushed into the room, hurrying to their father, to hug him tightly.

"Oh, my dears, my dears," he blubbered, "what shall we do?"

Bertha stepped outside the tent. *There has been enough running about and searching,* she thought. *Someone must think. Apparently, no ill has befallen Rotrud. There's no evidence a villain has spirited her away or drawn her blood. I must believe she is only missing. This may well be her own choice. I must try to think like my sister.*

Rotrud has been much subdued since the fiasco with Janus." Bertha muttered, considering Rotrud's state of mind. "And, then, Poppa reprimanded her, criticized her interest in Count Norico."

Over the years, Bertha learned she thought more

clearly if she spoke her thoughts aloud. "Dear Ma-mam recognized that," she remembered. *Ma-mam always told us, when she was confused by someone's actions: 'Put yourself in the person's shoes, Bertha, and much will clarify itself.'* So, Bertha tried to imagine she herself was Rotrud.

Within moments, Bertha surmised this was impossible. She and Rotrud were too different. She could never predict her older sister's actions. *I don't even understand her daily behavior, much less something out of the ordinary.* Bertha shook her head suddenly. She walked to the tent's entrance and entered quietly. She knew Gizzie and Charles were comforting their father. She caught Gizzie's eye and motioned to her. Gizzie gently whispered for King Charlemagne to lie down while Charles helped him. Charles began removing his foot coverings and leg bands as Gizzie came to the entrance. Bertha motioned for Gizzie to exit the tent. Both girls sat on a large boulder outside, holding hands to comfort each other.

"Gizzie, do you have any idea where Rotrud may have gone? It's clear she's no longer in the court's camp. If you know anything, you must tell me - for her safety."

Gizzie looked into her older sister's face. She squirmed, pushed her sleeve up and down, constantly smoothing her hair out of her eyes. "I don't know where she is, Bertha," Gizzie finally answered.

"I know you don't know her location, Gizzie. But if you know where she might be...or anything about her not being here, please tell me." Bertha repeated. "She, I'm sure, has some plan, disappearing like this. If there were no plan, she would be easily found. But, I do fear for Poppa; he's distraught. Pray he stays sad because, if his anger rules him, everyone in the court will suffer." Bertha stated emphatically.

Gizzie was caught. What must I do? She wondered. *I promised Rotrud I wouldn't tell a word. But I see how sad Poppa is…and how afraid for her.* Gizzie was torn.

Rotrud was the closest to a mother she'd ever known. It was Rotrud who comforted her after a bad dream, Rotrud who spent time telling her the tales and stories she so loved. It was this sister who chose her clothes, told her it was time to bathe, begged for her late nights at the banquet table. The nurses Gizzie generally ignored; the ladies-in-waiting, one and all, were distractions to her daily concerns. Rotrud was her true heroine, her one sibling who could do no wrong.

What should I do? Gizzie wondered yet again. *If Rotrud's in trouble, I'm the only one who might help her.* She looked into Bertha's face. "I gave a sworn promise, Bertha, a 'truly-true' promise." Gizzie replied. "I know just a little. Mayhap, telling it cannot hurt." She nodded, making her decision and spoke.

Rotrud, Gizzie said, left two days ago-after the midday meal. Gizzii admitted she saw Rotrud when she went to the stream to catch frogs. Justin had dared Gizzie to be out earlier than he was, betting she couldn't catch a frog alone. But she did, of a certainty. She caught three of them but knew Justin would never believe she had done it alone.

"Gizzie, forget the frogs." Bertha begged. "Tell me what you know about Rotrud…or her ride."

"She was riding on Alcuin's mount, Bertha. She said he wouldn't mind if she borrowed "Nib." She and Alcuin are best friends, you know that." Seeing Bertha's frown of impatience, Gizzie hurried on. "I asked if I could ride with her; but she told me I couldn't come. She said that she would be gone for two or three days, riding for her health. I thought she had a good idea, Bertha. You know she looks bad and has been skipping meals. She ate only a pear the other day; and when we went swimming, she…"

"Skipping meals, Gizzie? Are you certain?" Bertha, surprised, questioned Gizzie. "I know her clothes no longer fit as the dressmaker made them; but I didn't realize her health was suffering." She paused, her forehead wrinkled with concern. "That doesn't matter now, though." She recovered herself. "Do you know her destination, Gizzie? Tell me, if you know." Bertha commanded her little sister.

"Bertha," Gizzie screeched. "I can't! I gave Rotrud my oath! I won't betray her; I won't! She took Poppa's little Foxer with her. I know she's safe," and she ran from the room and Bertha's questions. Gizzie ran into Angilbert's legs as he pushed open the tent flap.

"What is this?" Seeing Gizzie's face shining with tears, he asked her. ; "Are you injured, Gizzie?" At the negative shake of her head, he responded. "Oh, don't worry about Rotrud. We are taking an escort to find your sister. She can't have gotten far. We'll find her. It will be fine, Gizzie," he added as he stroked her back.

"Where will you search?" Bertha demanded, glaring at Angilbert as she walked up. "I daresay you know less about Rotrud than any one of us! Don't be so sure she will be found easily." And, then, she, too, burst into tears. Angilbert moved quickly to her side and grabbed her arm.

Tilting her head to look into his eyes, Angilbert answered. "I know nothing of her destination, Bertha. That's true. But when King Charlemagne King commands me to search, search I do…until I drop from the effort. Don't frighten Gizzie needlessly. She looks like a lost puppy. Think of her despair, not just your own." Angilbert shook his head, realizing he had spoken harshly and reached to smooth down Bertha's hair.

"Do calm yourself, my love," he whispered. Bertha's eyes blinked, her face warmed suddenly and more tears gushed forth. She dropped her head on Angilbert's shoulder and sobbed.

Gizzie raised her eyes to the poet's. "I don't know where she is now, Master Angilbert," she offered. "But she went out riding; she left before mid-day; that was the day before yesterday. I saw her ride out. She made me promise not to speak to anyone else about it. Bertha was demanding I break my oath, my oath to Rotrud." Gizzie closed her mouth firmly, offended by the pressure from her sister.

"Gizzie," Angilbert answered. "If that's the case, then we all need your help. I respect your vow to Rotrud; but she may need us. Riding alone is not wise, especially for a beautiful, young woman. There are brigands on the road who'll knock her off her horse, to steal it. They'll think nothing of leaving her lying on the road. Bad things can happen to one traveling alone... I've an idea. You come with me on this search. Mayhap, a nudge to your memory will lead us to her destination."

"Rotrud is an excellent rider, Gizzie. Fear not for her riding skill," he added, seeing Gizzie's eyes widen. "Still, the horse may stumble, wedge a rock in its hoof, shy at a quick rabbit and she be thrown. Come with me. We'll saddle your horse and begin our search." With that, he kissed Bertha softly on the head and sat her on the nearby sleeping bench.

"You go to the library, Bertha," he directed her. "Everyone has gathered there to wait together. Tell them Gizzie is with me." Summoning a guard, Angilbert asked him to escort Bertha to the library tent. He took Gizzie's hand and rushed to the horse line.

***

A few breaths later, Angilbert, Gizzie, three guards and Alcuin were mounted, riding out of the camp. Alcuin had promised Charlemagne to look for his daughter. Only on that condition would the King remain in camp.

"Now, Gizzie," Angilbert said to her as they rode, "do you remember anything Rotrud said as she left?"

Gizzie felt caught. She was beginning to fear for her

sister. She now remembered tales of thieves and brigades on the road and wondered why Rotrud had not considered the danger.

"Master Angil," Gizzie quietly mumbled, "I got a feeling Rotrud wanted to see Peppin's old home, the one where he stayed when his mother died? She was ever curious about the manor. I don't know why."

Gizzie snuggled against Angilbert's chest, hoping somehow he could set things right. She felt Angilbert's arm lift as he motioned to the other riders. Then, Angilbert's horse turned slightly to the right, followed by the rest of the horses. Master Alcuin rode from behind and put his hand on Gizzie's shoulder. She smiled. With Master Alcuin riding with them, all would be well. Angilbert spoke.

"Gizzie feels Rotrud may have gone to Peppin's old home. Do you know where that is, Master?" Alcuin shook his head negatively but dropped back to consult with one of the guards. The two spoke together as Angilbert talked softly to Gizzie until Alcuin rode back.

"Stennis here," Alcuin said, nodding to the guard just behind him, "was in the escort which took Peppin home for his visit. He knows the way, says the journey is a less than a two days' ride. But, with speed, we can be there by tomorrow. It is best we move quickly…to confirm her presence there or not. We've no other possible destination; let's ride, Angil."

***

Unaware of all this consternation miles away, Rotrud was preparing a snack for a rather late mid-day meal. She and Count Norico of Maine met in this wonderful, old-fashioned house only last night. But, already, it felt to Rotrud that they had lived here for weeks. She gave little thought to home, believing no one would miss her for days. Gizzie vowed she would tell no one of Rotrud's 'ride.' Gizzie does love me well, Rotrud thought. *She won't announce to the court that I'm away. This 'affaire de coeur' may take place in utter secrecy. What a delight...and what a wonderful setting for romantic dreams.*

All of a sudden, Rotrud burst into tears. Tears coursed from her eyes, splattering her purple tunic, as if she were caught in a sudden rain squall. As she was dabbing at the wet splashes, Count Norico came into the cooking room, begging for nourishment. "Rotrud, I'm famished. What are you doing in here—growing a chicken from a chick?" he asked. Then, seeing Rotrud sniffing and blotting at her clothing, he hurried to her.

"My dear, what is it?" he asked as his hands circled her waist. He heard her intake of breath, felt a shudder, and wondered as she smiled up at him. The sadness on her face faded immediately, replaced by a bright, lilting smile as she looked into his eyes. "You're standing here in misery! What is it? Weeping? My precious one, what is it; what can make you so unhappy?"

"Norico, I don't know," Rotrud answered in amazement. "I was standing here, thinking of this perfect place and out perfect night," she added, blushing a little. "And the tears flowed down. I'm *NOT* unhappy! On the contrary, I am full of joy. Isn't it strange that I weep? But the boundary between joy and sorrow is very close, isn't it? Mayhap, my tiredness is the cause...and my hunger!" She laughed. "Aye, I'm famished as well. Here, food is ready." She pointed to the meal she just finished preparing.

"I am just so amazed...that we're here together. How on earth did you know to come here, know I was to be here? Now is the time to answer this question. It's not possible you just 'happened' to journey in this direction; this is not even the direction of your manor. Nay, don't deny it! I must know how you came to be here! I told no one of my destination. I wasn't even certain I could find this place."

"But almost upon my arrival, your horse trotted up. Was this the direction of your journey? And why, why would you come to Peppin's old home? This is a mystery you must explain. Now! I demand an answer," she teased as she motioned for him to bring the two trenchers to the table.

"I must confess, Rotrud. I followed you from the King's court. Seeing you dressed for riding, remembering your sad look the previous night at the banquet when the King bade me 'adieu;' I had to see you! Seeing your face made me listen to my own heart. I knew my existence was incomplete without seeing you every day. I was compelled to end my uncertainty! As I confessed last night, you hold my heart within your hands. What could I do? Not knowing if you had any regard for me was driving me mad! I couldn't imagine a life without you. If you had no feelings for me, I had to know. Knowing would be preferable to this damn uncertainty, even if I must bury my dreams in the dust. So, I followed you, my dear one. I followed you! It never occurred to me that you might be meeting another."

Rotrud laughed and jumped to her feet. "You would surely have spoiled a rendezvous, don't you think?" she asked as she nibbled the Count's ear. Norico laughed.

"How could I know? Mayhap, there was someone, someone unknown at the court, who had somehow attracted your eye. I had many fears, many fears that my love for you couldn't possibly be returned. Aye, aye I realize now you were trying to let me know. But when in doubt, we often deny all our senses tell us!" He took her into his arms. "Aye, I did follow you, having no idea of your destination. And now that impulsive moment will define my life forever." With this confession, Count Norico pulled her close to his chest and kissed her deeply.

He stood holding Rotrud and she him for many minutes. Then, they both remembered their food and sat down to eat.

"Norico, how about an adventure?" Rotrud asked, after cleaning up the remnants of their meal. "How would you like to swim? Peppin once described a small pool on the east side of the river we crossed yesternight. He declared that, while it was not nearly so warm as the waters at Aachen, he preferred the refreshing, rather than lulling, feeling that it produced after a swim. I know you swim," she added. "I've watched you dive, when the court had its picnics."

Rotrud didn't add how much she loved to watch his sinewy strength, as his body arched in perfect posture for diving. *No matter, were he diving off a high river bank or off the edge of the flowing water, he looked magnificent.* Norico looked up to see Rotrud smile. Her blissful smile assured him that, for her, seeing him swim was a very pleasant memory. With his nod of assent, Rotrud took his hand and exited the house, trying her best to remember Peppin's description of the path to the hidden pool.

They walked only a minute or two before coming to the river. Norico and Rotrud eased into the pool in the shallow run-off. It was cool, much more so than Peppin had described in his tales. Rotrud immediately began rubbing the goosebumps on her arms, deciding to head for shore. As she began to swim, Norico came up behind her and held her close.

Rotrud had never been unclothed before a man before; but after last night, the idea of wearing clothes--for bathing-- had seemed ridiculous. Despite the cool water, Norico's body was warm against her back. *I wonder that the water doesn't boil between us,* Rotrud thought. Her breasts ached for Norico's touch, so she turned to face him. She gently held his face and kissed his lips, the kiss coming all the way from her feet. His answering response fired her body, as she arched her back into the water and he entered her. She didn't notice the sting of the water as his thrusts moved her beyond the water, the day, and the cold near her feet.

Rotrud smiled. "You have made the water boil, my love," she whispered in Norico's ear. "I feel completely warm now," she giggled.

He took her hand and together they returned to the house, caressing and examining each other in the light of the firepit. Later, in its warmth, Rotrud and Norico lay curled around each other, secure in their newly shared love.

***

As Rotrud and Norico slept, the little band seeking Rotrud drew closer. Gizzie slept against Angilbert's chest. Alcuin recommended they ride through the night. He rode beside Angilbert and Gizzie, alert that Angilbert not falter and sleep himself. The other three men, long guards and used to night-time vigils, rode comfortably, alert to additional dangers posed by the dark. Ere the moon set near the horizon, the small group sighted a lone manor, some two leagues to their northwest.

"That'll be Peppin's house, Master Alcuin," Stennis confirmed. "It's not lighted up, as I remember it, of course; but that's his mother's manor. I'll recall all my day's Prince Peppin's delight in gazing at the place. He did stop, right about here as I recall, and looked at it, fussing to himself for being away so long." Stennis' face shone with warmth. "Ahhh, and the greeting they all gave the lad, it'd do your heart good to see it. I cannot think how lonely he must have been at the King's court. Helps explain things, some," Stennis added. "What a waste of a fine lad."

"You speak true, Stennis," Alcuin agreed. "This life is

full of such tragedy. The world does call out against these events and the loss they represent. Of a certainty, I agree with you. Your words won't move beyond these people and this place; but do be wary elsewhere when you speak."

"Thank you, Sire," Stennis responded. "I understand your warning and thank you for it."

***

Of those in the group searching for Rotrud, it was Alcuin who knew her best. As his tenure in King Charlemagne's court lengthened, he and Rotrud grew to be devoted friends. She didn't argue from the philosophical base which so strengthened her Aunt Gisela's speech; but she'd benefited greatly from her studies in the Palace School. And her arguments often made Alcuin proud, in both her thoughts and in her ability to speak. He knew, also, from her confidences that she felt alienated from the King, principally because of his dictum on marriage.

'Why does he condemn us to this kind of life, Master Alcuin?' she asked him repeatedly. 'How can he be free to have as many wives as he can get the Church to allow; but I may not have even one husband? I've no respect for him; do you hear? He neglects us all and limits our choices as well. I so wish I had another home, some location away from him!' Rotrud had spoken so for months, much more often in the past few weeks. He'd believed her long sorrow over the unpleasantness with Janus was conquered; but in the last two days, Alcuin changed his opinion on that. *She gave us constant warning...or, at least, she did so tell me. But I didn't imagine she'd flee the court. What will we find at this manor?*

Norico heard the horses' hooves from afar and rose to look out of the window. Dawn was pushing the night away. He woke Rotrud and urged her to go to a bed chamber.

"I shall stay here," he said, "and answer any summons.

173

It may be these coming are travelers, like ourselves, moving by night, for some reason. If they are from your father's court, I'll ease their minds, let them know you are safely abed and under my protection."

"Nay, Nay," he told her. "There'll be no questions asked this night, no recriminations about your being in this place. That will come on the morrow. I'll protect you now and then. Please, my dear one, please," he begged. "Remove yourself to your bedchamber and rest easy. At day's light, we'll understand this visit, if that, in fact, be what this is." He walked Rotrud to her bedchamber, kissed her lightly, and closed the door. That done, he walked to the manor's door. *I've no doubt this group is from King Charlemagne,* he thought. *I've little to say which the King will not question and dismiss. I, in fact, may easily lose my life. Mayhap, I should ride out before they draw any closer.*

Norico considered his probable fate at the hands of the King. *He will, at the worst, remand me to my father,* Norico decided. "That, too, will be an uneasy fate; but I've chosen my wife. Father will accept that - the daughter of the King. Of a certainty, he'll be delighted."

Alcuin approached the front door of the manor. Before he could knock, the door opened. Alcuin startled. He had seen this man before, a noble by his bearing; but he couldn't recall his name.

"Please enter, Master Alcuin," the tall, elegant man invited. "And summon the rest of your escort. All must be in need of food and rest, being so late on the road. I suppose this is the end of your journey?" Alcuin nodded imperceptibly and turned to take a few steps toward the men and Gizzie, waiting on their horses. The man at the door walked outside and accompanied Alcuin to the waiting escort.

"Come inside, do," the man invited them all. "I bid you all come in and eat. Anyone traveling with Master Alcuin is

welcome in this hall. Please come and refresh yourselves."
He stepped aside, waiting to follow the visitors as they
entered. Norico couldn't understand the presence of the
child, a small girl of, mayhap, eight or nine years. Had
she been visiting at the court and been summoned home
quickly? That didn't seem likely. *She's very weary; her head's
drooping and her clothing is covered with dust; but she doesn't
seem distraught nor worried about the break in the journey.*
Norico followed the group into the entry and preceded
them into the receiving room.

"I've just arrived myself," he acknowledged. "There's
no one about, so I have no one to receive travelers. But,
worry not. I can make you comfortable. Please – sit, rest
while I go to the cook room for refreshments." With that
said, he left the travelers to fend for themselves and
went to the cook room. There he found adequate food to
offer the wayfarers. *Rotrud has cooked for a family*, Norico
decided. He smiled to himself. *Mayhap, the dear prepared
as much food as she found, earlier this day. But, who knows?
Maybe she didn't wish to cook again! We may have been here for
a week...and have had a sufficient amount, though a great deal
of the same dish!*

Norico knew he was still smiling, thinking of Rotrud,
when he heard steps behind him. Turning, he saw Angilbert
in the arched doorway. Angilbert left Alcuin and the others
stretching and walking the kinks out of their legs. He felt it
was preferable for him to speak initially with Norico. If this
affair was as he suspected, he, himself, would have more
understanding of it than Alcuin. Angilbert noted Rotrud's
unhappiness more than two seasons ago. If she were here
with Count Norico, she must have found a way to curb
her loneliness. He smiled reassuringly, he did hope, at the
Count and introduced himself.

"I am Angilbert, assistant to Master Alcuin and
fledging poet of the King's court," he began. "I must first

make a serious inquiry, Sir. Is Rotrud here and, if not, do you have any knowledge of her whereabouts?" Seeing a startled lift to the Count's eyebrows, Angilbert continued. "The princess is missing from court...to the fear of everyone. We're but one party searching for her. We took this direction on the opinion of her little sister, Gizzie. I ask only if she's here and if she's unharmed." Angilbert ceased speaking. He shouldn't say overmuch to this count of whom he knew so little.

"Why, aye, of a certainty," the tall, self-possessed man replied. "She's sleeping above. She's unharmed. Do you wish me to wake her?" He asked, moving toward the door.

"Nay, nay. That's not necessary." Angilbert replied with a sigh. "We have, mayhap, been over-worried for her safety. We'll see her on the morrow. After all, the sun's rising won't require a lengthy wait." And he smiled at Norico. "Then, let's get this food to your escort. They must all be hungry. I am Norico," he added, "middle son of Count Brandt of Limonges." Count Norico picked up a trencher and a bread loaf. "There's no one to serve," he apologized, "we must take care of ourselves." He was almost into the corridor when Angilbert's voice stopped him.

"Sire," Angilbert began, making some rapid calculations of the situation in the manor, "don't speak of your presence here or your business to anyone, no matter who requires an explanation of you. I must speak to the King first. Do you understand?"

Norico looked at Angilbert quickly, taken aback by this directive. Although not completely understanding the offer, he knew his precarious position in being discovered here and assented with a dip of his head.

"Thank you, Angilbert," he replied. "I will be led by your direction."

Angilbert replied. "Thank you for the food, Norico. Don't take it amiss that I suggest you return to court...

alone and tonight."

Norico nodded, picked up a tray of food, and smiled. "Of a certainty, Master Angilbert, I shall do that, if you think it wise." Both men returned to the others, providing them with food and drink. Then, Norico led the men to the bedchambers. Gisela was taken to Rotrud's chamber and sent inside. She climbed into bed beside the sleeping Rotrud and fell immediately to sleep.

Thinking of the morrow, Norico searched through the cook's stores, luckily locating stored oats, a cased ring of cheese, and dried fruits. This will suffice to break their fast, come the morn, he thought. He left the food on the large table in the cook room and went to the small stable to saddle his horse. *I should be on my way before sunrise, as Angilbert suggests. If it appears I were but passing through, the King's judgment will go better for me.* He went to Rotrud's bedchamber and knocked quietly. In a moment, roused from sleep, Rotrud's head poked out of the door. She smiled immediately, stretching a hand to caress Norico's cheek.

"My love," Norico acknowledged her touch. "Did you see your little sister in your bed? Nay? She's just arrived with a small escort. Nay, nay. All seems to be calm at the moment. Your father has sent them, searching for you. I gave them refreshments 'ere the dawn was breaking and left food to break this morning's fast. But, being found here with you, alone, is far from positive...or acceptable. I'm going home, to my father's lands. Don't despair. I'll return to the court within a fortnight." To Rotrud's amazed stare, he smiled. Then, he took her hand and kissed it.

"Have no worry for me, dear. Master Alcuin and Master Angilbert are in this group. They do have your and our — it would seem — best interests at the forefront of their thoughts. Put yourself in their hands. I urge you to this course. Master Angilbert does appear to understand much, very much. I don't like to leave you, thus; but it is the best course at this point. Have no doubt; I love and adore you. I leave to speak to my father." With this, Norico kissed Rotrud, gave her a tight hug, and left.

Rotrud could sleep no longer. Norico's hasty farewell, his serious demeanor had banished sleep from her head. She returned to the bed, kissed Gisela who smiled slightly, and examined her clothing for a change of dress. Clothed for her expected journey home, she went to the cook room and began preparing food for the morning meal. Within a short time, Alcuin entered the room.

"Good morning, Rotrud," he greeted her gravely. "Before the others are here, do you wish to tell me anything, anything at all about this run from your father's court, about your sojourn here?" He gazed at her with compassionate eyes, understanding she realized the difficult situation she had provoked. To forestall her weeping, Alcuin held his arms open for her and kissed her head as she snuggled to his chest.

I'm not lost, Rotrud thought. *Master Alcuin is here. Mayhap, he can make a plan...one that will soothe Poppa. But I will be strong, too. This time I have a love I will not forego! Norico has given me his pledge and vowed he cares for me. Poppa must make some accommodation. I will not be deterred. Norico is the man I want. I will have him...no matter what Poppa says!*

"Master Alcuin, protect me from Poppa's wrath, please," she murmured. "I didn't plan to leave the court. Suddenly, I just couldn't stay there. In its midst, I was filled with pain and longing, for what I couldn't explain. I fled here to Peppin's house; his eyes always shown with happiness when he talked of this place." Rotrud smiled peacefully.

"I knew there would be no one here. I just yearned for some kind of peace, peace away from the court, away from Poppa, especially away from Fastrada." She slapped the table with her hands. "She cares for no one but herself, Master Alcuin. I can't accept that she can have a man's love, his care and concern, a life of luxury and contentment. And I'm to have no one. Poppa would deny me children and a home of my own! No longer, Master Alcuin; I will accept his strictures no longer. Mayhap, he'll banish me. No matter. Even if Norico will not share such banishment, I shall leave Poppa's kingdom. Mayhap, outside of it, I may live the life I choose."

"We shall fight for your life together, Rotrud," Master Alcuin assured her. "But you must speak to no one; admit nothing. Say nothing. Don't speak of this at all. If the court quotes my words, agree with all of them. I will speak with the King. He will give some concession; I shall demand it—on pain of my leaving his court." Alcuin replied.

"Oh, nay! Nay, Master Alcuin! You must not jeopardize your place at court! I cannot bear the guilt, should Poppa turn against you. I cannot allow it," Rotrud screamed.

"It's not for you to allow, my dear girl," Alcuin replied. "This is my choice; my choice for the young woman I know. God means for women to marry, else the Christ would not have blessed the wedding wine. It's normal and right for you to wish to follow the destiny God meant you to have. Don't despair! All your wishes won't be realized, but that does not mean some of them can't come true. Yet, you must say nothing—of your own volition. Do you understand me?"

"I do," Rotrud answered. "I'll be led by your advice. Now, I must seek out Gizzie and obtain her silence." She smiled as she quietly kissed Alcuin's cheek and returned to her bedchamber.

Gizzie was cleaning her teeth at the water basin and ran to Rotrud as she entered the room. "Oh, Rotrud!" Gizzie exclaimed. "Thank the saints; you're safe! We rode and rode yesterday night. The court was a jumble with Poppa like a thunderstorm. I was very frightened for you; Master Angilbert said you might be in danger, beset by thieves or worse!" And Gizzie burst into tears, sobbing at Rotrud's breast and hugging her desperately.

"My dear, my dear," Rotrud muttered. "All is well. Don't imagine horrible things! I'm safe, though I see now I was unwise to run from the court. I've no defense. I felt so buffeted there - alone, misunderstood and unhappy. But, Master Alcuin promises to intervene with Poppa. He assures me all will be well, despite my hasty disappearance.

Rotrud laughed; she felt better than she had in months. She knew much of it came from her feeling for Norico, of course; but much also sprang from Alcuin's love of her, of that she could only marvel and thank God for His blessing. "But you and I must talk, Gizzie. Although you may not understand now, Master Alcuin directs us to volunteer no information about this incident. We must tell no one what happened on this trip. Are you able to do that, Gizzie?" Rotrud asked. "Master Alcuin can put a positive explanation on this, if we don't contradict his account. My life and others will be well-served, if he's successful."

"I shall do whatever you ask, Rotrud," answered Gizzie. "I love you and Master Alcuin. Much of this I don't understand. Even Master Angilbert seems to know more than I. He has been SO kind to me, Rotrud. Do you know him?" At Rotrud's negative shake of the head, Gizzie continued. "He was very good...to bring me to help in the search for you, to hold me on his horse... Oh, Rotrud! Where is little Foxer? Is she with you? I saw her riding on your knee as you left the stables. Has she been hurt?" Gizzie was looking around the room frantically.

"Do you think I would risk Foxer, the way Poppa dotes on her? She's in the stables, protecting my mount!" Rotrud laughed. "All is well with both of them. She was a fine companion on my wild ride here. She's a fierce guard dog,

Gizzie, alert and feisty. And how is little Splotch?" Gizzie adopted Spotch when Peppin was imprisoned, promising herself to get the dog to Peppin at his monastery... whatever it took.

"Rinaldo helps me take care of him but still talks of taking him to Peppin. He wrote to ask the Bishop if Peppin might have Splotch at the monastery, there in Prum. I do hope so, Rotrud. Splotch's heart aches for Peppin; I can see it in his eyes." Gizzie answered, her eyes filling with tears.

"We shall ask Alcuin to prevail upon the holy father in Prum, never fear, Gizzie. Now," Rotrud continued briskly, "change your clothes so we can break our fast. We'll have a long ride back to the court. I've no doubt that Master Alcuin will wish to return forthwith."

As Rotrud predicted, the small band set out before mid-day for King Charlemagne's court. Sending one of the guards ahead to alert the King Rotrud was found and unhurt, Alcuin decided to slow the journey somewhat. He and Angilbert conferred steadily as the mounts' hooves ate up the miles.

***

"Let's give these two an outing, Angil," he suggested. "Neither Rotrud nor Gizzie ever has a change from the relentless moving of the court. The days march one after another, week in and day out. They are constantly moving with only the two or three week sojourn at Easter or Christmastide to provide a change. Queen Hildegard was ever planning little sorties, recreations, and gatherings for them. Not so, this queen... For too long, the younger children have had little delight in their lives. The King neglects them greatly." Alcuin sighed. "For all the concern about heirs and alliances, this King does not think about his offspring overmuch." *Without Rotrud, Gizzie would've had no mothering whatever.*

"A more restful journey will be good for you and me, as well," Angilbert replied. "I'm fascinated to watch these sisters. Even though there're years between their ages, their relationship does pleasure my heart. Rotrud is loving and wise, providing direction to her sister but injecting fun and laughter into the activities they share. She does seem like her mother, the tales I have heard of Queen Hildegard, I mean to say, Sir. And Gizzie, how full of life and laughter she is, despite the sadness, the loss, in the court—almost since her birth! It is remarkable—the ability of the human spirit to survive, and do so with lightness and hope?" Angilbert smiled at his teacher.

Alcuin glanced at his favorite person. *Aye*, Alcuin mused, *Angilbert is going to become a great poet. He has the sensitivity, the knowledge of words, and the feelings to write from his heart. But, most importantly, he is not ashamed of his sensitive nature. He doesn't hide it from others but, readily, shares himself with all around him. How proud I am of this boy.* Remembering the King's mistakes with his offspring, Alcuin turned to Angilbert.

"Angil, I must tell you how very proud of you I am. You have grown into a fine man, one with whom I would trust my life, my books, and my hopes. You're responsible, well-educated, and worthy of the respect which you're now receiving. My boy, my life has been immeasurably enriched by your parents' gift, and I am thankful to them...for the gift of yourself." Angilbert was so startled by Alcuin's words that he stopped his horse.

I know, of a certainty, Alcuin loves me, he thought. *And I knew he approved of my conduct; but to hear he's this pleased is well beyond my expectations. I hoped to bring him joy. How wonderful to understand I have.* Angil moved his mount close to his teacher and hugged him tightly as the tears rolled down his face.

"My father, my friend," he whispered quietly.

Rotrud and Gizzie saw Angilbert's tears as he and Alcuin looked around to decide about tonight's camp. They cantered immediately to the two men, dismay mirrored on their faces.

"Master Angilbert, are you ill?" Gizzie hurriedly asked. "Do you have a fever; is there anything we can do to ease your pain?" She looked at Rotrud, beseeching her help. Rotrud turned a bewildered face to the two men. They were just laughing together. She didn't know what to think.

"Nay." Angilbert protested. "I'm not ill! I was overcome by Master Alcuin's praise of me. He has ever bolstered my heart, as well as my mind. I was but thanking him for his words." He looked down shyly. Rotrud and Gizzie smiled and, then, broke into laughter, all of them enjoying such a misunderstanding.

"And, now," Master Alcuin added, as he chuckled one last time. "We should stop for our mid-day meal. I propose we delay our return to the court by examining the progress of spring through the kingdom. To verify our study to the King, we'll return to court with plant specimens: new leaves and buds, eggshells broken as baby birds hatched, shed snake skins, and cocoons burst open with no one inside." Rotrud and Gisela looked at him in horror.

"But, Master Alcuin," Gizzie cried. "Poppa will be angry with us! He won't understand! I don't understand. No one wants to rouse Poppa's temper. He's not pleasant at all!" She stopped, horrified her words were disloyal to her father. Alcuin smiled as Angilbert chortled good-naturedly.

"Oh, Master Alcuin is fooling you, Gizzie!" Angilbert almost giggled. "Of course, we wouldn't take those things before the King. He is just suggesting we find a reason to decrease our speed in returning to court. We shall say we were busy examining spring's progress across the King's realm. He'll want a report, you see."

"If you'll make the report while Rotrud and I sneak to our room, that'll be fine with me," Gizzie responded dubiously. Alcuin and Angilbert laughed again at Gizzie's doubtful face and assured her all would be well.

"Master Alcuin is giving us an excuse, Gizzie, to linger on our journey," Angilbert grinned.

Alcuin assured Gizzie that he would talk with her father and explain the great educational value of their journey. The king would wish he had joined them, he told her. But, right now, they needed to go fishing. Aye, he acknowledged, only Charles and Peppin had previously enjoyed that pleasure. But that lack in their education would be changed very soon. He directed Gizzie and Rotrud to cut willow saplings for fishing poles. He had twine in his bags and Angilbert knew the worms' hiding places. His eyes twinkled with mischief as he winked at Angilbert.

Spying plums on the near-by trees, Rotrud picked as many as she could carry in her shawl while Angilbert and Gisela dug up worms. In less than twenty minutes, the little group marched on, eating tart plums, and watching Alcuin look for a 'likely-looking spot.' Alcuin and Angilbert baited their hooks while giving copious instructions to the girls. They settled down and waited for the fish to bite. Alcuin complimented Rotrud's efforts to bait her hook but allowed she needed practice. Still, he assured her, she would make an excellent fisherwoman. He had no doubt.

***

Some several days later, the small band arrived at the King's camp. Alcuin went directly to the library upon their return. Although he took great pleasure from their desultory journey home, Alcuin knew he must report to Charlemagne immediately. Despite Stennis's rapid return and his report to the King, Charlemagne would be eager to know the particulars of their journey. Adequate time had passed for the King's fear to dissipate and for his anger to build.

"Dear Lord, help me," Alcuin prayed. He resolved to be firm with his comments and to speak passionately for the future of the princesses. "This must be the speech of my life." Alcuin muttered as he gathered his courage. *I will not be overtalked by the King this night,* he vowed. *I'm fighting for the girls' happiness. The King's so resolute in his opinion no one dares defy him. But I shall...if on this misplaced idea alone.*

He cannot deny his daughters the love God, the Father, clearly expects – the love God directs His people to embrace. No matter the King's love for them; no matter his fear of their being trapped or mistreated, the princesses deserve caring husbands. Alcuin rejected the King's argument. Charlemagne must understand that not allowing his daughters to marry would encourage his enemies to accuse him of sinful behavior, of sexual knowledge of his own daughters.

"I will not allow it!" Alcuin spoke aloud. "I must not allow this accusation to arise, to float through the court like a noxious mist, to spread throughout the realm. "How can he forget rumor and innuendo so quickly?" Alcuin asked with all the strength at his disposal. "I shall argue in God's name. HE would so command it."

Chapter 10

THE WORK CONTINUES.

King Charlemagne awaited Alcuin, reading a parchment at his library desk, seemingly lost in its pages. But, as Alcuin entered the room, the King rolled the parchment and set it aside.

"Welcome back to court, Alcuin." the king greeted him. "I worried that you had set out on a year-long tour of the realm." He checked his resentful retort and nodded to the scholar. "As you imagine, I'm much relieved at both Rotrud's safe return, as well as the rest of you. None of you had permission to leave the court, by the way. But I appreciate your efforts in this rescue; I am forever in your debt. You cannot know the fear, the worry that galloped through ..." He stopped speaking. *Of a certainty, Alcuin knows exactly. He loves my daughters, just as I do and, probably, understands them better.*

"Ask anything you wish of me and I shall do my best to supply it. My daughter has come to no harm. God be praised." Alcuin immediately saw his opening and greeted the King.

"All is well, Sire. Our fears were unfounded, as I'd predicted. Rotrud is safely back in the arms of the court. There were no maurauders, no confrontations, no threats. After finding Rotrud, we undertook our springtime journey and received nothing but pleasant and peaceful results."

"But, it was entirely an unnecessary journey," the King

growled. "...wholly unnecessary, brought on by a slip of a girl, selfish and with no thought for our worries! I am angry beyond words, Alcuin. And wish you to help calm me, help me make sense of this behavior."

Alcuin deepened his frown, deliberately balled his fists, and moved his head an inch forward. He often watched the King, as his anger mounted, and so was well-aware of body changes in the face of anger or exasperation.

"Nay, Sire." he said in cold, static tones. "I'm not here to calm you. Mayhap, you should offer something to calm me! My temper is fully aroused; I warn you. The words you hear from my lips will *NOT* be calming." Alcuin glared at King Charlemagne, slowly shaking his head from side to side. He stood ramrod straight, looked directly into the king's face. "I'm amazed at your stupidity, Sire. I cannot accept that your eyes can be so dull or your heart so cruel! Have you given no thought to Rotrud's flight—the reason for it? Nay, it had nothing to do with selfishness. On the contrary, Rotrud fled to improve her chance at life. Have you no understanding of the hurt which precipitated her leave-taking?" The king physically took a step backward, his face a mask of shock. He clearly did not expect this reaction.

"What kind of father are you-- so unfeeling you cannot imagine your daughter's pain; so certain in your pronouncements you treat her like a book: to be placed here and there, to be beautiful, to be used, and to be controlled? What possible excuse can you concoct for killing your daughter's spirit?"

Alcuin spewed the works, enhancing his sarcasm. He hoped to shock Charlemagne, shock him with a verbal attack so he would be vulnerable. The king stared at Alcuin, clearly stung by the cutting words but unable to believe the Scholar uttered them. Alcuin spoke again, using the momentum to make his points quickly.

"Rotrud fled because she no longer wanted to live in your world, in this sacrosanct court where the lives of only two people are served: you and your queen. Neither you nor Fastrada, God help you, has concern for your children. You imprison yours and know little of hers. Fastrada's even worse. She dresses her young girls as princesses, sits them in some ridiculous pose, and leaves them for hours. They learn nothing; they enjoy no society. They're no more than plants around a pool, molded and static for others' viewing. Your children? She pretends they don't exist unless she can criticize and harass them. Then, she criticizes them to you, further undermining your interest in them. Have you no mind left – thinking this a healthy environment for any of your children, Sir?"

"You know nothing of them, Charlemagne. I ask you: which one has an overwhelming love of Greek poetry? Identify the child who talks with the shepherds about wildflowers. Name the daughter who walks around a worm, rather than step on it. And, yet, you believe you have a right to control their lives…a father who has no knowledge of them at all? You may not decide everything your own way! God forbids it! Do you hear me, Sire? God forbids it!" Alcuin's eyes bulged, his face was red; his arms waved in the air.

"Let me explain things to you. You forbid your daughters to marry – not your sons, just your daughters. There's the explanation for Rotrud's flight. She is unable to continue living here. She wants a husband, a family of her own. You, Sir, at least have a life-mate. The kind of life-mate you have chosen is of no consequence." Alcuin plowed on, over-riding the King's effort to interrupt. "You have a wife. The court revolves around her wishes. She has little positive feelings – for the children you fathered or, God help her, for your children by another mother. Still, Fastrada is pampered, obeyed, catered to. The same describes your life. How, then, can you deny a home and family to your female children? It's blasphemous, I tell you. Blasphemous! You deny them a God-given directive: be fruitful and multiply. You deny them! And who are you to make such a choice? You are **not** God. You do understand that, Sire?"

Seeing the King listening intently, Alcuin continued. He reminded Charlemagne of disturbing incidents from the past. Alcuin knew the gossip which arose, again, from time to time. Again, he asked the king about the talk which accused him of unnatural acts with Rotrud! "Describe Hildegard's horror for me, Sire. Do you forget Abbot's Fulrad's pain? Do you imagine the rumors are squelched? If such horrid suggestions were made when Rotrud was but a child, what speculation do you think runs rife now... when she's a beautiful, young woman? Can you be so dull, so thick-witted, so secure in your place, that those rumors are forgotten? Will you have your realm destroyed by unsubstantiated talk which undermines the very basis of your rule, that of Christian precepts? Don't deceive yourself!" Alcuin raised his voice.

"Your kingdom will be nothing! Your efforts will scatter to the winds! Your hopes for your people will die, if there be any hint of lust in your behavior with your daughters. And a father who rules, who declares to everyone his daughters won't be allowed to marry, is suspect—many, many times over!" Alcuin licked his lips. He was exhausted.

The emotion of this topic, for the King and for his daughters' futures, was almost more than the scholar could endure. He knew the effect of his words would be minimal if the King didn't feel threatened, if he thought people supported his actions. The only hope for Rotrud--and for Bertha and Gizzie as well--was Charlemagne's fear that he, himself, would be harmed by his refusal to allow them to marry. *I have spoken as well as I'm able,* Alcuin thought, *the rest is in the hands of God.* And he was silent. King Charlemagne continued to look into his face. Alcuin stood resolute, staring back, not moving an inch. After many moments, the King waved him away.

"Leave me, Alcuin," he muttered. "Leave me. I must think on your words. Harsh words they be, Scholar," he added. "…harsh words, indeed, from a friend to his King. Be gone!"

***

Alcuin walked slowly out of the library, pushed open the door at the end of the corridor, and disappeared into the edge of the forest. Rinaldo, suspecting Alcuin's errand in the library and watching the outside door, followed him into the trees.

"He did his best," Rinaldo whispered softly, "fighting for the King's future and for the happiness of these daughters. What a burden for a scholar, one who merely wishes to teach the great thoughts. This one has become an adviser, an instructor, even the conscience of a king! In Alcuin what a loving heart the King brought to this court!" Rinaldo felt overwhelmed by Alcuin's duties. "This may be King Charlemagne's realm, but its future rests in Scholar Alcuin's vision."

***

Though it was still deep in the night, Rotrud waked. A courier summoned her to the library, at the King's request. As she opened her chamber door, the church bell tolled 2:00 am. Making her way down the corridor, she searched the turns and alcoves frantically for Alcuin but couldn't find him. Fearing in being late she would anger her father even more, she hurried to the library. She felt completely unprepared for seeing her father alone but wanted no one but Alcuin. Just as she steeled herself to enter the library, she saw Alcuin hurrying around the corner. Very relieved, she waved in greeting, waiting for him to join her.

"Rotrud, the king has summoned you?" Alcuin inquired.

"Only a bit ago," Rotrud affirmed, reaching for Alcuin's arm. "I'm not certain I could've entered without you, Master," she added as she gave his arm a small squeeze. "I do so dread this. My explanation will never satisfy Poppa. And I am so afraid of his questions - judgmental and unpleasant, delivered with dark, angry looks and shouting."

"If he asks questions, ignore them," Alcuin advised. "I've a feeling the King will have much to say. Most of it, nay none of it, will require an answer. He will not expect one. Pay attention; don't let your mind wander. Try to show no emotion. He may be harsh, Rotrud; so keep your feelings well covered." Alcuin advised. Rotrud felt but did not completely understand Alcuin's tension. She knew nothing of Alcuin's discussion with King Charlemagne. They walked into the library tent together, drawing strength from each other's presence.

The King looked up from his writing desk as they entered. He nodded calmly to Alcuin, rose and came to Rotrud and kissed her cheek.

"Thank God you are unharmed, Rotrud," he began. "I know I over-react when my children seem to be threatened. The last few days have been trying, indeed, for me — your distraught father. But, happily all has ended safely. We shall speak no more about it." Rotrud's eyes bulged with this statement. She looked at Alcuin, a question mirrored in her eyes. Alcuin did not respond to the look or to the King's words.

"I wish you to know, before I continue. You have an undisputed champion at this court. I know now — without a doubt—that if I ever need an impassioned defense or heartfelt pleading, I will call for Master Alcuin. He is eloquent in defending those he loves. And his love for you, Rotrud, is mind-bending. I have always admired his disciplined mind; his prodigious ability to think, analyze, and conclude; his command of classic Greek and Latin literature. But he has done himself proud in his pleas for your future and those of your sisters." The King nodded at his eldest daughter, then raised his hand to both her and Alcuin.

"Nay, do not look upon me with hopeful faces. I haven't changed my mind about your marital choices. You won't have the choice of becoming anyone's wife." Alcuin stirred, took a step forward, ready to protest. King Charlemagne halted him with a look. "I have not finished, Scholar Alcuin." He gave them both a grave smile.

"I have closely examined my distaste for marriage for my daughters," he continued, involving them both in his glance. "I've not changed my views, though I do believe some joinings can be lifetime commitments. In fact, some few may well last beyond a lifetime. I've only to remember my life with your mother, Rotrud, to know this kind of love. And, just last night, I realized she was, indeed, younger than you when our love began. It was Hilde's love for me, Scholar Alcuin, which caused me to re-evaluate my position." The King twisted the signet ring on his finger, back and forth. "I will admit your impassioned speech reminded me of our relationship; but it was Hilde's love alone which moved me."

Alcuin nodded, knowing the King would never protest his influence if, in fact, it had been inconsequential. He returned his attention to the King as he continued.

"Rotrud, I don't know if you have a man whom you've thought of marrying…or of fleeing the court for. I do not ask that you so inform me. I won't allow you to marry; I absolutely will not allow you to choose such a vulnerable position...no matter that the Christian Church requires it. None of you will be Christians, then, in this situation." The King shook his head, then looked directly at his oldest daughter.

"But, I will not judge you in any liaison you wish to enter," he smiled briefly, seeing Rotrud's shocked face. "I ask you to be discreet in your loving. Choose your lover so there never need be an apology for his behavior nor the need for a tale to cover any subterfuge or embarrassment which might result from his actions. I would urge you, should you take a lover, to have no more than one. Loyalty and faithfulness are as important in a paired union as they're important between father and child." He rubbed his eyes, remembering the Church's judgment of his and Hildegard's 'barbarian union.' The King shook his head slowly and returned to the present.

"If you will but indicate your preference in location, I shall provide a tent or bedchamber separate from the communal one you share with your sisters. I don't wish you to have difficulty in sharing your time and life with your mate; but neither do I wish you to flaunt your relationship to the court." The King held up his hand to forestall any speech.

"Should any child result from such a union, that child will be as dear to me as any of my other grandchildren. And such as I can do for your offspring, I shall do happily. Because of my position in the Church, I will treat you and your mate as the single individuals you are, not acknowledging your relationship. But never will I criticize or denigrate the union to anyone, most importantly to your children. I know this is not an ideal solution. Certainly, it's not a solution that delights Alcuin." King Charlemagne glanced at Alcuin, aware of the surprise and sadness reflected in the man's eyes.

"But, with my very real concern for you and for this realm, it's the best I can offer. I hope it's enough." So saying the King kissed Rotrud once more, this time on the forehead, grasped Alcuin's shoulder and turned to leave. His steps faltered; he stopped.

"Know that I love you both dearly," he added as he left the room.

***

As he promised, Norico returned within the fortnight. He went directly to Rotrud, having arrived in mid-morning. She recounted her father's words. Norico re-iterated his love for her. Because he was a third-born son, his father's blessing was not required for their joining. He was due nothing from his father that he'd not already received. He and Rotrud bound themselves, each to the other, and were united as one — making their own vows and beseeching Master Alcuin to bless them.

***

Settling affairs with his children, improving court conditions for their benefit, were never grievous for the King. He always believed he maintained his authority and his control of them; and that was enough. Only Queen Hildegard had managed to apply his broad concern for his people to specific concern for his sons and daughters. When she died, no one reminded him of his fatherly duties. Only rarely did Gisela prevail upon him to consider Fastrada's children's needs, and her pleas, for the most part, fell on deaf ears.

The king loved his daughters dearly but his kingly duty, and their duty to him, were the basis of their joint relationships. As the King acknowledged to Abbot Fulrad many years before, he never thought of a man's (or woman's) feelings, just the choices which proved advantageous for the realm.

***

Despite the challenges in his personal life, King Charlemagne used his prodigious energy to strengthen and expand his realm. Ever did he plan and fight, both to conquer more peoples and expand his kingdom. Years before, he concluded that the Saxons would ever prove intractable, rebelling and plundering, almost as often as the seasons changed. And, thus, he was constantly fighting them. His hatred of the Saxons and, later, of the Avars (sometimes called Huns) consumed his thoughts.

The Saxons rebelled against King Charlemagne with consistent regularity. Their raids, characterized by strike-run tactics, continued to antagonize King Charlemagne and his army. At news of each uprising, the King himself led the march against them; or, if busy elsewhere, he sent one of his sons to crush the perpetrators. Even the capture of the Saxon leader Widukind in 792 had not produced peace for long. The year after Widukind's capture, the northern Saxons rose once more against the Franks and almost annihilated Charlemagne's army.

Charlemagne responded with his now legendary brutality toward the Saxons and removed them from their ancestral lands, replacing them with Frankish and Slav settlers. Although it appeared he would never completely subdue them, or—at the least—keep them loyal, he continued to fight. He, also, led the Frankish army against a new invader, the Avars. Additional support from a Slav army strengthened his successes. He defeated the Saxons and Avars repeatedly; but there was always another day for battle.

"King Charlemagne!" Rinaldo called, "King Charlemagne! We have a missive." He waved it as he got within talking distance of the King. "One of the Avar's leaders has turned against their ruler, the khagan. This man, now a traitor to the Avars, wishes to become your vassal. His oath is here on this parchment. Orag, that's his name." Charlemagne was taken aback at first but, then, laughed gleefully.

"By the grace of God, can this be true?" he asked Rinaldo. "Recount to me once more this Avar's message." And he reached for the parchment in Rinaldo's hand.

Rinaldo denied any specific knowledge of the Avars or of the khagan's change of heart. But he answered. "Orag swears he intends to become a Christian, Sire; at least that's his message to you. I can't say if the khagan himself is dead or overthrown." Always suspicious, the King, hoping some rift was developing among the Avars, decided to wait to return to the Danubian Plain. He suspected this message and the declaration itself might be a trap. So, he decided to do nothing — to wait.

Months later, Charlemagne received additional information from Erich, the Duke of Friuli. Erich reported the Avar leader had been undermined by his own supporters; and, as a result, the entire Avar army was in disarray. Accordingly, in 796, the Duke led his soldiers against the Avar capital and sacked a camp on the banks of the Danube River, the very river Charlemagne tried to link with the Rhine years before. The Frankish war against the Avars was then in its fifth year. The Duke of Friuli broke into the Avar capital and discovered the 'rings' (strongholds of treasure), full of riches completely unsuspected. The Duke met with such little resistance that he sent couriers to both King Pepin in Italy and King Charlemagne, urging them to overrun the entire Avar region.

King Pepin, acting on this information from his vassal, took a larger Lombard army into the Avar lands, attacking and ravaging them again. He appropriated all that was left and, then, made a special journey to Charlemagne's court to describe the riches.

The destruction of the Avar continued until 802 when the Avar Khanate was completely annihilated, decimated unlike any other of Charlemagne's enemies.

***

"Poppa, Poppa!" King Pepin rushed into Charlemagne's tent. "The Avars are pushed beyond the Danube, beaten and defeated! But I must acquaint you with additional news. Might we retire to the library?"

"Aye, my boy, of a certainty. I'm relieved you're unharmed. Was it a difficult battle?" the King replied, as he gave Pepin a welcome home--congratulatory hug, all in one. "What is so pressing? Don't you want food, ale, time to catch your breath? We've many hours to talk and discuss your battle. Your men, are they bedded down?"

"Of a certainty; all is well. Hasten, Poppa, do! I have amazing news, undreamt of news." King Pepin was disheveled: his helmet scarred and bent, his cloak frayed and stained. "Poppa! I couldn't linger; I had to come to court myself! You have the good news."

"I can think of no news more positive than this—the Avars are defeated! Pepin, you are a fighter after my own heart!" the King praised his son. His comment brought a rousing laugh from Pepin.

Closing the library door, Pepin grabbed his father, his hands on his father's shoulders, holding him still. "We are rich, Poppa! Do you hear? We are dripping in gems... and gold...and beautiful, absolutely stupendous things— crowns, jewel-encrusted knives, exotic woods, vast stores of embroidered linens! Do you understand me, Poppa?

Can you believe it?"

"My son! My son! What are you shouting? Rich...but by what means? Nay! Truly I don't know what you are saying! Rich? Rich....by whose account? The last time I inquired, the coffers were housing spiders!"

"No, No, Poppa! From the Avars...from the booty we took! We have wealth beyond imagining. It'll take me weeks to describe all we have taken. Do you know what this means, Poppa? Now, you may easily realize grandfather's promise to the Pope. You are now able to fulfill grandfather's expansion of the Holy See, more property for the Church! The Pope will be amazed!"

"Pepin, my boy! What are you saying?" Charlemagne asked. "Rich, Rich? Can it be true?"

Pepin began dancing around the room, swaying from side to side, encouraging his father to dance with him. "It's true, Poppa. It's true!" Pepin jumped and shouted, letting his enthusiasm out, delighted to tell his father the good news.

***

King Charlemagne received Pepin as a conquering hero. The court celebrated both the defeat of the Avars and the wealth King Pepin and Erich had taken. Despite the happiness generated by the Avar wealth, death again cut short the King's merriment.

In Frankfurt in the summer of 793, Queen Fastrada died. Although she died with the King's court surrounding her, the King was her only real mourner. Among the courtiers, the nobility, the King's children, the court workers, few could be found who were not relieved she was gone.

"We shall, again, prepare food as we have not done in years," the royal cook announced. "Queen Fastrada has died. We must uphold the reputation of the court and honor the King's view of his mistress." Several young servers snickered, noting the cook's use of the word 'mistress,' rather than 'wife.'

"Oh, that we could show our true view of her," one of the servers commented. She turned quickly away when she saw the chief cook staring, shocked at her temerity.

"I have heard the rumors," the royal cook acknowledged. "There's little sorrow lost in the court. But we must not speak so. Increase the heat in the ovens, knead the dough! Everyone to work!" He hurried the kitchen helpers to their work benches. "Here in Frankfurt, many people will come to observe the courtesies. We must be prepared. Work hard and honor the King. We will all pray we'll return to Aachen by Christmastide. This sadness will be behind us!" Seeing the excitement on people's faces, he moved their minds toward the future. "I do hope construction of the palace is moving forward…in these days of good weather. Soon, the rains of winter will force a break in the laying of bricks and curing of wood."

All members of the court prayed, did penance, and provided comfort to the King. The much disliked Queen was buried in honor, much to the disgust of Hildegard's children. Within a few months, Charlemagne had taken a concubine, Liutgard, into his bed. The entire court, now used to the comforts their King demanded, made no comment at all. As for his daughters, they no longer cared.

***

Charles, long having struggled to please his father, was often in battle, still attempting to prove his mettle to the King. When home, he was tutored and schooled, examined and trained so he'd be prepared for his kingship. Pepin in his Lombard kingdom and Louis in Aquitaine were, of course, equally schooled; but the latter two sons were in someone else's hands. The King had little direct influence on their upbringing or with the training experiences in their lives.

His daughters were, however, the toast of his court. They were endlessly entertaining to their father, found favor with him in most endeavors, and were blessed by his approval. As time passed, Rotrud delivered a son, Louis, fathered by Count Norico. She was ever loyal to him and appeared to have not a modicum of interest in any other man. Although the court talked and rumored, Rotrud did as she pleased...with the blessing of her father.

***

"Be the King deterred or concerned about the morals of his daughters, my sisters?" Louis inquired of Paul the Deacon during Paul's latest visit to the Aquitaine court. "It does seem strange for a Christian court, doesn't it, to countenance children with no father acknowledged? Poppa acts as if nothing is out of the ordinary in these arrangements. I cannot suffer it, Master. I can visit only when necessity requires my presence. The entire realm is tainted by my father's perverse ways!" King Louis' face reddened as the muscles in his jaws bulged.

"Your interpretation is your own, King Louis," Paul responded. "But your father is our King. His word is our law. I can assure you Rotrud is doing no harm. She and Norico love each other. They are restrained and discreet in public. No one's harmed by this arrangement, certainly not the court! On the contrary, their union seems to have produced a great deal of happiness and height of positive feeling."

"Nonetheless, by the laws of God and the holy Church, their actions are despicable, Deacon!" Louis' face turned from red to a distinct shade of gray. His yellowed skin, the permanent lines in his forehead, the slight sneer to his mouth, lent gravity to his judgmental words. "Ever has my father done just as he chooses—notwithstanding all the praying, chapel attendance, fasting, exhortations to God or his dedication of battles to Christ. This is blasphemous! I cannot abide this type of hypocrisy. You understand now, this very day, that there will be massive changes when I take over my father's part of the realm. I shall influence him...to uphold Church law and injunctions." Louis intoned.

"You may conduct your realm's affairs as you wish." Paul the Deacon replied. "Your Poppa's lands will not be yours. The king controls the realm. Mayhap, he'll be open to your suggestions but mayhap not!" Paul suggested. "You're more blessed than he, Louis. Your realm has come to you early and, so far, you have been allowed to govern as you choose." So saying, Paul gathered his parchment to leave the presence of the proud, ineffectual son of a great king.

"Oh, if only you could make your father proud, Louis!" he intoned. "Only then might you suggest minor changes to your sire." Paul hurried out of the tent, clamping his lips shut so he would make no additional injudicious remarks.

***

To bury Louis' acidic remarks from his memory, Paul the Deacon recalled the last 'studies' night he shared at the King's court. The regular discussion group had met in the library, as was their habit. Certain court members gathered regularly to share ideas, debate philosophies, and stretch their minds. Never did they agree with each other, but neither did they enjoy any other company so much. In keeping with their respect for each other and in acknowledging each one's contributions to the 'studies' effort, they gave each member of the group a name different from his/her own.

The King, acknowledged leader of the group, was most often referred to as King David, an appellation first suggested by Scholar Alcuin. Alcuin's 'studies' name was Flaccus—for the famous poet. Angilbert was called 'Homer;' and Eberhard' was Eppinus. Often, one of the group would request that poems or dramas or, even, recitations given to the group be shared again at an upcoming evening meal. Because of the great amount of time required to consume the food, 'entertainments' for special banquets were assiduously planned, all of them for the pleasure and the diversion of the guests.

What a wonderful court to visit, Paul thought. *And all the more for those of us who live here. We all journey away from time to time; but no one can control his excitement over his return. How many times have I seen travelers delay greeting their friends and families in order to join the 'studies' in the library? And not just the glories of the mind or of the table are provided. The parks and grounds around the palaces are cultivated with all manner of growing things, plants as well as animals. I recall my delight in the peacock which the King brought back from a distant realm! The yellow, green, and pink birds which dart among the trees; the many-hued salamanders and frogs hiding in the pools, all are there for our delight. We each eagerly anticipated the 'elefant' that the King, that is King David, finally received from the caliph. I can't imagine a heaven any more glorious than this dear court.*

Paul recovered his good spirits, just in remembering his daily life's blessings. He let Louis' caustic forebodings wash out of his mind and, joyfully, went to the stables. He had persuaded the visiting Bishop of Orleans, Theodulf by name, to accompany him for a ride. Theodulf would be another welcome addition to the studies' group. Paul was delighted to urge him to consider joining them. *I must remember to describe the scriptorium to Theodulf,* he thought. *He'll be amazed at the Greek and Latin texts being sent to the monasteries all over the kingdom. How like King Charlemagne to share these wonderful writings with everyone!*

What a gift to the monks and nuns in remote locations – the wealth of classical literature in their own libraries!

***

Paul did not imagine the care with which another poet was, at that very minute, composing a message. Angilbert was writing a summons to Bertha which requested her presence in the herb garden. He wished to discuss little Gizzie's 'worries,' he wrote Bertha. He requested she meet him as soon as possible. Angilbert and Gizzie concocted their story last evening after Angilbert confessed he never was able to talk long enough with Bertha. Liking him very much, Gizzie thought the condition should be quickly remedied and suggested a plan to Angilbert.

A courier delivered the summons to Bertha in the 'little ones' teaching room where she was replacing a teacher who was ill with a stomach ache. Receiving a written summons was unusual. Bertha was eager to read her note. She told the 'little ones' to sit in groups and draw pictures of a rodent, a fowl, and a predator. She hoped to increase both their vocabularies and their animal knowledge with the three new words. She read the summons and was immediately concerned.

Gizzie has worries? What in the world does that mean? Does Rotrud know our sister is troubled or has some problem? Bertha repeated her instructions to the young children, hurrying to respond to the summons immediately. Luckily, she spied her brother, Charles, outside the room and insisted he come inside to assist the 'little ones' with their drawings.

Then, she practically ran to the herb garden. She stepped on the stone path as she moved through the garden, doing her best not to bruise the delicate plantings. A few steps ahead, she spied Gizzie and Angilbert talking together. When Gizzie saw Rotrud, she whispered something into Angilbert's ear and clung to his arm. Bertha increased her speed and rushed up to the two of them.

"What's the matter; are you ill, Gizzie?" she asked as she placed a hand on her sister's forehead. "What problem can you have Angilbert can solve more quickly than I or Rotrud?"

"Oh, that," Gizzie dismissed the problem. "I've talked all about it to Angilbert. He's made me feel better," she added. "I guess there's no problem now. See you at the evening repast!" and she skipped away.

"Wait, wait, Gizzie," Bertha called. "Are you sure?" Gizzie waved strenuously with both hands and hurried down the path, following it around to the vegetable garden where she had her own little plot of earth.

"How very strange," Bertha said to Angilbert. "Might I know about this problem or is it a secret between the two of you?" she inquired.

With a serious expression, Angilbert replied: "It's solved now, Bertha; I believe Gizzie and I would prefer to keep it private, now that she's feeling better." He smiled to forestall Bertha as she began to protest.

"I'm very glad to see you," he added quickly. "Mayhap, we could talk a bit and, while doing so, enjoy this wonderful garden. I've been wondering about you these past weeks. How can you be so busy? I never see you. You never appear where I hope you'll be. How can you be such a sprite?" Angilbert smiled kindly.

Bertha, displeased over apparent secrets between Gizzie and Angilbert, answered impulsively. "See me, why ever would you wish to see me? I'm about my usual routine; I can't imagine you aren't able to find me from one day to another. I'm not a phantom, you know." She looked at Angilbert with undisguised hostility, he who had stolen her sister's confidence. *How dare he!*

Angilbert was shocked. "Why are you so angry? Have I done something to offend you?" Looking at her furious face, he was dumbfounded. "What? Do you object to Gizzie and me talking, here in the garden? Surely, Bertha, our talking cannot be a problem!" He hesitated and, then, decided to say no more. In that instant, Bertha saw her words surprised him, maybe stung him a little. She flushed in embarrassment at her lack of manners and noticed the lines of tension around his eyes.

"Oh, forgive me, Angilbert. I'm just hurt--that my sister confides her worries to you and not to me. You...you're not even family!" Bertha fumed. "But I apologize for my reaction. We each are free to have the friends we choose. Please forgive my bad temper, Angilbert." She looked closely at his face. His eyes were hurt, his mouth held tightly. And his body was set to flee. *He looks like he wants to run away!* Bertha thought to herself. Angilbert gazed at Bertha. It's been days since I've seen her, he thought.

"Bertha," Angilbert took her small hand in his. "I just want to spend some time with you. This concern for Gisela was all a ruse. I could think of no other way to get your attention. Do you know how beautiful you look, sitting there in the sunlight? Your lips are perfect little buds, just like tiny roses on the wall, before they're ready to open. Please forgive me; I must touch your face." And with that, he stroked her cheek, the one bright with sunlight.

"You are so lovely. Your hair's like a halo, catching the sun's rays. The anger in your cheeks infuses your face with life and energy. How can you not realize how much I care for you?" Bertha stared at Angilbert in amazement. She was still holding his hand and, all of a sudden, realized she was squeezing it with vigor.

"Oh, forgive me," she exclaimed as she pulled her hand from his. "I... I did... I did not mean..."

"Didn't mean what?" Angilbert asked. The squeeze of her hand set his heart beating much more quickly. At least, he was getting some response, one different from the anger of her previous words. "I do so want you to speak, Bertha. I need to hear your voice. Did you know I've been dreaming about your voice...hoping it might admit some feeling for me? Am I being too bold? Oh, my love, speak to me. Say something from which I can take a tendril of hope." Angilbert grabbed both her hands again and brought them to his lips.

Bertha was overwhelmed. She had been dreaming about Angilbert for weeks. She longed to have him close. His eyes, his voice, his golden hair burned into her memories. He was ever with her, wherever she went about her daily business. His presence walked beside her every action. *Was he saying all that she'd dreamed...or was she imagining the words, willing the words so hard they seemed to be true? I must listen carefully,* she told herself. *I must be positive he's speaking the words, not that I'm imagining them.*

"I don't know if I can believe your words," she whispered softly. "Might these words be the ones I long to hear and not the ones you speak?" She pulled one of her hands from Angilbert's grasp and gently touched his lips. He smiled at her and kissed her hand.

"Bertha," Angilbert began, "will you share your life with me? Will you be my soul mate? I know your father won't agree to a formal joining, to a Christian marriage. But that is of no consequence to me. I love you, dearest. Please be my love for life; I will dedicate myself to your happiness." He squeezed her hand with enthusiasm and smiled all over his face! "My feeling for you is beyond the warmth of the sun, the depth of the sea, the height of the heavens. I wish to define my life with yours. Is it possible, my little Bertha?"

Bertha's legs trembled so she sat, pulling Angilbert onto the bench beside her. His arm went around her waist. He sat quietly, his question hanging in the air.

"Oh, my love," Bertha answered, "All things are

possible...all things. Between us two, all will come true." Angilbert folded her into his arms. They sat quietly together.

Chapter 11

EFFORTS FOR THE FUTURE

King Charlemagne sent envoys throughout the world, seeking to enhance the intellectual base of his court and to increase the educational quality of his schools. Despite such peaceful concerns, his armies continued to fight, conquered more people and, thus, appropriated additional lands. He continued his never-ending fight with the Saxons, quelling another Saxon uprising the next summer, much the same as in years past. His commanders' success in overtaking the Avars and in discovering their riches was a boon for the King and his court.

But, even though Charlemagne could enrich the Church with generous gifts, he could not prolong the life of his friend, Pope Hadrian. Charlemagne and the Pope knew and liked each other for more than twenty years. Together, they watched the growth and influence of Charlemagne's empire, as well as the growing sweep of the Church – one hand helped the other, as it were. But Pope Hadrian's trials and his accomplishments were over.

Pope Hadrian was succeeded by Leo III in 795. But Leo III was immediately disliked. Many nobles searched for a way to remove him from the Church. The Pope quickly realized his precarious position. Reflecting on the manner in which Charlemagne's support had strengthened Pope Hadrian, he sought to increase Charlemagne's allegiance to the Roman Church and, in so doing, to obtain a champion for himself.

Leo discarded the previous system of dating chancellery documents. Instead, he began to date the chancellery documents by the number of years which Charlemagne had ruled in Italy. He maintained a regular correspondence with the King, one in which they argued theology and suggested additional reforms of the church to each other. Charlemagne spoke eloquently of revising court procedures.

When the controversy over the use of icons in the church swept the Christian world, Charlemagne resolutely opposed the use of icons. The King was as engaged as ever in the doctrinal foundations of Church policy and in its everyday workings. Although his support protected and strengthened the Pope, Leo III was, nevertheless, a weak Pope. And the king himself was not helped by his loyalty and concern for Leo.

***

Tales of Pope Leo's sexual proclivities spread throughout the land. Powerful people in and out of Rome wished to replace him. In 799, Roman court officials instigated an uprising against Leo, planning to blind him and cut out his tongue. He would, then, be unable to defend himself. This was the Byzantine method for removing an official from office.

***

'Get thee to Spoleto, Father. I cannot protect you here. From there, I don't know. Mayhap the Duke will remove you in secret. If caught, your life is worth nothing!' Leo read the letter from his king and stiffened. Next to him, the courier - a man in rich robes - pushed Pope Leo into a covered cart.

"Go! Go!" He called to the driver who was accompanied by a lone man on horseback. "Keep to the back roads, you hear!" The cart lurched forward and was soon moving at a frightening pace. To better secure his place, the Pope wedged himself between the wine barrels in the cart and silently cursed. He could only hope the note was from the king. It looked like his hand but Leo could not be certain.

Within a few minutes the cart pulled into a small church's courtyard and he was hustled out. A monk he did not recognized bade him go in to the church. As he entered and looked around, his arms were bound from behind. A swarthy man walked him quickly to a horse, mounted himself and pulled up Leo behind him. He draped a long cape over the Pope and told him to lock his legs tight around their mount.

"Let's ride," the mounted man shouted to a second man on a horse nearby. They raced down the road for miles, finally stopping in a thick wood where another, covered cart was waiting. The Pope was stupefied but dissented not a moment. His life, if he kept it, depended on his acquiescence to someone else's plan. *I cannot save myself.* He repeated over and over. *You must trust someone, Leo, or you will die. Do not complain; think of the alternative.*

The men rode deep into the night, gave him bread and meat when they stopped and a wool linen to wrap himself in as he slept. At the sun's rising, they began riding again, taking turns with him as a riding companion. There was next to no talk, just a nudge with meat or drink and the Pope's quiet 'thank you.' Late in the third day of their journey, the men reined in at the gate of a walled courtyard near Spoleto. The town itself lay in the distance.

"We've brought a visitor to the Duke." The older of Leo's rescuers said to the guard at the gate. "Nay, we - Han and I - will not come in. We've a long ride back. Aye.

Expecting him? I do hope so!" He turned to Pope Leo and motioned him from the horse.

"This is the end of our journey, Father. May God protect you." He bowed to the Pope, took his elbow, and walked him to the gate which opened to admit him. The Pope, exhausted from his escape from Rome, walked unsteadily through the gate. Once inside, a guard took his elbow and escorted him to the beautiful manor inside. The Pope noticed the splendid bougainvillea climbing the walls, its dark green leaves resplendent against the creamy beige of the manor.

Ahh, Pope Leo thought, what hope there can be in a bit of color. The purple flowers almost gave him hope…hope for considerable more breaths before he died. The guard walked him around the house to a covered room near the back.

"Make yourself at home, Father. The Duke will see you promptly." He said as he backed away and returned to the front of the manor. Pope Leo stepped into the shade of the roof and saw the Duke of Spoleto come from the manor. The Duke came to him, went to one knee, and kissed his ring.

"Father." He said. "Welcome to my house."

"My son," Pope Leo answered. "You have my eternal gratitude. I don't know what…" The Duke of Spoleto raised his hands.

"Nay, nay, Father. No thanks, if you will. I can do little for you. You are still in danger. A contingent of armed men are riding this way. Forgive me, but I must send you to one better able to protect you." He turned, motioning to a sheik who came from inside the manor.

"Take him immediately. There is not time to linger or…" The Duke turned back to Pope Leo. "…no time to welcome you, Father, or, even, to inquire as to your comfort. You must be on your way. Abdul-Hafiz takes you to King Charlemagne. May you have a successful…a safe journey. Forgive my haste, Sire."

Pope Leo bowed to the Duke, folding his hands together in blessing. He felt ever more hopeful as his guide helped him into a bedecked cart, one with silk pillows and ornate window hangings. He sat back on the seat, thankful for his escape from barrels and a flimsy cart. As Abdul-Hafiz gave the signal to move forward, the Pope extended his hand in blessing to the Duke of Spoleto. The Pope's journey was, again, hurried and furtive; but in time, he was sitting in King Charlemagne's castle in Paderborn, limp with exhaustion but more than ever aware of his friends.

"My Grace, are you well?" Charlemagne inquired, taking a hurried inventory of Pope Leo's physical body. "I don't understand your unannounced arrival; but I'm delighted to welcome you to Paderborn."

"My son, my son," the Pope greeted King Charlemagne. "I felt it was past time for a visit and hurried, with Duke Spoleto's help, to reach you before you began moving again. I appreciate your welcome."

"I know you must be weary, Holy Father. Please follow this guardsman to your chambers," Charlemagne welcomed him graciously. "We shall talk before our evening meal. I'm ruling on a particularly ugly assault case and must return to court at this moment," the King answered. He turned at a commotion in the corridor.

"Nay, stop! Do you hear me? Stop! Stop in the name of King Charlemagne!" The Captain of the Guard shouted. "Who are you…that you overlook all courtesies? You will lose your head, entering a court by force. Halt! Who are you? I shall not ask again." Charlemagne took a step forward, his brow wrinkling.

"Go no further, Sire! Nay! I don't know who you are. Stand firm." The Captain's voice rang out.

Charlemagne hurried forward, followed by the Pope.

They waited as steps approached their chamber. Leo sank to a bench, trembling, his face in his hands. He could not speak.

"What is the difficulty, Lothar?" the King asked his captain. "Is someone violating the security of the hall? Bring the culprit to me."

"Sire, forgive me. He refuses to respond." the Captain answered. "He dashed into the hall and made directly for your chamber." Lothar replied as he held the man's arms behind his back. The man struggled, muttering under his breath.

Frowning, Lothar explained. "As he barged through the door, he said he's a noble from Rome. If so, Sire, he has no patrician manners," the guard reported in a disgusted voice.

"See to the security of the holy Father," Charlemagne directed the guard. "I shall attend to this boor myself." And he entered the corridor to walk toward the incensed man waiting with the castle guard.

"What is your business here, Sire?" the King demanded. "You have made my captain of the guard very angry. That does not contribute to a long life in this kingdom! I hope there is a sound explanation for your rudeness and highly unorthodox behavior--unwise behavior in my courts. Who are you and what do you want here?"

"Ahh, King Charlemagne, I beg your pardon! I didn't mean to give offense. But in my hurry to subdue the Pope, I have let my mission undermine my courtesies. Please, forgive my haste and, sadly, my bluster!" The tall, erect man apologized, pulling his fur-lined cloak odd his shoulders.

King Charlemagne hadn't expected so profuse an apology. He walked directly in front of the man, looking into the red, perspiring face of someone who appeared to be a Roman noble, if quality of dress and regal demeanor could be equated with that position.

"And you are?" the King asked, as he approached the man.

"I am Campulus, treasurer of the papal court, your Majesty. I'm accompanied on this journey by Paschalis, introducer of the papal guests. Forgive my indiscretion, Sire!" He flicked imaginary dust from his clothing. "We, of a certainty, should have consulted you before rushing to take Leo. He is accused of high crimes in Rome. We shall return him there for trial and punishment." Campulus stepped to move around the King toward Pope Leo.

"Of a certainty," King Charlemagne replied, "Pope Leo will return to Rome, be these charges of sufficient merit. But, he shall return with my escort, respected as the true Pope until such time as a commission shall try his case." Charlemagne placed both hands on the man's chest.

"Leave this hall. You will accompany my guard to a chamber. I recognize your brooch. Welcome to my realm!" The King offered. "Refresh yourselves and join us for the evening meal. I shall send Paul the Deacon to lead you to the banquet hall." So saying, King Charlemagne bowed regally, turned on his heel and returned to the Pope whose hands were trembling, his eyes bulging from their sockets.

"It does appear you have charges to answer, Leo," Charlemagne King said. "Come, we must talk," and he led the Pope into the library.

***

Several weeks later, the Pope began his return journey to Rome, escorted by Archbishop Hildibald of Cologne and Archbishop Arno of Salzburg. Accompanying the party were also five additional bishops and three counts. Assenting to the demands of the delegation from Rome, Charlemagne formed a commission himself to escort Pope Leo back to Rome. Only with such an escort did he believe the Pope's life could be guaranteed.

Several hearings were held in Rome in 799 AD. The ten person commission determined Leo was innocent of all charges. Leo sent his accusers, Campulus and Pascahalis, to Frankland, knowing they would be punished by King Charlemagne. Charlemagne's will and his power protected Leo. Now, all of Rome awaited a visit by the King. Obviously, the king was the true ruler of the Church.

***

When Pope Leo was safely back in Rome, Charlemagne journeyed to Aachen to spend the 799 Christmastide season there. His castle, under construction for many months, was finally completed. All members of Charlemagne's court anticipated moving in, their permanent court finished at last.

Once in Aachen, King Charlemagne mourned the deaths of two of his most beloved commanders. Gerold, duke of Bavaria and Hildegard's brother, was recently killed by a troop of revolting Avars. And Eric, the Duke of Friuli, who, years before, devastated the Avar 'rings' was also lost - killed in an ambush by encroaching Croatians.

Sorrow ever follows my footsteps. King Charlemagne wept. *God, please, I beg you. Don't let me outlive all of my friends! It's at these times I doubt the holiness of my cause. May I not have long-known companions into my old age, friends with whom to share remembered times and conquests? I fear I will be an old man, alone and looking back at the ages, lamenting these deaths!*

***

Once more, though, the battles of the summer brought

good news to the King. Rinaldo delivered the reports, hoping they would relieve Charlemagne's despair over the deaths of his Peers.

"Sire, our armies have had great success. Just listen to these reports!" Rinaldo exclaimed. He listed the battles won. "The Celts of Brittany have been taken and are under your control. The Moors are now pushed out of Majorca. And the emir of Huesca, on the Iberian peninsula, bowed to the inevitable and offered you entrance to his city." He handed the parchment to the King. "We now control even more lands. And King Louis is eager to bring Iberia into the realm." Rinaldo assured the King.

"Aye, Rinaldo; we have done well." Charlemagne agreed with a vague wave of his hand. "Let's call the armies home. Thank God, it is time to tend our wounded and prepare for the winter. I am weary, this year, of the fighting!" he added.

The King was preoccupied with his thoughts. *I must journey to Rome,* the King reminded himself. *This threat to Pope Leo, though he was absolved of the charges brought against him, is not eliminated. I so worry! If Leo is investigated or accused again, it will be impossible to clear him. The man is a damn fool! How can he risk his holy position? And, if I am to save him again, what will be the price?* The King rubbed his temples, hoping to relieve the tension around his eyes. *Must there always be trouble?* Charlemagne asked himself.

***

The following spring, King Charlemagne traveled down the Meuse, sailed to the mouth of the Somme and stopped at the monastery of Saint-Requier. Here, Angilbert was the head of the monastery. He was, also, one of the king's unofficial sons-in-law.

Charlemagne was seeking information. He hoped Angilbert's spies were successful, obtaining information on the activities of the Northmen, as well as names of boatmen who might build a fleet for him. Up and down the coast, the Northmen were attacking. *They do threaten my realm!* Charlemagne worried. *I must develop defenses but I need more information about these people.*

Angilbert did not disappoint the King. After his reports, Charlemagne left Rinaldo at the monastery, urging him to study the Northmen's tactics and their style of fighting. Angilbert promised to help Rinaldo as much as he could. The two of them assured King Charlemagne they would travel to him with their report within a fortnight.

Charlemagne was eager to leave Saint-Requier to travel towards the monastery at St. Martin of Tours. It was now the home of Alcuin, the new Abbot at St. Martin. He left Charlemagne's court and his employ, releasing the education of the young to more 'worthy' souls, as he put it. Every soul in the Aachen castle sorely missed the scholar. They begged the King to bring him back. But Alcuin even declined the King's invitation to travel with him to Rome. If he could not entice Alcuin away, King Charlemagne was determined to visit his old friend, if only for a short time.

***

I shall seek his advice and his thoughts before leaving for the Holy City. The King decided. He greeted Alcuin very early the morning after his arrival at Saint Martin's. They spoke about Pope Leo's difficulties in Rome and the extent of the damage done to the church...and to Leo's rule.

"Alcuin, what do you think?" the King continued the conversation. "You watched events in Rome, even before you joined our court. What is Leo's future as Pope? Has he the strength to defy the Byzantine ruler, if that becomes necessary?"

The King gives me a clear opening. What is my view of this Pope and of his understanding of Charlemagne's support and

217

his needs? Alcuin did not reply immediately. It was true; he hoped and planned for Charlemagne to be crowned emperor. But he was not sure it could happen quickly enough. For years, he felt the king had the strength for the task. His compelling defense of Christianity earned him the position. Alcuin wrote Pope Hadrian often when he lived: complimenting the king, bolstering Hadrian's knowledge of Charlemagne's conquests, and carefully setting the stage for a power shift to the western realms of the Church's jurisdiction. He continued this correspondence with Pope Leo after Hadrian went to his eternal reward. He looked into Charlemagne's face.

"Ever have I hoped the Church in Rome would crown you, Sire; you know that," Alcuin said to Charlemagne. "But, I've not asked any other soul to predict the likelihood of it. Let me talk with some people, especially Paul the Deacon. Surely, he'll have some wisdom on this subject. I do pray for that happy day!" He smiled at the King. "As to its likelihood, I absolutely don't know. I have little insight into Pope Leo, his thoughts or his values. He was almost unknown to me before his meteoric rise. But, remember, Sire; the Lord's will must be done. We should have faith in HIS wisdom."

***

As promised, Alcuin talked with Paul the Deacon about the state of the Christian Church in Rome, especially in light of Pope Leo's worsening reputation. To clarify his thoughts, Alcuin discussed Charlemagne's view of the Church with Paul.

"The King sees no difference between the Church in each man's life and each Christian's place in his Carolingian empire. He sees his empire and the church as one, Paul. Can you see the simplicity of it?" Alcuin asked Paul.

"Do you honestly believe Pope Leo will give this much power to the King?" Paul the Deacon asked in astonishment. "You're suggesting the power of the Church be subsumed under the power of our king? If this comes to be, there will be even greater fear of us from the Byzantine court: fear of the western Church's power and fear of King Charlemagne himself." Paul shook his head, trying to understand the reason both Charlemagne and Alcuin would want such responsibility.

"Can Pope Leo exalt King Charlemagne above the empress?" Paul questioned. He had honestly given this possibility no thought. "I don't know, Alcuin! No one in the Church is comfortable with a woman heading the Byzantine faith. That is partly because of Queen Irene herself, of a certainty. But what will happen? If our King becomes the head of the church, will the Byzantine nobility leave Irene in place, a woman who has dethroned and blinded her own son? I dare not imagine! What is to come, Master Alcuin, what sense can be made from all this? Do you think it possible for a military king...for a fighter... to be the Christian religion's pre-eminent man of God?" Paul was astounded. He needed time to puzzle out the consequences of such a thing.

"I cannot explain my feelings, not right now. But it does frighten me very much." Paul answered.

"I believe the King has earned this place, Paul. He's the only sovereign who has labored to build a Christian kingdom, to convert the pagans, to bring Christianity to all peoples," Alcuin replied. "The Church itself has not converted the number of pilgrims our King has brought to the Christian faith. Aye, he is worthy of this honor!" Paul looked dubious.

"But, Master!" he objected. "Does becoming a Christian, at the point of a sword, represent conversion? You know yourself. There was a period when hundreds were killed, hundreds who did not obey Church law! The king made no distinction between breaking a fast day or stealing! Do you think people so frightened would choose to become Christians? Who knows if any of these conquered peoples embrace the religion willingly? I don't consider this 'winning people to the faith,' Sir. Nay, not at all." he added.

"But his success is obvious, Paul," Alcuin argued. "He must be free...free both to continue the work of God and the building of our Christian kingdom."

***

Alcuin himself felt so strongly King Charlemagne should be emperor that he dismissed Paul's doubts. Days later he assured the King that he was worthy to be Emperor, even though he told the king that Paul would not comment on his hopes.

"You give me much support, Alcuin, in this question and in the wise suggestions for dealing with Pope Leo." Charlemagne thanked his scholar. "I shall keep your advice in mind. And I do put some little hope in your views. I like the sound in that change of title! Pray to almighty God it will be as you describe. I, for one, have doubts. The Pope is ever self-serving. I know his commitment to his own personal advancement. His dedication to the Church is the commitment I question. He must realize the immediate consequence of my being crowned emperor-- the diminishing of his power, I mean." King Charlemagne controlled his smile, hardly daring to believe he might become the head of the Church.

"Leo is, as you say, in a poor position, brought to his knees by his own weaknesses. He may see my support, my elevation, as his only salvation. Let's not speak of this to anyone. It would not be seemly." The King closed all conversation related to an expansion of his authority and of his power.

***

"Alcuin, I yearn to see my Bertha," Charlemagne changed the subject. "Her time is near and I wished to ascertain her health, now the babe is ready to enter the world. Before journeying here, we sailed down the Meuse, then to the Somme and stopped at Saint-Requier monastery. Angilbert had some knowledge of the Northmen's activities and acquired other reports from inland. He and Rinaldo plan to meet me on this journey with more specifics." Remembering his mention of his second daughter, Charlemagne turned back to that topic.

"Bertha wished to deliver her babe...with the child's father close by. I did not have it in my heart to deny her request. Weeks ago she journeyed to Saint Requier to join Angilbert there. She hadn't birthed the child before we left, but no matter. Bertha is well and very happy. I must find her a small manor close by. She does not wish to be separated from Angilbert, though she did agree to spend time in my court...after the babe is born." He smiled at the anticipated birth and hoped for a girl.

"I shall ever be indebted to you, good friend, for your advice on my daughters those years ago. How blind men are to others' needs...or, mayhap, it is the blindness of kings."

***

Fortunate it was that the King and his family were visiting at Tours. It was here in 800 AD that Queen Liutgard (who was first a concubine, much like Queen Hildegard had been) took ill and died in the early summer. This death brought condolences from everyone, for this Liutgard was well loved and, consequently, much mourned.

After a longer stay in Tours than he originally planned, Charlemagne announced he would travel to Rome in the autumn. He returned to Aachen via Paris during the late summer, organized his vast army and began the journey to Italy. An army was necessary because Prince Grimwald of Benevento, whom he previously conquered, was making mutinous noises against the Franks. Perhaps because of the King's large army, Grimwald only growled. Charlemagne arrived in Rome peacefully.

***

Pope Leo met the King outside the city and shared an evening meal with him. The following day, King Charlemagne entered Rome and walked up the steps of St. Peter's basilica. It was December 6, 800 AD. The people of the city, including the Roman nobles, welcomed him with praise and thanksgiving, just as they had welcomed Pope Leo home the previous year.

The King prayed and fasted, hoping to instill confidence in Leo's leadership by his own presence and piety. Within a week the Roman ecclesiastics and Frankish nobles convened in a synod in St. Peter's basilica. King Charlemagne exhorted all to investigate the Pope's crimes.

"Let there be no hesitation," the King began. "We are here, we are all gathered here, at this blessed Christmastide to convict or exonerate Pope Leo of the crimes of which he has been accused. Time enough has passed for those who charged him and for those who subscribe to these charges to present their evidence. This is a worthy undertaking; one for which the Church itself is in our debt." He looked around at the men who would decide the Pope's fate. Charlemagne expected them to support his wishes. *But men being men,* he said, *I can never be sure.* He turned to them all.

"Let any man come forth who would submit evidence to support the charges against Pope Leo, the Third. Come forth, all with evidence, with testimony, with proof of his misdeeds." The King stood majestically, looking neither right nor left, patiently waiting for a response. In fact, no one moved and no one brought forth evidence against the Pope. Nevertheless, Pope Leo himself swore a holy oath, an oath of innocence, that the charges arraigned against him were totally and utterly false. This oath appeared to weaken everyone's doubts, even if those doubts weren't completely eliminated. Pope Leo was exonerated.

On the same day, there arrived a small delegation from the caliph Harun-al-Rashid. He sent two monks to give the keys of Calvary and of the Holy Sepulchre to King Charlemagne, implying Christendom's holiest sites were under the King's protection.

***

Some weeks later, on Christmas morning, 800 AD, Charlemagne came again to St. Peter's basilica for his daily devotions. Frankish courtiers and many Roman citizens accompanied him. Some joined him in his walk down the street to St. Peter's. This morning, Charles no longer wore Frankish clothing. He dressed in a long Roman tunic, a scarf thrown over his shoulders. I do pray I can manage this scarf, the King thought to himself. *If it gets between my feet, I may find myself bottom-up on the floor.* He smiled slightly, amused at the figure of the King of Christendom tangled in a scarf! He kneeled at the *confessio* of St. Peter.

As he rose, Pope Leo approached and placed a golden crown upon his head. At that, the Roman citizens acclaimed three separate times: "To Carolus Augustus, crowned by God, mighty and pacific *emperor,* be life and victory."

King Charlemagne was overcome. He could scarcely stand. *Is it true?* He asked himself. *Am I truly crowned Emperor?*

Catching Alcuin's delighted eyes, he found the answer there. The people of Rome declared him emperor on Christmas day, 800 A. D. There were now officially two empires, the Eastern Roman empire in Byzantium and the Western Roman Empire in Rome. And for the Church's blessing, Pope Leo III also crowned Charlemagne King of the Frankish realm and named him emperor as well!

***

The King spent the rest of the winter reorganizing the realm, pouring more life into the empire's internal organization, and emphasizing the interests of peace and righteousness. He no longer fought on the battlefield; his commanders and his sons accepted that duty. He spent his time in the much more difficult task of integrating his wide-spread domain and improving the lives of his people. Although his organizational skills served him well once again, his personality, exuberance, and physical strength continued to maintain and protect his beloved Frankish realm. The core of his kingdom came from his father, but Charlemagne carved out the rest himself – one battle at a time. His Carolingian kingdom stretched from the southern shores of France, into Italy, to the Elbe River in the east, and along much of northern Europe's coast - the ongoing vision of a thinking king.

Ever hardy and seemingly indestructible, Charlemagne outlived three of his adult children. Both Pepin, the King of Aquitaine, and Rotrud, beloved daughter, died in 810. Charles, the intended heir of the King's part of the realm, died in 811. His brothers' early deaths left Louis, the son most unlike his father, to rule the entire empire.

The End